How to Lose a Prince This Summer

Wedding Fever, Book 2

Sara Adrien & Tanya Wilde

ARE YOU SIGNED UP FOR DRAGONBLADE'S BLOG?

You'll get the latest news and information on exclusive giveaways, exclusive excerpts, coming releases, sales, free books, cover reveals and more.

Check out our complete list of authors, too!

No spam, no junk. That's a promise!

Sign Up Here

www.dragonbladepublishing.com

Dearest Reader;

Thank you for your support of a small press. At Dragonblade Publishing, we strive to bring you the highest quality Historical Romance from some of the best authors in the business. Without your support, there is no 'us', so we sincerely hope you adore these stories and find some new favorite authors along the way.

Happy Reading!

CEO, Dragonblade Publishing

For my little son, who thought the first time on a boat was like floating in space. May the prince in this story show you to find love and truth in people.

~ Sara Adrien

As always, for you, dear reader.

~ Tanya Wilde

Preface

Dear Readers,

Welcome, and thank you for opening the pages of this story. Whether you're a long-time fan of these characters or stumbling upon their world for the first time, we're so happy to have you here.

Before we step into Miss Seraphina Lyndon's tale, allow us to guide you through the world of our series. Sera is the sharp-witted, big-hearted heroine of this book. Her love interest is none other than Prince Alexander von Hohenzollern-Sigmaringen—known simply as Alex. He carries his title and responsibilities with grace, but his story is filled with mystery, charm, and a romance that will sweep you away.

If this series is new to you, you might want to meet some familiar faces who weave in and out of these books. Lady Ashley, for example, was the heroine of the first story in the *Wedding Fever* series, *How to Tempt an Earl This Spring*. Her love story blossomed with Thomas, the Earl of Linsey, and began the web of love and friendship that ties these stories together.

Prince Alex, as gallant as he is, isn't the only royal you'll meet in these pages. His younger brother, Prince Stan, stars in *The Sound of Seduction*, book four of my *Miracles on Harley Street* series, while his clever and spirited sister, Princess Thea, claims her own tale in *A Touch of Charm*, the third book of that series.

Looking ahead, Lady Charlene, another one of our quartet of leading ladies, will take center stage in the next installment, *How to Seduce a Duke This Autumn*. And for those who love cozy, snowy settings, you'll look forward to Maddie's romantic adventure in book four, *Ways to Kiss a Marquess This Winter*. This final chapter in the series will return us to the Earl of Linsey's castle, where familiar and beloved characters—including the earl's best friend, Sebastian—will reappear to kindle our hearts.

Of course, no love story is complete without a villain to stir the pot, and Baron Wolfgang von List fills those shoes here and in other novels. A scheming Prussian baron who revels in corruption and intrigue, he challenges our virtuous characters at every turn. If his ignoble adventures leave you curious, you'll see more of him (and his well-deserved comeuppance) throughout Sara Adrien's books. Find out more at www.SaraAdrien.com.

Next, fans of Tanya Wilde's delightful romance *Ladies Who Dare* find unexpected connections between her characters and the world of Charlene's story. Be sure to visit her online to explore more about her novels; the links between our works mean there is even more Regency magic waiting for you at www.author tanyawilde.com.

Now, dear reader, we invite you to find a cozy spot, perhaps with a cup of tea, and disappear into this tale of fierce love, sweeping landscapes, and the enduring hope that brings our characters together. Sera and Alex's story awaits, full of heart, longing, and the promise of happily ever after—which we all deserve, don't we?

Yours sincerely,
Sara Adrien and Tanya Wilde

Chapter One

Cornwall, 1818.

I NEED TO lose a dratted prince...
What a conundrum.

Most women would give anything to marry a prince. But Seraphina Lyndon, known to friends and family simply as Sera, bent down to pick up a seashell that was clamped shut. She didn't want to marry a stranger, regardless of his royal title. Two halves fitting perfectly together protected something precious inside like an oyster harboring a pearl; that's what love ought to be—a genuine connection, not the cold arrangement her betrothal promised. She held the shell to her ear momentarily and then tossed it back into the ocean.

She watched as the ocean spat the shell onto the shore, the waves crashing and leaving white foam across the beach. Overhead, the sky was a hazy gray, with fog clinging stubbornly to the horizon. Something far in the distance caught her eye, moving slowly across the horizon. Sera squinted. Part of a creature emerged from the sea.

A whale!

Excitement bubbled up inside her as she spotted the small tail of a baby whale following close behind. How extraordinary! Her gaze swept the beach, but, of course, there was nobody. Alone, she grinned and strolled along the shore, occasionally glancing back at the whale and its calf until they completely disappeared. The sand was cool and firm beneath her feet, and the occasional splash of water was a welcome relief. Cornwall's water was often warm despite the fog, or maybe her love for this place made it feel that way.

If only I could be as free as those whales.

She'd swim far away from this blasted engagement! Engaged since birth to a prince of a foreign land she'd never even visited.

A prince!

Why would she ever want to marry one? It might seem like something from fairy tales, but it was a royal travesty in real life. First, he'd whisk her away to his distant kingdom, and she'd rarely see her friends and family—only on rare, brief occasions. Second, there was no fairy tale aspect to it—no love, tender kisses, or romance leading to a happily ever after. Third, and most importantly, she didn't even know him.

Sera hadn't agreed to blindly marry a stranger who would seize control of her life... but her agreement didn't seem to matter to her parents. No, she had to wriggle her way out of this arrangement. And that's where her conundrum came from: How could she lose a prince this summer and forge her own life?

The very thought made her stomach twist.

The rules, the restrictions, the life of a princess in some distant European country where she might not even speak the language? No, thank you! It had been easy to ignore her betrothal—and her betrothed for that matter—as the years passed. After all, out of sight, out of mind. But now, with the date fast approaching, she could feel the cords of this weighty arrangement pulling tight.

Like a noose around her neck.

He ought to have arrived in England by now, right?

Urgh!

Sera's feet left fleeting footprints in the sand, soon washed away by the waves, leaving only shallow imprints. If someone whisked her away to a place she didn't want to be, would

Cornwall forget her? She traced a line in the sand, wistfully thinking that she'd have to say goodbye to her beloved summers at the beach if she had to live in some faraway region in a distant country. Did they even have beaches in Transylvania?

Snap out of it, Sera! You are a resourceful woman!

Indeed. All she needed was a plan. Her mind raced through various ways to escape the announcement of her impending engagement. Could the book that Ashley had given her help? What was its name again? *Matters of the Heart.* She should look for strategies to repel royal fiancés later.

Because one thing was clear like the Cornwall sky: she would not succumb to her parents' pressure to marry a stranger, no matter how important his family was to her father's business connections! That prince would have to drag her away, caged and chained, before she would let him take her from her beloved England! She walked faster, nearly stomping, as she pressed her feet into the sand to leave a deeper imprint.

She understood that her father had his reasons, but she only wanted a choice—a say in her own life. However, she couldn't simply break off this engagement. Too much was at stake for her family. But if the prince were to end it… wouldn't that solve her problem? Then the backlash wouldn't fall on her family but on his, right?

Sera suddenly laughed.

Yes, she would rid herself of this prince by becoming the most unappealing creature in his world! Then he would be forced to find another match to take her place. All she needed to do was figure out how to become the most undesirable prospect for such a man. She glanced at a large rock formation in the distance, shaped almost like a sleeping bear, resolute and unmoved by the powerful waves crashing against it. Sera would be that rock! Determination coursed through her as she marched on, her feet pressing deeper into the sand with each step. She wasn't about to let some prince dictate her life. No, she'd ensure he saw her as the most unsuitable bride imaginable!

Sera squinted.

The mist made everything appear like a dreamy watercolor painting against reality. Hah! Much like the view before her, her future seemed just as obscured—uncertain and brimming with possibilities she couldn't begin to predict.

Who enjoyed predictability anyway?

The waves roared louder as she approached the rock, and she spotted a distant figure on the beach—a young man in breeches and half-clothed, performing some form of peculiar exercise. She watched as he dropped onto his hands, his body a long plank, pushing himself up and down with powerful strokes.

A shiver swept over her as she imagined the strength in those arms.

Shaking her head, something else caught her eye—a seagull fluttering low, so close she nearly jumped out of her skin. Sera blinked in surprise, watching as it struggled past her, a rusty object dangling from its beak. Curiosity piqued, she followed the bird's erratic flight. It landed on a large rock jutting from the cliff's edge, its wings tangled in a long, thin thread leading to a metal fishing hook. The sight tugged at her heartstrings.

Poor thing!

Without thinking, she rushed over and clambered up the low slope of rock, edging around to the part of the rock that disappeared into the sea.

She glanced down at the waves crashing up the rock.

Perhaps this was not a good idea, but she refused to turn back now after having come this far, so, once close enough, she reached out to free the struggling bird. But as she neared, the seagull fluttered away, just out of reach again.

Frustration bubbled up inside her. "I'm trying to help you!"

The bird settled higher up on the rock, and Sera tracked it further. She carefully maneuvered closer, reaching out again. She tried to catch the thrashing bird, but it was always just out of reach. Another seagull flew past her, its cry almost in her ear, as if warning her away from its friend.

Her foot slipped.

Sera cried out, losing her balance on the precarious edge of the rock she held. Only then did she realize she'd scaled almost completely around the formation, farther and farther away from the beach. *No!* Her fingers dug in deep as she tried to regain her footing, but the world around her tilted, and in a blur, she tumbled into the icy waters below.

A cry left her lips.

Only one thought filled her head.

I can't swim…

PRINCE ALEXANDER VON Hohenzollern-Sigmaringen stood on the beach, gazing at the waves crashing against the English shore. England had always felt foreign to him, a place he had only known through detached discussions at court. Yet, he hadn't crossed the channel to appreciate its customs. His purpose was far more pressing: locating his younger brother, Prince Stan, whose diplomatic mission in England had stirred rumors that their family could not ignore.

In truth, Alex hoped to delay his search for Stan as his brother had sent reports of various difficulties—none of which Alex wanted to consider. Pressing matters, particularly those concerning lifelong partners, led him to seek out Miss Lyndon, the wealthy merchant's daughter, his betrothed since age four. He had never met her, or any member of her family for that matter. Economic significance had necessitated the match, and at four and twenty, he was prepared to fulfill his duty.

They may not hail from aristocratic circles, but they are richer and more resourceful than anyone I have ever met, his mother had said before he left Vienna three months ago.

He wondered whether Miss Lyndon had been raised to embrace the role expected of her—the role of a princess. Yet, he knew that elevating a woman into aristocracy was no easy task.

And royalty? That came with its own set of expectations and challenges. Would Miss Lyndon suit him? The fact that he was marrying a commoner was remarkable in itself. That his parents allowed it. Anything for business.

Another point of question, would he be suitable for her? Did that even matter, given that marriage was a decision made for them? He was a prince, expected to command, to search, to succeed. But beneath all the swath was just a man.

Yet he was determined to embrace his duty.

I must prove myself.

It was *expected* of him to prove himself. Returning with Stan and a wife would accomplish that to a degree. It would prove he was capable. It would prove his unwavering sense of duty. It would prove him worthy of the title of *prince*. Of course, he knew little about Miss Lyndon, but it was entirely possible she could be the anchor he needed to return to his home country with solid shipping influence, especially since his brother required his support in conflicts with the Prussians. Still, Alex had lived in Vienna since University, and he wasn't ready to return to Bran Castle empty-handed.

For now, he was at the beach.

The shore of England spread before him like an uncharted map, and his mission was to chart its course—starting with Miss Lyndon. Then he would find Stan to confront him with whatever truths had led him to flee.

He lifted his face to the sky and inhaled deeply.

He loved the smell of the ocean.

How could he not, growing up in the countryside at Bran Castle, surrounded by the lush landscape of the Carpathian Mountains. Rivers were lovely, but the ocean was a whole different kind of wonderful.

Cold water lapped at his toes as he stepped onto the damp edge of the shore. He'd discarded his boots some yards back; if he was lucky, the sea wouldn't swallow them by the time he returned.

His hotel valet might throttle him otherwise.

His gaze followed the endless expanse of the ocean, the sound of the waves, a symphony that could almost lull one into a trance-like state. Perhaps the possibilities in England were as vast as its blue sea in Cornwall. He raised his arms over his head, stretching out the muscles that had just had a thorough workout. The beach here felt like a slice of heaven.

Just then, a flash of white in the water caught his eye.

The fog hadn't entirely lifted, so he squinted, trying to discern the shape. A slender arm. Panic shot through him as he realized it must be a child or a woman.

Why weren't they swimming?

The head suddenly vanished beneath the surface.

With a surge of urgency, Alex sprinted toward the water. The head resurfaced, but the person's flailing limbs made their desperation clear. His heart thundered as he dashed into the waves, the chill biting into him as he waded deeper. Only that person mattered at the moment. He was certain if he didn't get to them soon, they'd been swept into the ocean and beyond his reach. Purpose sharpened in his mind. He wouldn't let someone drown, not while he was capable of acting.

He dove into the waves and swam, the cold seizing his muscles, but he pushed through the resistance, each stroke carrying a purpose, each heartbeat a countdown, and each breath a reminder of the stakes.

It didn't take that long to reach the person—a woman.

"Hold on!" he shouted.

His fingers found her arm, and he pulled her up against his body. Her fingers bit into him momentarily before they went slack.

Please, no!

Had she lost consciousness?

Alex's arm wrapped around her waist, her body slight and delicate under his grip. Dark hair clung to her cheeks as he kicked toward the shore, her weight almost lifeless against the pull of the sea tide. The shore seemed torturously distant, each stroke bringing exhaustion as much as progress. But he refused to falter.

Just a little longer.

Finally, his feet struck sand, and they washed out, sprawling onto the shore, the woman on top of him. He lay there for a moment, catching his breath before he rolled over, settling her on her back while he rose to his knees, his fingers shaking as he searched for a pulse. Alex placed his ear near her mouth, relief flooding him at the faint wisps of breath. His training, both in Vienna and from his youth, kicked in, and he began chest compressions, his movements steady and deliberate. If there was any water in her lungs, it needed to be addressed. He pressed his lips against hers and blew air into her lungs.

"Come on," he urged. "Let it all count."

She let out a strangled cough.

He pushed her hair back from her face. "That's it, cough it all up."

Her eyes suddenly fluttered open, and Alex found himself gazing into a set of startling green eyes, and it felt as though he was the one submerged in water.

Had he just saved a siren?

Chapter Two

S ERA'S EYES FLUTTERED open and shut again.

They still stung from the salty water.

Her body shivered, and she coughed again. Someone—a man—was speaking to her, but the words were a jumble she couldn't untangle. But she did know this person had saved her life.

A hand touched her cheek.

The comfort that small action brought eased some of the biting chill that clung to her bones. And had she imagined it, or had his lips touched hers?

Did she perhaps die?

Why else would a man kiss a near-drowned woman?

No. No, no, no! A seagull flashed in her mind. That… that… blasted bird! No attempted good deed went unpunished, right?

She tried again to open her eyes, but they still stung fiercely from the salty water, forcing her to keep them closed until the relentless burn eased a bit. Then a mouth met hers once more, urgent and hot. A burst of air rushed past her lips as Sera coughed again, this time a strained, spluttering breath. The man gathered her into his arms, and she didn't utter a protest. The strength of his body was too comforting, even though she had no idea what on earth he was doing.

At that moment, his hold became her lifeline.

Who was he? She wanted to ask him, but her voice failed her. It was as if the command of her brain couldn't reach her tongue.

She wasn't dying—was she?

No.

I refuse to die.

Her eyes finally managed to flutter open to meet his—a pair of dark, intense eyes that smoldered with both worry and relief.

"You..." She choked.

"Breathe," he commanded, his voice laced with authority.

Sera took a deep breath, then another, her body gradually calming as her eyes remained locked on his. Was he the man she saw on the cliff? How did he find her? But as each breath steadied her, so did the storm of inquiries steady, too—except for one: *Who are you, and why did you risk your life for me?*

Words still failed to pass her lips, yet something flashing in his gaze held her as securely as his arms. Something that set all her senses on alert and brought awareness back to their situation.

Scandalous, a stray thought whispered.

Well, wasn't this... perfect?

She managed to smile despite the ache in her limbs. Saved by a handsome man—could a girl ask for anything more?

The man's brows drew together. "Are you in pain?" His tone was firm, almost a rebuke, as if he were frustrated, or perhaps angry, that she'd nearly succumbed to the waves.

"I..." The burn of his gaze sent a shock through her already trembling body, nerves firing as warmth replaced the cold, igniting beneath her skin.

Not pain. Just... heat.

The heat coursing through her body seemed to emanate from him, melting away the lingering chill. Which was rather odd since he should have been just as cold as she, right? He wasn't the sun, was he? A deity from the heavens?

She focused on his face, his features rugged yet oddly refined, as if he belonged to both the earth and something far removed from it. Blond, thick hair clung to his forehead, droplets of water dripping onto her. Sharp cheekbones balanced by a slightly square jaw, and dark brows framed eyes that were unexpectedly watchful, as if he were accustomed to taking in every detail around him. The gaze that held her was intense but not unkind, a quiet command lingering that suggested he was no stranger to dangerous situations—or to leading others out of them. His hand, steady and strong on her shoulder, contrasted with the wet, disheveled state of his clothes, which clung to him, revealing the lines of a lean but powerful build. Even in his soaked state, there was a sense of discipline in the way he held himself, even as he looked her over, assessing her condition after the rescue.

Handsome.

In an otherworldly sort of way.

Honestly, Sera! This was not the time. She could have died today. But then, was there a better time to notice a man's beauty other than right after death? A surge of humor bubbled up, and she tested her voice again. "Are…" She cleared her throat. "Are you my prince?"

Wait, no.

That wasn't right. It should have been a knight, not a prince. Her tongue still felt heavy, as did her mind, and she tried to shake the muddle from her head when he answered.

"No, I'm not your prince." Firm.

Of course not. "So honest." Her prince was probably an arrogant, pot-bellied man with none of this stranger's stoic grace. The thought was ridiculous yet amusing, given her current predicament. She squirmed in his embrace, strangely reluctant for him to let go. "Please… help me sit up."

He nodded, shifting his arm behind her back, helping her to her feet. Every movement of his was careful, as though he feared hurting her. "Honesty saves lives," he finally said.

She wanted to laugh at that.

He also saved lives. She drew in a deep breath, taking stock of her body, leaning on one of her arms. "Thank you for saving mine."

He dipped his head in a slight, respectful nod. "It was fortunate I was nearby. What were you doing in the water?"

Sera sighed. "Would you believe me if I said I tried to save a bird on that rock over there?" She gestured with her chin to the gray stone, half of it jutting innocently from the ocean, the other half merging wickedly with the beach as the tide licked at its edges.

She'd been reckless.

He followed her gaze before turning back to her, a half-smile twitching at the corners of his mouth that didn't quite reach his eyes. "And you never considered the dangers?"

"Did you?" she shot back. She watched his face, intrigued by how various emotions flashed across his features. There was depth to his gaze, holding as many untold secrets as the ocean bore. And Sera felt the need to learn to swim—not in water, but to learn more about her savior.

How strange, this feeling.

For a heartbeat, they were silent, observing each other. Sera felt her pulse quicken, not from fear but from a strange thrill. She had to fill the quiet, the way his eyes, too observant, too knowing, held her gaze.

"Did no one accompany you to the beach?" he asked.

She awkwardly brushed a stray curl from her forehead. "I slipped out." At his look, she added, "I like to stroll on the beach alone. I suppose that wouldn't make sense to most people."

He sighed, dragging his hand through his wet hair. "On the contrary, I understand much more than you might imagine. I enjoy the quiet, too."

Her pulse skittered again at the way he spoke to her, not patronizingly, and not as if he was trying to puzzle her out like some intricate riddle. Just normal. And despite herself, she wanted to know more about him, this mysterious stranger who'd pulled her from the water without fear of death. "I suppose I owe you something, though I'm afraid I have nothing to give you." She laughed lightly. "Except a word of advice: steer clear of impetuous young women with a fondness for saving creatures they can't actually catch."

He gave her a half-smile. "Consider the lesson learned." There was a lilt to his speech—something unusual in Cornwall. Perhaps English wasn't his first language, but he spoke as if it came naturally to him.

"Good," she murmured. "I'd hate for you to risk your life again on my account."

There was a pause, his eyes glancing toward the waves, then back at her. "You're sure you're well?"

"Only a little bruised in body and pride, rest assured," Sera answered, her voice almost fully recovered, just a slight scratchiness remaining. "And perhaps a bit grateful. You don't meet someone who saves your life every day."

And being kissed—or a version of a kiss—as well.

Wait, did that count as her first kiss being stolen?

ALEX WATCHED THE girl a moment longer, her pale skin almost ghostly against the rising sun. She was breathing, her chest rising and falling with slow, steady breaths. That was all that mattered. However, she did look a tiny bit comic with her hair, tangled and damp from the water, clinging to her face like seaweed, but as she pushed it aside, she revealed her features fully, and he felt a sharp intake of breath.

Her eyes were still dazed yet vivid—a shade of green he'd never quite seen before. Her face, despite its pallor, held an undeniable strength beneath its softness. The kind of strength he knew all too well from the women of his homeland. But this— this was something different. Something more… profound.

Rebellious, even.

She slowly shifted her body, and he searched for any sign of distress.

"You stole my first kiss," she suddenly accused.

"I beg your pardon?" He did no such thing!

"You pressed your lips against mine. What is that if not a kiss?"

"It's saving your life." When her eyes narrowed, he continued, "I vow, I speak the truth."

She studied him for a moment before nodding. "I shall believe you."

Thank saints.

"But lips touching lips, in my estimation, still remains a kiss."

Alex cursed, ready to launch into an explanation when she said, "I suppose I should return home."

Yes. Before more comments on kissing. But he found he didn't mind all that much. Besides that, for a woman who nearly died, she showed no sign of hysteria, and his heart felt almost distressed for her. The thought of this girl, this stranger, gone from this world… strangely unsettled him in a way he hadn't anticipated.

She began to push herself upright but faltered.

"Steady now," Alex said softly, rising to his feet and holding out his hand to her. "Here, let me help."

She placed her palm in his, slowly attempting to stand again, and let out a breath when she succeeded. "Thank you."

"I'll escort you home."

She shook her head. "No need."

He didn't argue. "Very well. At least I'll escort you to solid ground."

Alex thought she'd decline again, but to his relief, she nodded. "That might be best."

She took a few steps but then stopped again, hunching over. Her apologetic gaze found his. "Sorry, I'm afraid this might take a while."

Alex stood still for a moment, his gaze moving over her from head to toe. Her soaked dress clung to her form rather scandalously, leaving little of her curves to the imagination. His gaze swept the beach, suddenly worried. The longer they tarried, the greater the chance of being found and complications arising.

Without a word, he dropped to one knee and effortlessly lifted her into his arms. The motion was seamless—his muscles barely straining under her weight, even though they still burned from exhaustion.

"Then I'll carry you."

She blinked at him, her green eyes wide as her arms wrapped around his neck. "That's not necessary!"

He shifted her slightly in his arms. "Your legs say otherwise."

"My legs?" Suddenly, she laughed. "Are you a fisherman and I a mermaid?"

Alex raised an eyebrow, glancing down at her. "No," he replied, a hint of a smile tugging at the corner of his lips. "I'm no fisherman."

"A shipbuilder, then?" she asked. "You do seem built like one."

Oh? "And how are they built?"

"Strong," she replied, though he sensed an undercurrent of appreciation.

"Well, I'm not a shipbuilder either," he said, shaking his head slightly. "I'm just an ordinary man."

"Too cavalier for ordinary." She tilted her head, and for a moment, he wondered if she would ask again if he were something else. Instead, she simply sighed. "Can you let me go? I think I've caught enough of a breath."

"No," Alex said firmly, his eyes locking onto hers, challenging her to argue further. "You're in no condition to walk on sand."

"It's just sand."

"It's uneven."

She huffed, sounding exasperated, but he caught a glimpse of her upturned lips. "You are stubborn, aren't you?" Alex said nothing but adjusted his grip on her, holding her securely against his chest. He had already made up his mind: she wasn't going anywhere on her own, at least not on the beach. Once they reached solid ground, he'd reassess.

She pointed to a spot in the distance. "You can set me on my feet over there."

He nodded.

"Are you visiting Cornwall or are you a resident?" she suddenly asked.

"Visiting."

"You're not a man of many words, are you?"

"Our breath is precious."

Especially since she had almost lost hers. She chuckled, and he could feel her breathing softly, her head moving slightly with each of his steps. The closeness was undeniable.

"You're a foreigner, right? I can't place your accent; it's too faint."

"Yes. And thank you, I'll take that as a compliment," he replied, his tone evasive. The truth was, he didn't know what he wanted to say about himself. His life and his reasons for being here weren't subjects one brought up in polite conversation, especially not to a woman he was carrying in his arms. And certainly not when she was looking up at him with those sharp, intelligent eyes.

The distance between them didn't seem to matter to her. She seemed content to ask her questions. Perhaps this was her way of coping with her near-death experience.

"Where are you from?" she pressed, her curiosity relentless.

He chuckled. "Far from here."

"Fine, keep your secrets." She scratched her nose. "You must be getting tired, carrying me all this way."

"Not yet," he lied. Just a small one.

She scoffed. "You're not very convincing."

"I can still carry you, tired or not."

"Commendable."

The path ahead narrowed, leading toward the base of a small slope where the beach transitioned into a rugged trail that could only be the quickest route to her home. Alex had no doubt this woman was far more capable than most he had met, so when they arrived, he slowly set her down on her feet, his hands lingering for just a moment to ensure her balance.

"Are you sure you don't need any help from here?" he asked.

She offered him a determined smile and began to make a series of small marching movements, lifting her knees in a show of strength. "See? My legs have almost completely recovered. I'll be fine, I assure you."

He couldn't help the faint smile that tugged at his lips as her gaze met his, her eyes sincere. "I don't know how to repay you, but… again, thank you."

Alex inclined his head. "Just don't do something so dangerous again."

A small laugh escaped her. "I'll do my best." She adjusted her clothes, though nothing seemed to adjust. Still, she took a few confident steps back toward the path and glanced over her shoulder one last time. "Then I shall be off," she said, giving him a small nod. A farewell?

Protest welled within.

Alex returned the nod, though his eyes remained fixed on her retreating form until she disappeared into the landscape. It wasn't until she was entirely out of view that he realized he'd never asked for her name. He frowned slightly, feeling an unexpected pang of regret at the thought.

But then, he reminded himself, there was no need.

He would never see her again.

Chapter Three

S ERA SANK INTO the soft cushions of the settee, gripping the small book, *Matters of the Heart,* in her lap as she tried to focus. But the memory of her near-drowning kept bubbling to the surface. She could still feel his arms steady around her, his mouth on hers, pressing air back into her lungs. Her cheeks flushed at the thought. And, of all things, she had asked whether he was her prince!

Her prince! No.

I'm not your prince.

She grimaced. No, he was not. What on earth had possessed her to say something so absurd? She was engaged to a prince—a real one, with a castle, a title, and everything. And she wanted to get rid of that one.

Determined to distract herself, she flipped open *Matters of the Heart* and paged through, her eyes skimming each headline, each piece of ridiculous advice and Ashley's scrawl as she penned her own thoughts on certain matters. Her friend hadn't found the book helpful, but maybe it could provide the ammunition she needed to scare off her betrothed.

Her gaze landed on "Dance With Your Beau As Often As Possible." Perfect. She could refuse to dance or—better yet—dance atrociously. Perhaps she'd wax the soles of her slippers and slip on the parquet. Sera pictured herself stomping around a ballroom, her arms flailing like a drunken sailor, her partner aghast. Yes, that might work. But was it enough?

She paged through some more.

"Become a Mystery Wrapped in a Riddle." Hmm. She could be an open book, sharing every trivial thought with a cloying enthusiasm. Maybe chew loudly with her mouth open. Surely, even the most patient prince would falter at the sight.

A grin crossed her lips as she read, "Steer Clear of Obscure Subjects." Oh, this had potential. She could fill their conversations with peculiar, irrelevant topics—migration patterns of Swedish bats or theories on how fish scales influenced the tides. She hardly knew a thing about such subjects, or if they even existed, but she could concoct all sorts of nonsense with the flick of her finger!

But still, was it enough? What she needed was that one big thing—along with these little things—that would skid the prince to a halt and make him shake his head, oh, no. No. No. No. That was what she wanted.

And yes, Sera felt a pinch of guilt when she thought about her parents and breaking such a big engagement, but having almost died today cemented her resolve. After coming face to face with death and witnessing how quickly one's life could be nipped in the bud, she had become all the more determined to live it, to enjoy it, on her own terms.

Her parents would understand. With time.

A loud clatter jolted her from her schemes. Isabella, her twelve-year-old sister, had entered the room, plopping onto the bench by the pianoforte, eyes gleaming with the mischief of a young girl. "You look like death."

"How would you know what it looks like?"

Isabella grimaced. "I just wondered whether you were well. You don't seem like yourself since this morning."

Sera sighed. That's because she nearly came face to face with death today. "So, you are saying I'm looking like death? Thank you, Isabella."

"Perhaps some music will make you feel better?" Isabella flashed her a quick smile before her fingers crashed down on the pianoforte keys, creating a racket throughout the library.

Sera cringed, waving her hand. "Please, I beg you, have mercy on my ears! You're killing me with those notes."

The music mercifully stopped, and Isabella laughed before saying, "You know, Mama and Papa are going to hound you again. Not just because you're sprawled out like a peasant, but because you look positively ghostly."

"Perhaps they'll send me to a nunnery, then." At least it would be better than marrying her off and sending her to a foreign country to live without friends.

Isabella laughed. "If anyone's going to a nunnery, it's me—not that I'll be going. A life without adventures sounds dreadful." Her face twisted into a mock-serious expression. "Mother believes you are meant to be a princess."

Her mother couldn't truly think she wanted to spend her days confined to court in a foreign country. But what her mother thought didn't matter. This was, after all, a business engagement—one her father arranged.

Sera groaned, flopping back against the cushions. "Mother Mary, please save me from this family." Her eyes narrowed at her sister. "Would you like to marry a prince?"

Her sister's eyes widened. "Me? Wait, do you mean the one you're engaged to? No, thank you."

"Why not?"

"Well, for one, he's probably terribly stuck up. Or arrogant! And secondly, not all girls dream of becoming princesses. Some dream of becoming a prince."

Sera snorted. "Only you would think that way."

"So then, do you want to become a princess?" her sister asked.

"No," Sera muttered sourly. "If anything, I'd rather be the rebel."

Isabella's brow furrowed, her voice incredulous. "The rebel?

Sera, they always lose."

Sera's gaze hardened, a fierce glint sparking in her eyes. "That's only because they haven't had me as their rebel yet."

Her sister's laughter filled the room, her small fists thumping against the pianoforte keys in delight. "Mother would faint if she heard you say that! You, a rebel!"

"Yes, well, don't you dare tattle on me."

"Oh, I shall never!" Isabella paused thoughtfully. "You never mentioned anything before. Why not? I'm sure if you spoke to Papa…"

"I have, but he won't listen to anything," Sera muttered. "So, I gave up and pretended this engagement didn't exist. But I can't pretend any longer." She hadn't even told her friends because she didn't want to burden them.

"Then break it off," her sister said simply.

That was her plan and hearing it from her sister as if it were the most logical next step made her heart lurch. Would she truly dare to try and lose the prince this summer? Talk was one thing; action was quite another.

Scandal might erupt, depending on how everything transpired. Her father would be held responsible. Unless he broke it off… then it would be the prince's fault, and she'd be nothing but the poor jilted damsel.

She could live with that.

Sera cocked her head, pointing out to Isabella, "You do realize that it might affect your chances of finding a good match?" Which was the main reason why she hadn't truly acted before this and pretended her engagement didn't exist.

"Top match? Sister, I have no dreams about becoming leg-shackled to any man in any life. So, please, if you are worried about me, don't. In fact, I want nothing more than to help you out of this predicament."

Sera's heart swelled. "Thank you. You are far too wise for your age." And far too curious.

Isabella shrugged. "I think everyone expects us to do certain things, but…" She hesitated, then smiled. "I think it's still our choice, Sera."

How wise. "You're right, Bella. And if I have to turn this whole engagement upside down to claim my choice, then so be it."

Isabella's eyes gleamed with pride. "Now that sounds like something a rebel would say."

NO MATTER HOW grand the hotel bed or how fine the linens fit for a prince, sleep eluded him. The velvet-soft pillows had long been discarded, unable to numb the sharp edge of his unease. Alex turned again, the mattress groaning softly beneath his weight, but the ghost of cold water clung to him. The nightmare always found him, curling in the corners of his mind, regardless of the walls surrounding him.

His hands gripped the silk sheet, damp and tangled at his sides. The muted glow of a dying fire cast restless shadows across the room, flickering like the fragments of his dream. He opened his eyes to the intricately carved ceiling above—a far cry from the ribbed beams of a ship—but it didn't ease the ache in his chest, nor did it stop the echo of Anton's name from slicing through the stillness. Sleep had slipped away from him now, as it so often did after the nightmares…

The deck tilted sharply beneath Alex's feet, the ship wavering as if caught on the edge of the world. The air around him was thick—too thick—like trying to breathe through wet wool. Shapes blurred and sharpened unnaturally, the sails above swollen with a wind that howled like a wounded beast. He couldn't find the admiral or the crew, only endless shouts, their voices warped, the words slipping through his grasp.

The rope whipped around then. Anton grabbed it without him noticing. Too absorbed in his task, the sharp warning shout failed to register with him. One moment, the boy stood there, a goofy grin plastered on his face as his clumsy fingers fumbled with the latch. The next, the great boom swung wide, the crack echoing like a gunshot in the heavy, foggy air. Against his will, Alex was drawn forward; he desperately wanted to look away but couldn't.

Anton's head snapped to the side, his body folding unnaturally before disappearing over the edge of the railing. Alex shouted—his voice raw and broken. Around him, the world shrank. The railings loomed impossibly high, and the mast was tangled with ropes that reached for him, serpentine and sinewy. A flash of blood smeared across the deck, fresh and glistening "Man overboard!" The words echoed endlessly, each syllable stretching into a taunt.

Alex climbed over the rail as the ship groaned beneath him, the sea below shimmering like living silver. Someone grabbed his arm—a faceless shadow that faded into the mist as Alex threw himself into the darkness.

The water engulfed him completely.

It was colder than the frozen ponds at home, a salty and biting emptiness that gnawed at his bones. He kicked furiously, but the currents dragged him deeper. He couldn't discern which way was up— not with the gray sky and the gray sea merging into one another. His limbs felt heavy, burdened by unseen forces.

There. A flash of blond hair in the shadows.

"Anton!" His voice emerged garbled, the water pressing in on him. Alex dove blindly, arms outstretched. He clawed at the void, fingers grazing something soft. A sleeve. A shoulder. No, it slipped away again.

Shapes twisted in the water. Faces emerged from the darkness— Anton's pale eyes wide and staring. Alex kicked harder, faster, his lungs burning. He reached for the vanishing figure as the sea seemed to scream around him.

And then—

Anton was gone.

The weight of failure crushed Alex deeper into a pitiless silence. He surfaced into blinding light, gasping. But he wasn't in the sea anymore; he was in his cabin, tangled in damp sheets, his skin slick with cold sweat. His chest heaved as he blinked the dim room into focus. Moonlight filtered through the narrow window, painting faint patterns along the floor.

The roar of the waves remained in his head, deafening, even though the sea outside the ship was calm. Alex sat up, running a trembling hand through his hair, which clung to his forehead, soaked. His throat ached as if he'd screamed himself raw.

He couldn't shake the weight pressing down on his chest—or the phantom chill of the water. The dream wasn't just a dream; it was Anton. Always Anton.

And he hadn't saved him.

When the valet gently stirred Alex awake, he had already fought to steady his breath and collect himself. It wasn't Anton this time—it was the imprint of her hand, the glimmer of white fabric pulling him back into the dream's clutches just before waking. The cold sweat still clung to him, refusing to ease, even as the morning light filtered in, and he sought refuge in a bath.

But nothing—neither the cleansing water nor the day's bright promise—could banish the heaviness on his chest. Remarkably, she had crept past his defenses, weaving herself into the very seams of his thoughts. And now, she haunted him as potently as any memory of Anton. Once again, Alex found himself adrift, held captive by ghosts he could not outrun.

At three o'clock in the afternoon, his stomach growled, and Alex needed to escape the loneliness of his nightmares. Light danced through the curtains of the dining room windows at the Royal Duchy Hotel as he walked through the double doors into the garden. The salty sea air blew comfortingly across the flowers in the garden, so he'd given the valet instructions for a quiet meal outdoors.

But the image of her face beneath the water haunted him still—those wide, terrified eyes, the way her arms had flailed before they went limp. He could still feel the strain in his shoulders from pulling her through the waves, the icy sting of the water cutting through his flesh like knives.

Almost.

She'd almost lost her life.

His breath caught at the mere possibility of it. No one, not on his watch, would meet such a fate. He clenched his jaw at the thought. It was his duty—no, more than that. It was who he was. To act, to protect, to ensure the cruelty of this world didn't swallow the weak. That was his responsibility, whether on a battlefield, aboard a ship, or even here in the quiet destruction of his mind. For what good was a prince who could not guard even one solitary life?

Alex steadied his breathing, gripping tightly to the ideals that had governed his every decision—principles carved into him by blood, loss, and expectation. He told himself it was this alone that drove him. It had to be. Anything else would unsettle the fragile balance he so carefully upheld. Anything else—no, it could not be.

He strolled to the small, round table draped in pristine white linen awaiting him, set for afternoon tea under the shade of a flowering cherry tree, whose branches fluttered gracefully in the summer breeze. His gaze flicked over the table, the three-tiered cake stand displaying an assortment of delicate sandwiches, scones, and pastries.

Lord, he could just about eat it all.

Alex settled into a wrought-iron chair while the footman, clad in a well-fitted tailcoat, bowed slightly as he served the tea, pouring a rich stream of black tea into his cup, and the aroma of bergamot immediately enveloped his senses. He reached for one of the round puff pastries, which resembled an éclair but was filled with yellow cream. He popped it in his mouth. Hmm, lemony delight. Delicious.

"Sir, we recommend starting from the bottom tier and working your way to the top," the waiter announced with a decorous air, gesturing to the three-tiered stand.

"Are you both the footman and the waiter here?" Alex asked, unsure what to think about the same man being assigned as his footman and valet. It might be an English thing.

"I'm whatever Your Royal Highness requires," the man replied humbly, lifting his chin as if he were immensely pleased with himself. "I'm always at your service."

Alex raised an eyebrow. "I am at ease."

The man inclined his head and left him to his lunch. Alex reached for a cucumber sandwich, its soft bread yielding to the cool, crisp filling on the first bite. Each sandwich was a work of art, cut into dainty triangles and arranged with geometric precision. While he typically preferred heartier fare, he appreciated the craftsmanship and subtle flavor of these miniature creations, despite being able to fit a whole sandwich in his mouth at once, watercress decoration or not. He wolfed down the food while his gaze drifted over the garden.

Peaceful.

Especially when roses were in full bloom, their petals splashing against the hedges in red, pink, and white. Butterflies flitted among the blossoms, and the air buzzed with life—the lively song of robins and the chirping of chaffinches filled the space. It was a scene as if drawn from a painting. Almost too perfect to believe.

And it was indeed too good because Alex knew he was running out of this... whatever it was called: freedom? Time? He wouldn't linger much longer in Cornwall, perhaps just a few days while he confirmed that the lead on his brother was false, then he would return to London to meet his bride.

He swallowed hard, his chest tightening.

He didn't know her.

They may have been betrothed as small children, but how could he be sure she was the one? This silly romantic notion he'd harbored since... since he realized a woman was waiting for him, someone fated for him, kept growing in his mind. But he couldn't stop thinking about the siren he'd rescued from the waves.

Could there be more to fate than a mere transactional match?

He'd always felt it was his duty to liaise with the most powerful tradesman in Europe, who happened to be Marcus Lyndon. However, his own heart seemed to possess a rather romantic nature—a secret he kept hidden from his family lest he be laughed out of court.

Green eyes filled the spaces of his mind.

The girl again.

He wondered what it was about her that refused to leave him.

What was it about her that lingered and haunted him? She wasn't just a girl so much as a woman in his arms, haunting him since this morning. Even when her long brown hair, tangled and damp, framed her face and life had nearly faded from her, she'd been… He couldn't quite put it into words that made sense. She had looked like a vision from one of his mother's old stories, where the prince kissed a princess back to life.

I need to take a stroll.

Get his mind off her. He rose and made his way through the garden, slipping past a hedge of rose bushes onto a secluded path. The lawn soon opened to a meadow beyond the hotel's gardens, sprinkled with summer flowers and clover. He turned toward a tree-shaded area and heard the gentle sound of a little river—a creek, he realized as he approached. But his heart began to race with anticipation as he drew nearer.

No, surely it couldn't…

It was *her*.

He would recognize her profile anywhere. She lay on her back, her chest rising and falling, a book open on her stomach. His gaze drifted to the swell of her breasts before he quickly looked away. He should turn and walk away.

He should let her be.

But his feet were frozen to the ground.

And then, they slowly inched forward.

She seemed lost in thought, unaware of his approach. As he drew closer, he noticed her eyes were closed, a blade of grass held between her lips, swaying gently from side to side. She appeared to be part of this untouched world on a warm day.

Turn around and go.

The blade of grass in her mouth seemed to tickle her nose,

causing her to twitch and blink. Her eyes fluttered open, widening slightly at the sight of him.

Alex bent down instinctively to smile at her, casting a large shadow over her. "Forgive me for startling you," he said softly. The proximity allowed him to catch the subtle scent of wildflowers and sunshine clinging to her.

So beautiful.

Against the blur of green, she stood out with a breathtaking and intelligent gaze that set her apart from any woman he had ever known.

"Ah, my savior."

His smile widened. "I suppose you could say that. My apologies for the intrusion."

A smile played at the corners of her lips as she regarded him with curiosity. "It's quite all right. The view is quite delightful."

You mean me?

He couldn't help but chuckle. *Turn around and leave, Alex. This is nothing but trouble.*

"I'm Sera."

And now trouble had a name.

Sera. A pretty name, too. "I'm—" He paused, thinking whether he should give his full title—Prince Alexander Friedrich Wilhelm Leopold of Hohenzollern-Sigmaringen—but discarded it. In this setting, with this woman, he simply wanted to be himself. "Alex."

❧

Chapter Four

A LEX.
The name suited him well.

And she hadn't lied. The sight of him… Truly reminiscent of a Greek mythology hero! She had thought him handsome before, but seawater didn't do a person any justice. Except in his case, it flattered him even more. Sera propped herself into a sitting position and set the book aside. "It's a pleasure to meet you, Alex."

His gaze fell on the book, and he arched an eyebrow. "*Matters of the Heart*? Interesting reading material."

She closed the book with an audible swish and left her flat hand on it, as if pinning down evidence of a crime. Heat rose to her neck, burning her cheeks, and she dared not meet Alex's gaze. "It's not what you think," she blurted, although his raised eyebrow suggested otherwise. Though, why she felt the need to defend herself baffled her. She wasn't committing a crime, after all. "It's supposed to help me catch the attention of the man I have my sights set on."

"That's exactly what I thought." He gave a lopsided smile that stirred something within Sera, as if swirling her insides around. "And have you such a man?"

"There's a man," Sera admitted slowly, word for word. "My

sights are set on him. But not for the reasons this book might suggest."

She probably shouldn't be so forward with a stranger, but then, she was betrothed to a complete stranger. That logic would deem this—whatever time spent with Alex—harmless. Society would consider this scandalous, while her betrothal to a man she'd never met would be considered ordinary. And the man had rescued her from the ocean! At the very least, he wasn't a total stranger. With those warm eyes of his, he deserved far more than her gratitude.

Her heart, she mused, though it was a notion she wished to bury in the sand like a little crab.

And she could make him less of a stranger.

What did the book say again?

A lady must always conduct herself with the utmost propriety in the company of a gentleman, ensuring her manners are impeccable and her demeanor reserved. Above all, she should never find herself alone with him, for such indiscretion might cast a shadow over her reputation.

Sera bit her lip—she needed to ensure they could be alone.

"Come with me," Sera said, reaching for his hand as he followed her over the slippery rocks in the shallow creek.

"Where are we going?" he asked, grasping her hand with a moment's hesitation.

Feeling the urge to be closer to the refreshing water, Sera slipped off her shoes and stepped onto the smooth rocks in the shallow creek. The cool water lapped at her ankles, bringing an immediate and delightful shiver.

She turned and smiled at Alex, who watched her with an amused yet baffled expression.

"Not joining me? Too attached to those Hessians?"

"I'm joining you," he replied with a grin, but his eyes connected with hers in a way that tugged at her soul. He removed his boots, set them aside, and rolled up the hem of his trousers before following in her footsteps.

He still looked so handsome, she kicked her foot and splashed him with water, disturbing the small fish that swam by.

"Minx," he muttered. "As if getting drenched this morning wasn't misery enough."

Sera's laughter rippled through the air like a melody, infectious and bright. She walked a little ahead of him, her fingers dancing through the tall grasses along the bank. "You'll survive," she teased, nodding toward a patch of swaying white flowers with sunny yellow centers. "Those are oxeye daisies. They thrive this time of year—June to August is their big show." She didn't wait for his reply, already pointing to a cluster of rich blue blooms tucked farther down by the water. "Bluebells. They're usually gone by May, but isn't it delightful to imagine them lingering? Like little rebels refusing to stick to the schedule."

"Rebels, are they?" Alex raised an eyebrow. "I'll try not to trample their cause."

"Better not." Sera grinned, moving toward something new. Giddiness filled her as she gestured toward a stretch of soft pink flowers spilling over the edge of the path. "Cornish Heath," she said with evident affection. "They're famous on the Lizard Peninsula, but look—here they are, playing tourist like the rest of the us."

"Oh, how special," Alex drawled, his tone dripping with enough fake interest to make her scoff.

"You know, for someone following me around gaping at flowers, you lack proper enthusiasm."

He smirked. "I wouldn't say gaping."

"Fine." She tilted her head. "Would it kill you to pretend I'm an excellent tour guide?"

"You've memorized some names. Congratulations." His voice was flat, but the twinkle in his eyes gave him away. "That said, you're passably… diligent."

"Oh, passably? Now I'm intrigued." Heat rose to her face. She shot him a look but couldn't quite suppress her laugh. She wanted to impress him. Really impress him. He had an air about him that seemed to draw her ambitions out.

Kneeling to pick a bright orange-red blossom, her tone softened. "And these," she said, brushing her fingers over delicate scarlet petals, "are common poppies."

Sera suppressed the impulse to slap her hand over her face. Common poppies.

There was so much more to say about their delicate flowers adding a splash of color to the rugged landscape along the cliffs. But when she looked up at him, the bright sun illuminated him from behind, and he cast her such a warm look that even the sun felt cold. Sera forgot what she wanted to say. "The seeds taste wonderful in scones."

"I know poppies. Also, poppy strudel." His voice was lower now, his accent curling warmly around the word. "They grow everywhere in Europe."

Her breath hitched slightly as she glanced at him. His face was angled toward her, but his eyes... they weren't on hers. They were fixed somewhere else—maybe on her mouth?

Sera blinked, suddenly aware of the way the moment stretched between them. Her pulse quickened, a warm flush creeping into her neck. "Then you'll appreciate them as much as I do."

"Oh, I'm appreciating something," Alex murmured, almost to himself.

She turned away quickly, her fingers trembling slightly as they grazed the petals again. She didn't look up this time, not trusting herself to hold his gaze. But she could feel it—his eyes on her, intent and unguarded—making her heart stumble over itself in a way that no flower ever had.

Sera wasn't sure what to make of it. It was as if a thousand butterflies had entered her belly and fluttered about madly.

Their eyes met, and she swore the summer sun bathed his dark eyes in a golden hue, making them sparkle like crystals.

How romantic of you, Sera!

Which was ridiculous, even to her. She considered herself the least romantic person on this planet. Her voice tried to remain steady, but inside, her heart raced each time their hands brushed or their eyes met.

He's a "somewhat" stranger, she reminded herself.

Sera retreated a step, and to her horror, her foot slipped on a moss-covered rock. She gasped, her arms reaching out instinctively for balance. Before she could fall, Alex's strong hands caught her, pulling her close against his chest.

For a moment, time seemed to stand still.

Their eyes locked, and Sera felt all those butterflies fluttering to her lungs. The heat of his hands on her arms sent sparks shooting through her body, igniting something—a sort of thrill, she thought, that she had never felt before.

"Are you all right?" he asked softly, his voice filled with concern.

"Yes," she whispered. "Thank you. You keep saving me from near disasters."

"You seem rather prone to them."

She laughed. "I promise, I'm not usually this way. There must be something in the air this season."

Perhaps it's you.

"Well, whatever it is, I hope it passes by quickly." She rather hoped not, especially if this man was there to catch her each time.

Too bad he wouldn't be.

The loss of him surprised her—mattered more to her than she'd anticipated.

"Are there other, less watery places that are just as pretty?" he asked.

Sera's mind raced over all the options. The market was lovely, but there were too many people. The new library? Too many books. "There's the cherry orchard."

"Orchards? That sounds rather intriguing."

"I'm happy to be your guide. I'm glad I get to share my knowledge."

"You make it sound like you'll never share it again."

Sera shrugged. "You never know what the future might hold." She was unsure where the prince would take her if she failed in her plans. "But for now, I'm here. You're here. We're here."

"I quite like the sentiment."

So do I.

ALEX FOLLOWED SERA through the orchard; the soft murmur of leaves dancing in the breeze filled the warm afternoon air. He had only ever been to local apple orchards with his brother and sister before, so this was refreshingly different from the area around Brașov where he grew up.

This young woman was spirited and sweet—and so pretty.

Yet, she didn't carry her beauty with artifice or flirtation; it simply threaded through her like the warm light of the Cornish sun glinting off the waves. It wasn't long before Alex realized something much deeper shimmered beneath that outer grace. It was the way her eyes sparkled with life when she spoke of a plant or a half-forgotten tale. He found himself watching her more closely than he intended, captivated by how she seemed made of the very landscape they wandered together.

In her presence, every detail of the countryside became vibrant. Talking to her, Alex didn't feel like a prince—he felt much smaller, much more human. Yet, in her world, even that smallness felt significant. There was a wonder in how she saw Cornwall that made him ache to see how she looked at him. She didn't treat him like a prince, didn't lower her voice or glance nervously at him as others might. Her laughter often came at his expense, ringing sharp and clear in the crisp air, but he could never mind that. No one had dared challenge him like this before, and perhaps more surprisingly—he liked it.

"So how is it that you're such a good swimmer?" Sera asked

as they walked together, her eyes focused on the narrow path while her bonnet shielded her from the afternoon sun.

"I worked on a ship for a time," he said, his stride slowing slightly. "We spent long days at sea. Swimming wasn't a choice, really. It meant life or—"

"Death? Like you prevented mine?" Sera turned her head toward him, eyes glowing.

"Not exactly the same, but yes, life or death."

She nodded thoughtfully. "What was it like? Sailing the seas?"

"It was work," Alex murmured. Duty. He could feel the tension curling in his chest, the weight of memory coiled too tightly to release, begging for release. He'd never told anyone before. Not even his family. He paused, before admitting, "One of the men went overboard."

She gasped. "That must have been terrible."

It had been terrible, yes. The only life he'd ever lost while he was in charge. After a pause that felt far too loud, he spoke again, his voice firmer now. "It was my task to pull him out. I couldn't. The sea… was too strong that day. It took him before I could reach him."

"I'm sorry to hear that," Sera said, her voice barely a whisper. "It's not your fault."

Alex glanced sideways, unable to stop himself. It felt rather strange that somehow, for some unexplainable reason, he needed her to know this about him before anything else. A man died on his watch, whether he was to blame or not. "Since that day, I've made a promise that no one dies on my watch. Not if I can prevent it."

Then came her response—soft, tentative, but certain. "What happened to that poor man is horrible, but know that I'm not your responsibility, Alex. Not back at the beach, and not if this tree here decides to fall and flatten me."

The corner of his mouth twitched. She had a way to brighten the mood. "I'll still claim responsibility."

She laughed, her gaze drifting over him. "How heavy must

those shoulders be."

Not so heavy when you are here. "I can manage."

She laughed again. "You're a better man than you give your-self credit for," she said simply, stepping closer. Her voice carried no fanfare, no excessive sweetness. Just honesty. "So, give yourself some more, will you."

He met her gaze, his chest stirring with a sensation he couldn't quite name. "I shall try."

Their elbows brushed, but he didn't shift away. Neither did she. If anything, he allowed the space between them to shrink, and he thought, perhaps, she did the same. He recognized this kind of closeness, having felt it before in many ballrooms when women tilted their heads just so, turning toward him with hardly any concealed expectation. He'd always stepped back—polite but distant. He had never welcomed such attention before.

But here, now, the thought of distance between them unset-tled him in a way he couldn't articulate. He was close—just a day's ride from fulfilling years of obligation and expectation to meet his intended bride. Yet at this moment, with Sera's presence beside him, all those duties felt abstract and far removed. When her hand brushed lightly against his, the touch sent a ripple through him. He didn't stop to think. He turned his palm and took her hand in his, curling his fingers around hers.

Her breath hitched audibly, a small and fleeting sound, but she didn't pull away. Alex felt the faint tremble of her fingers. He glanced at her, catching the faintest flicker in her expression—surprise, hesitation, but something else, too.

Something shared.

They continued walking, her hand resting easily in his now, impossibly natural, as though it had always been there, waiting for him to reach out. How to explain this? How to explain *her*? There was only one answer. He couldn't.

Cherry trees rose around him, their branches stretching to-ward the sky with an abundance of small, luscious cherries dangling just beyond his reach.

"Beautiful, aren't they?" she asked.

He smiled, glancing at her. "I don't recall if I've ever seen anything as beautiful."

She paused beneath one of the trees and turned to him. Her eyes sparkled like the sunlit dew on the grassy path they'd just walked and pointed to a cluster of cherries hanging above her. Alex didn't follow her gaze upward, instead, his gaze settled on the elegant curve of her neck, the way it sloped to her delicate chin. His heart quickened. He imagined the softness of her skin beneath his lips, the exquisite thrill of following a trail of kisses along her collarbone.

"Shall we taste them?" she asked, grinning at him.

Alex blinked away the splendid imagery.

I want to taste you.

"They're not ours to take, are they?" Neither was she.

"Do not worry. I know the owner," she replied.

"Well, if you're going to take liberties with his cherries, best do it properly." He stepped forward to offer his hands as a makeshift step. "Can you reach them if I lift you up a little?"

"I believe so." She didn't hesitate to place her foot into the cradle he created, her fingers settling on his shoulders for balance. "You're certain you can lift me, yes? I'm no feather."

She shouldn't take her shoes off, nor expose her ankles, he wanted to say, but then he was the one that offered to lift her. In any event, he'd done this countless times, lifting his sister, Thea, up in the apple trees in Brașov. "You're no sack of grain either."

"Oh, you have trouble lifting those?" she teased him. "How interesting."

He chuckled. "Would you think less of me if I'd say I never have?"

"I'm more relieved not to be a sack of grain."

Alex laughed. "If you were one, you'd be the most charming one I ever lifted."

"I'm ready," she announced. "You can lift me."

He did so, her skirts rustling against Alex's arms as she

stretched toward a branch. He steadied her, watching as her lips curled with satisfaction. "I can reach it. Wait. Almost—"

He lifted her a little higher. "What about now?"

Before she could answer, her body swayed slightly, throwing her off-balance. In a heartbeat, one arm gripped her waist while the other wrapped around her legs. She let out a small gasp as her palms pressed against his shoulders, steadying herself. Her face was inches from his, and all the nerves in his body sparked to life.

Their eyes met, and the orchard around them faded. He could feel the heat of her body through the fabric of her dress, the faint scent of her perfume weaving with the fresh earth and fruit. The moment was magnetic, a pull so strong he had to clench his jaw to keep from leaning in closer. This didn't feel like just a moment of physical support; it felt like the awakening of something deeper, something fundamental within him.

He cleared his throat, trying to shake the strange feeling that spread inside him. "Quite the unexpected adventure, picking cherries."

Her cheeks flushed. "Quite. Though I think I might need a firmer footing next time."

"Next time?" he teased, the words slipping out before he could catch them. "Planning to climb more trees with me, are you?"

She grinned. "Well, since it's this thrilling, why not?"

He smiled. Here, in the cherry orchard, away from prying eyes, he had to admit he felt free from the constraints of decorum, unburdened by the expectations that usually hovered over his interactions. In this secluded orchard, he was simply Alex, unmasked and genuine, reveling in the uninhibited allure of the moment.

He could savor this rare gift of intimacy that came with no expectations.

"You can set me down now," she said softly.

Oh.

Indeed.

He lowered her to her feet, surprised at his own reluctance. She lifted her hand with a triumphant smile, and he caught sight of the cherry between her fingers. "I got one."

And then, with a wicked little smile, she bit into it, letting the juice spill slightly down her lip.

Alex watched, entirely spellbound, as she slowly wiped the juice away with her thumb. "Quite the victory," he managed, the words coming out in a voice that sounded far too rough. "But what about me?"

Chapter Five

Matters of the Heart, Page 24: A refined lady must always keep her footwear, modestly conceal her ankles, and in the company of a gentleman, show grace and restraint to maintain her noble dignity. Page 89: She must never make the first move.

WHAT ABOUT ME?

How could a girl's heart not race at that question? Her pulse quickened as she watched Alex's eyes darken. There was something breathtaking about how he leaned in, bleeding confidence as if he commanded every situation. This moment, shared beneath the rustling leaves, felt wild and scandalous. She could sense the heat between them, an electric current ignited by the slightest glance, which had only intensified since they entered the orchard.

With each breath, she moved closer, drawn in by the gravitational pull of his scent—smoky vetiver blended with the creamy sweetness of sandalwood. Her future remained uncertain, but in this moment, she decided to throw all caution to the wind.

Let the wind do with it what it will.

She stepped closer, the grass soft beneath her bare feet. She had taken off her shoes somewhere by the creek, though she didn't know where, as she hadn't been able to tear her gaze away from Alex. Perhaps too greedy for cherries—and greedy for something more. Utterly unladylike!

"I don't mind giving you a taste."

She lifted onto her toes, closing the distance between them with a determined tilt of her chin. She leaned in, her lips meeting his in a confident kiss. It was straightforward, even practical, yet something about its simplicity—the way he responded without a hint of hesitation—held its own unexpected thrill.

Sera wrapped her arms around his neck, pressing closer, a shiver skimming down her spine when his hands cradled her waist. Every breath felt electrified, as if nothing could ever be the same after her first kiss.

She was crossing an invisible line.

And she crossed it gladly.

How magical.

She felt herself unraveling. She was no longer the cautious planner; she was a woman embracing the wild, scandalous side she had kept hidden for too long. He kissed like she imagined a prince might in a fairy tale—insistent, confident, yet gentle, with a touch that made her feel as if she were something rare and precious. There was something disarming about Alex. His touch was both foreign and familiar. She felt as if she were floating, each sensation heightened, her world condensing into the pure emotion of their connection.

Sera smiled against his lips. "Just who are you?" she whispered, half teasing, half sincere.

"Just a man," he murmured back.

When she pulled back, she noticed the surprise lingering in his expression. "That was delicious, wasn't it?"

"Exceedingly fresh." His response was low and warm, sending butterflies fluttering in her stomach.

She felt a rush of daring at his words. She stepped back, leaning against the tree, as the kiss had left her surprisingly dizzy. This man… He wasn't just any stranger; he seemed to be a catalyst for something she hadn't realized she craved.

She had always been the responsible one. Her weekends were

filled with to-do lists and careful plans, leaving no room for unexpected encounters. Well, aside from adventures with her friends. Those had a certain spontaneity. But for herself, deciding to lose her prince was about the most reckless thing she had done in years, aside from following birds onto rocks.

Their kiss should have left her feeling a bit lost, but how could she feel completely adrift when, with him, she felt as though she had arrived exactly where she needed to be?

Her gaze traveled over his features.

The way his hair fell across his forehead, the way his eyes were locked on her, and the play of shadows on his strong jaw. Suddenly, she laughed.

"What's the matter?" he asked, his brows raising as if unsure whether to be amused or concerned.

"Have you ever felt like you've known someone your whole life, even if you just met?" she asked, tilting her head to study him.

A flicker of surprise crossed his face, then he gave a slight nod. "Yes," he replied, though his tone lifted at the end, almost like he was asking himself the same thing. "It's strange, isn't it?"

"Not strange," she said, pushing herself off the tree. She brushed her skirts down, all prim and proper—yet given her bare feet and bold actions, she was anything but ladylike. "Perhaps just… inevitable."

"Inevitable?" he repeated, watching her closely like he was trying to decipher some hidden meaning behind her words. "So, what happens now in this inevitable story of ours? Since you are referring to us, aren't you?"

Yes, I am.

She flashed him a teasing grin. "Well, that depends. Can you climb trees?"

"Are you daring me, Miss Sera?" he asked, one brow lifting.

"Think of it as… encouraging you to keep up," she said before she turned back toward the cherry trees, casting him a glance over her shoulder. "Unless you don't want more cherries?"

I certainly do.

ALEX DRUMMED HIS fingers on the edge of the writing desk, his gaze drifting to the boots neatly placed in the center of his room. The valet had been unusually talkative that morning, rambling on about "the pristine boots, now desecrated with sea sand, grass stains, and suspicious smears of dirt that could only have come from rolling around."

It wasn't as if he had actually been rolling around with Sera—well, not in any scandalous way.

Very scandalous, indeed.

But he couldn't help but remember the way she laughed as she offered him cherries, the sparkle in her eye that made everything else fade away. He'd kissed her, and it was all he had thought about since.

The door burst open, and Charles, his ever-present valet at the hotel, stormed in, looking utterly disapproving. He picked up Alex's boots gingerly, as if they were contaminated.

"Your boots, Your Royal Highness," he said in a tone that conveyed the weight of someone delivering bad news.

Alex sighed, steeling himself. "What about them?"

"It's not my place to say, Your Highness," the valet began, which, of course, meant he intended to say quite a lot. "But when one is entrusted with the care of fine leather footwear, one doesn't expect to find them in a state that suggests they've been through a war."

"A war?" Alex raised an eyebrow.

"Apparently sand and seawater, grass, and—" His valet lowered his voice to a scandalized whisper, "—mud, sir."

"It's not mud," Alex replied, half-distracted as he recalled that moment with Sera, her lips soft against his. "It's just a little dirt."

"A bit of dirt, Your Highness?" the valet repeated, looking as though he'd swallowed a lemon. "These are finely crafted boots, made in Florence according to the stamp on the soles. And now…" He shook his head, looking skyward. "They're quite the opposite of what their creator intended them to be."

"He intended them to be worn."

"In style, yes."

"Is it really that bad?" Alex attempted to look sympathetic, but he kept picturing Sera in the orchard, her eyes bright and challenging, her laughter ringing through the trees. His boots, he figured, had been a necessary casualty of that adventure. Plus, he'd done worse to boots during his time in the navy.

His valet, sensing he wasn't being taken seriously, placed the boots on the floor with a thud. "Allow me to be frank, Your Highness. The soles are caked with vegetation. If there were a seed, it could sprout."

Were all British valets this sensitive? "Grass, you mean. That's just a little of it."

"And the heels?" His valet gestured with one gloved hand. "Unholy amounts of mud."

"Are you sure it's mud?" Alex asked, genuinely curious. "It might just be a variant of it." He stifled a chuckle.

His valet's face twisted as if he'd just tasted something particularly sour. "Dirt and mud are related, Your Highness. Both cling to your pristine boots, which I was hired to keep spotless."

Could he unhire the man assigned by the hotel?

"My apologies."

"There's no need to apologize, Your Highness, but I believe it's my duty to inform you that these boots were masterpieces of craftsmanship, designed for royalty, not for… horticultural endeavors."

Alex stifled a chuckle. "Horticultural endeavors? Really, Charles?"

But he quite liked the idea of other "cultural" endeavors with a certain girl from Cornwall. Though, she'd said she was visiting, just like him, hadn't she? He wondered where she was from. Also, the word "contaminants" was so perfectly dramatic that Alex had to suppress rolling his eyes. Wait. "How did you know I was at the cherry orchard?"

The valet showed him the sole of one of his boots, where a crushed cherry had lodged itself. But the sight only reminded him of that spark in Sera's eye, the rush of her breath as she leaned closer, her fingers threading through his hair as if she had known him forever.

This was a problem.

Because he couldn't make this last forever. He was the contaminant in her life, burdened by royal duties, a betrothal to a stranger, and then there was that matter of his honesty. Virtue—not that a man had any, he thought. Yet he had always imagined sharing certain intimacies only with the one who would be his wife.

And Sera couldn't be his wife.

Yes, she was the first girl—ever!—with whom he wanted to share this: himself—physically, emotionally, and if she kissed him like that again, then his soul.

The valet cleared his throat.

"Ah, yes, I stumbled upon the orchard by accident," Alex admitted, though he regretted nothing about that moment in the orchard.

The valet muttered something under his breath. "Might I suggest a more conservative promenade next time, sir? A stroll in town, perhaps?"

"I'll certainly keep that in mind. Though I don't believe the vegetation is the issue."

The valet's eyebrows shot up. "Oh?"

"Let's just say there were… distractions," Alex murmured. A distraction that made him feel like a boy again, forgetting, for just a moment, the family duty drilled into him from birth.

His valet, however, remained firmly planted in irritation, his mind solely on the sacrilege done to Alex's footwear. "Distractions, indeed," he muttered under his breath. "I suppose the young lady in question has little regard for fine leather?"

"Who says it was a young lady?"

"What other distraction could lure a royal into a cherry orchard?"

"Cherries?"

The valet harrumphed at that.

Alex nodded absentmindedly. "Indeed, you're right. And I'm not sure her regard for leather was the foremost thought on either of our minds."

This time, the valet seemed taken aback. "Oh. I see."

"No," Alex said, his tone softening. "I don't think you do. She makes me…" He hesitated, choosing his words carefully. "Forget things. My apologies, Charles."

"I see that, too." At Alex's pointed look, the valet cleared his throat. "Forgive me, sir, but what must a man of your royal station not forget in this specific instance?"

"My responsibilities, my duty," Alex replied, running a hand through his hair. "Forget that there's an engagement planned for me."

"Ah," the valet said with a nod. "One of those arrangements."

"One of those," Alex confirmed. "Since I was a child."

"And yet," the valet said, his voice surprisingly gentle now, "it seems that this young miss is a bit troublesome."

Alex let out a short laugh. "Among other things. She's fearless. Stubborn, likely to a fault. And funny. She makes me feel in a way I've never imagined…" He trailed off, observing the valet's thoughtful expression. "But it's not as simple as that. I have responsibilities I can't ignore, lest they catch up with me."

His valet was quiet for a moment, glancing at the boots, then back at Alex. "Sometimes, your highness, responsibilities and duties aren't necessarily the things that make a life… well-lived."

Alex blinked, surprised by the sudden shift in the man's usually theatrical character. It was almost as if he spoke from experience.

"But I am engaged to someone else."

"An engagement is just words, your highness. A lifetime is something entirely different. It's life. Time."

A lifetime…

Alex sighed, leaning back. "And what am I supposed to do about it? Break it off? Disappoint my family? Risk… well, everything, just for someone I might not have even known if I hadn't come to Cornwall."

"But you did, your highness. Perhaps that is fate."

"Are you speaking from experience then?" Alex pressed.

The valet's expression changed. It wasn't stern and judgmental for the first time but rather vulnerable.

"Yes." Charles avoided meeting his eyes and looked at his hands.

Alex rose and clapped his valet on the back with a grin. "Thank you, Charles. And I promise to stay out of the mud… at least until tomorrow."

His valet gave him a skeptical look, picking up the boots as if they were precious artifacts that needed guarding. "One can only hope, sir."

The valet left with the boots, and Alex stared after him, chuckling to himself. But as the door closed, his laughter faded, and his thoughts turned back to Sera. For just a moment, in the soft light of that orchard—and earlier, on the beach—he'd felt like he could be the man he wanted to be. He'd felt free.

He shook his head, wondering if he'd ever feel that way again. Deep down, he knew that if she was part of his life, he'd be a better man.

A lifetime. Fate.

Hadn't that already been set in ink on paper?

But not in stone.

Chapter Six

The next morning

I WANT TO *see him again.*

Sera wondered where she would wander today to catch a glimpse of the mysterious Alex. There was something exciting about remaining purposefully strangers, yet she wanted to know more. She longed to slowly discover the man beneath the mystery. For that, she needed to escape her parents' discerning eyes.

"What do you think, dear?"

Sera blinked at her mother when the lively chatter that filled the drawing room quieted, and three pairs of eyes turned to her. "About what?"

"Returning to London sooner."

What? No! That would be... horrific! "I want to stay a bit longer," she replied rather abruptly, perhaps even too eagerly, causing her father's brow to furrow.

"Why?" her father asked.

Well... She wanted to kiss a certain someone again.

Perhaps.

But not just once.

Ah! How bothersome one's memory could be! She hadn't planned on kissing him yesterday. But when she looked up, his eyes met hers with such an expression that even she could not explain but that sent shivers down her spine, all thought of propriety vanished. That is to say, propriety had never been there in the first place, but whatever little remained had scattered. And stars, the touch of his lips, confident yet subtly tender, was enough to set her whole world spinning. And the strangest part? For the first time in her life, she felt truly alive, as if her spirit had broken free from the cage of expectation that confined it. The cage that formed the moment she became engaged to a prince.

And it had solidified over the years to the point of restraining her in every way.

The low murmur of her family's voices drifted from the sitting room, but Sera lingered by the window, her fingertips brushing the cool pane. The sea stretched endlessly beyond, wild and unrestrained, so unlike the tidy fate laid out for her. Her stomach tightened at the thought of a prince she'd never met, his name a hollow echo of someone else's decision. Here, in Cornwall, she was herself—barefoot on the sand, salt in her hair. No amount of elegance could quiet the tempest inside her. She craved something real—love, fire, and…

Alex.

She cleared her throat and said to her father, "I wish to enjoy the breezes of Cornwall a bit longer."

Her father arched a brow. He was not fooled, even though he might be indulgent. "A few days won't do any harm, I suppose."

"What about a lifetime?" Sera countered.

"The royal family expects complete loyalty."

"But Papa—"

"I know your reservations, Seraphina," her father interrupted. "But this family cannot break an engagement on your whims. You haven't even met the prince yet. I'm sure he will be to your liking."

Isabella sent her a look before asking, "But what is he like, Papa? Is he handsome? Heroic? Charming?"

"He is a prince."

Sera made a face at that dry answer.

Sera's mother glanced at her with a small smile. "Darling, like your father said, he's a prince. Third son of a distinguished family with ties to the Imperial German Empire, Hungary, and even France. And marrying a prince is a rare and great honor."

"Then why don't you marry him?"

"Seraphina," her father warned. "That's enough."

Sera folded her arms, her brow creasing. "Fine, but has anyone asked me if I even want this honor?" She tried to keep the bitterness out of her voice, but she was certain everyone caught it anyway. "What if I don't want to marry this prince?"

"You deserve the best, dear," her father said.

"I don't want the best. I want what's best for me." Sera crossed her arms.

"I know what's best, and that's a prince." Her father had that tone he used when business was at stake. It was always about business, wasn't it? Not about what she wanted or matters of the heart. Even the book only served to foster lucrative liaisons, not the passionate and sincere ones like… Alex's warm gaze came to mind again, and Sera broke into goosebumps.

Her mother paled. "Sera, you know you can't simply break an engagement to a prince! Not even if we tried."

"Why not?" she challenged, not only feigning innocence but also mocking. "If these shipping routes are so important, why doesn't Papa marry one of the ships to him? Why me?"

Her mother gasped, clasping a hand over her heart as if struck. "Sera! That is an outrageous suggestion! What has gotten into you? You have never voiced any protests before."

Not like this, no. She had been able to pretend that something might happen on the royal family's side that would cut the engagement. After all, it was not a fairy tale. Princes didn't marry commoners no matter how rich their fathers were. She could practically feel the imbalance of power just with this betrothal. She didn't want to imagine how many times that would increase once she married the man.

She'd have no say in this union.

The weight of it pressed down like an undertow, pulling her farther from the shore of her life with every thought of the man she'd never met. No matter how fiercely she struggled, the waves would drown her voice, leaving her adrift and silent in a sea not of her choosing. Just like those waves sucking her to the bottom of the ocean.

If it hadn't been for Alex…

But there would be no Alex once she married. There would be no one to save her. She could only save herself.

Her father, clearly not in the least bit amused, cleared his throat. "I understand you feel a certain amount of reluctance. But your duty to this family is not to be trifled with. It is admiral, even."

Admiral her derriere!

"Oh, duty, yes," Sera mused, a faint smile teasing the corners of her lips. "How 'duty' so marvelously aligns with what benefits *you*, Papa. At the cost of my life and happiness?"

"Sera!" Her mother looked positively scandalized, and Isabella stifled a laugh.

"You don't know that the prince and his castle won't make you happy." Her father, on the other hand, appeared unperturbed. "What benefits me, benefits the family."

And lock me away as an accessory to some prince's life. I'd have to leave everything I love behind.

What an unpleasant truth—that her life was not her own to shape. That she was merely a gambling chip, moved strategically to secure alliances and wealth, her happiness an afterthought. It stung, bitterly so. And yet, it wasn't entirely unexpected. And it was a truth she might have accepted unquestioningly had she not nearly lost her life in the ocean.

However, her engagement to the prince loomed over her like a storm cloud. She couldn't simply break it. The repercussions for her family would be immense, the shame to her mother and father unbearable. But the prince could. And that, at least, gave her hope.

She had tasted the sharp edge of mortality and realized she didn't want to spend her life merely *accepting* and *settling*.

She wanted more.

On that much she was clear.

So, she would just have to make sure the prince broke their engagement.

She would have to give it her all.

"Of course, Papa," Sera murmured, deciding to let it go. Her father would never give in, so it was no use in arguing over the matter. "How irresponsible of me to forget."

Isabella winked at Sera. "We are all allowed one or two irresponsible moments."

Her mother scowled. "Not you, too, Isabella!" She puffed out a breath. "If you're going to be irresponsible, please keep it to Cornwall. In London, I expect you both to be on your best behavior."

Sera almost laughed.

She could do that... She could keep her irresponsible actions to Cornwall. In fact, that suited her quite well. And Alex... He might just be the very key for her to accomplish her goals.

And set her heart free.

ALEX PULLED THE brim of his hat lower over his eyes. He wore the plainest of his clothes—simple black trousers, a white shirt, and a black coat—not wanting to stand out as he strolled through the streets of Cornwall.

He had a mission—one that had proven frustratingly elusive.

He had checked the lake, circled the orchard, and even waited at the beach despite the chilly breeze. Not a single glimpse of her. The "her" in question, of course, was the enchanting water nymph who had stolen his senses—and his reason—back in the orchard.

Sera.

It was silly, really.

A single kiss had turned his Cornwall visit upside down. A kiss that still haunted him with its simplicity and its promise of more. A kiss he should forget, given his obligations. Yet here he was, wandering aimlessly through a bustling market in search of her, as if she might be strolling down the street with cherries in her hand and a smile on her lips.

There was something remarkable about how she moved through the world—entirely unencumbered by titles or formality. He had watched her stop to chat with a shepherd, her hands brushing over a lamb's wool as if it were the softest silk. She crouched beside a group of children to show them the proper way to whistle through a blade of grass. There was grace in her gestures, but no haughtiness—just ease. It was humbling to see a woman who carried herself with both warmth and dignity.

Alex hadn't known anyone quite like her.

And he couldn't wait to find her again.

He kept his head down, scanning the crowd beneath the brim of his hat. His gaze flitted from one woman to another. He couldn't quite say what had drawn him here, since he didn't believe this was the sort of place Sera would come to willingly, which was why he called her a water nymph.

There was no large or small body of water in town besides the Thames, and that was dirty—not at all a place for nymphs.

He paused by a stall selling ribbons and lace, his fingers brushing over a length of green silk that reminded him of Sera's eyes. The stall keeper, a portly man with a thick mustache, perked up immediately.

"A fine choice, sir!" the man said. "Perfect for a lady's bonnet."

Alex cleared his throat, taking a step back. "I'm just browsing." He had no business buying ribbons for ladies. And come to think of it, he had only once seen Sera wearing a bonnet before. Granted, he'd only ever met her twice.

The man's eager smile never faltered. "Of course, sir."

The back of his neck prickled. As if... Alex's brows furrowed. As if someone were watching him.

His gaze swept over the crowd.

Nothing.

Moving on, Alex found himself drawn to a small bookshop nestled between a bakery and a tobacco shop. He probably won't find Sera today. What a pity. The bell above the door jingled softly as he entered, and the scent of aged paper welcomed him. Shelves crammed with volumes of various sizes lined the walls, and a young woman sat behind the counter, engrossed in a novel.

Alex drifted through the rows, his fingers grazing the spines of books without truly seeing them, his mind elsewhere. A book caught his eye: *Mythes et Contes de L'Eau*. He pulled it from the shelf, smirking at the irony. *Myths and Tales of Water*. How fitting. Was she his water nymph, luring him into the depths with no hope of escape?

"An unusual choice," came a voice from behind him.

Alex turned to find the woman behind the counter had set her novel down, eyeing his selection with curiosity. "It reminds me of someone."

"Water?" she explained, glancing at him with a knowing smile. "Well, if she's from Cornwall, I wouldn't find that surprising."

He hesitated. "Who says there's a 'she'?"

The woman shrugged. "Your face."

Alex grunted.

The shopkeeper tilted her head, studying him as though trying to discern something. "Well, if you're looking for enchantment, Cornwall is full of it. The cliffs, the sea, even the market square—there's magic everywhere if you know where to look."

Green eyes swam to the surface of his mind.

Yes, he might have already found a bit of it. "And orchards," he murmured.

"Orchards?" The woman scrunched her brows. "I believe the ones around here are private property, all owned by a wealthy merchant. I'd steer clear of them."

"I see." Alex placed the book back on the shelf. Could the orchard be a clue to Sera's identity? "I'll keep that in mind."

As he exited the shop, the woman's words burned into his bones.

There's magic everywhere if you know where to look.

Magic…

The rational part of his mind urged him to return to the hotel, to abandon this foolish quest. He had obligations, a future carefully mapped out long before he'd met her. A future that didn't include stolen kisses in orchards or an impulsive search through an English town. Like a fool. Yet he couldn't shake the hope that he might turn a corner and find her there, smiling at him as if she'd been waiting all along.

A flash of dark hair caught his attention. His heart leapt, but the woman turned, and it wasn't Sera. He sighed. This was madness. He couldn't spend the entire day chasing shadows. He clearly didn't even know where she lived.

Alex admitted to himself that he knew nothing about her—but he knew himself well enough to want all of her.

A hand suddenly snatched his wrist.

Alex turned, his eyes locking with hauntingly familiar green ones.

Sera.

Finally.

"I've been—"

"Come," she interrupted him, pulling him down into an alleyway.

Alex didn't resist. After all, this was the little bit of magic he had been looking for all morning.

Chapter Seven

S ERA PRESSED HER back against the rough stone wall of the alley, still clutching Alex's wrist tightly, peeking around the corner to ensure her mother's bonnet had disappeared into the swarm of people buzzing about. Her heart raced—not with fear, but with exhilaration. Isabella had done an excellent job of distracting their mother at the fabric stall, giving her just enough time to slip away.

She grinned at Alex.

She hadn't expected to run into him here. She'd all but lost hope when her mother dragged her and Isabella into town. "What smashing luck."

He leaned his head close to hers. "Who are we hiding from?"

"My mother." When his eyes widened, she added, "And my sister. Do not worry about her. However, we should leave before they see us."

"I am at your command." And there was a mischievous glint in his eyes, a boyish lop-sided smile when his eyes locked with hers for an instant and then fell to her mouth.

She laughed, letting go of him but his fingers interlaced with hers. "Follow me, then." She led him down a series of streets, grinning when a large, rusty sign came into view.

"Where are we going?" he asked, stepping up beside her. "A

forest? A cornfield, perhaps?"

"A hole."

"A hole?" he asked skeptically.

She yanked the bonnet from her head and grinned at him. "Have you ever tasted a Cornish shrub before?"

He arched his brow. "I can't say I have. Wait, don't tell me the hole is a—"

"Tavern, yes. I am in the mood for a bit of adventure, aren't you?" And the *Piping Hot Pot* was the perfect place to find it.

"Well, there's a first for everything."

A little mischievous, Sera asked, "You've never had *shrub* before?"

"I've never been in," he eyed the tavern door from top to bottom, "such an establishment before."

Who has never been to a tavern before? He must be from a terribly rural place then.

"Well, there's a first for everything. I'm honored to introduce you to this new experience." She grabbed his hand again and pulled him into the tavern, the welcoming scent of roasted meat and fruity shrub hitting her all at once.

She inhaled deeply. "I love this smell. What do you think?"

"Not bad," the man beside her replied.

She pointed to a table against the far wall. "Let's sit there."

"Is that your usual spot?"

She laughed at his sarcasm. "Yes, fortunately, there aren't many people here at this time of day."

"So, you come here often? Aren't you afraid you'll be recognized?"

Sera shook her head. "What regular? I come here often in different disguises. Plus, I know the owner. They're quite fond of me."

"That seems to be a trend with you."

"Well, I'm highly fashionable when it comes to my connections."

He chuckled, holding the chair for her to take a seat. "How

gentlemanly of you, sir."

"What else am I to be?"

"A rogue in a tavern?" Sera offered, smiling as he slid into the seat across from her.

"You know, that doesn't sound too bad."

A serving girl promptly placed two tankards of shrub before them. Sera laughed when Alex's eyes widened. "They only serve one type of shrub. And their service is unparalleled."

The familiar scent of rich, earthy aromas, characteristic of ripe apples, mingled with a slightly yeasty or musty undertone from the natural fermentation of the added vinegar. Quintessential late summer aromas. Oh, how she loved this.

His eyes held hers, steady and unguarded, as though she were the only person in the world who mattered. Her chest ached with something warm, something terrifying, as if he'd reached inside and touched the rawest part of her. The way he looked at her—no judgment, no expectation—made her feel seen in a way that left her breathless. She hadn't known being with a man could feel like this, like stumbling off a cliff and choosing not to stop the fall. He was the wave carrying her heart, and she didn't mind drowning in the feeling.

"What exactly are we drinking here?" Alex asked, turning the glass without bringing it to his lips.

"Shrub. Apple shrub, specifically."

Seeing his confusion, she clarified: "The recipe calls for equal parts ground apples—even the damaged or spoiled ones are suitable. Then you add the same amount of sugar and the same amount of vinegar."

"You want me to drink vinegar with sugar?" Alex grimaced.

"Try it. It becomes a lovely apple syrup. Bubbly."

"Is apple even a word in English?"

Sera nodded but choked on her words. His gaze was so intense, innocent yet intelligent, that she got flustered. He hesitated but then brought the glass to his mouth, smelled the concoction, shut his eyes, and downed about a third of the glass.

Sera laughed out loud.

Where was he from if he didn't know taverns yet drank the shrub just to impress her? She leaned back, her laughter still hovering in the air like the last kiss of summer warmth. And yet it was the heat he brought to her heart that lingered.

Alex's earnest expression—those storm-dark eyes searching for why she found his words so hilarious—made her heart stumble in its rhythm. He was utterly unlike anyone she'd known.

There was a quiet honesty with him, a kind of guileless charm that made her want to share everything she loved, every secret joy, just to see how he'd react. The way he held the glass of tart shrub, laughably tentative but willing, as if the entire point of the drink was to please her—it was ridiculous, adorable, and wildly disarming all at once. It felt as though he was peeling back layers of her defenses without even trying.

Falling for Alex wasn't like the stories her friends whispered in drawing rooms—no single, dramatic moment when the world tilted on its axis. It was softer than that, subtler. It was the warmth in how he said her name, the attentive tilt of his head when she spoke about Cornwall, the way he seemed to be seeing something in her, which others had never dared to look for.

I am falling in love with you.

Sera's breath caught, her cheeks growing hot. She realized with a certainty that terrified her—it wasn't just that he made her happy. She wanted to make him happy, too. She gazed at him, and the three words she couldn't yet speak tangled warmly in her throat, as inevitable as the tide pulling toward shore. She was overwhelmed by her pull to him. And there wasn't a single thing she could do to stop it. "You love Cornwall, don't you?"

"Of course, it's my favorite place in England, though I cannot quite put a finger on why. I just enjoy it so much here."

"Have you ever longed to travel?"

Sera took a sip of shrub. "Do you mean abroad?"

He nodded. She shrugged.

"Not really. There are still so many diamonds to find here at home."

He chuckled. "That's true."

"What about you? What brings you to our shores? Wait, let me guess…" She studied the man. "You're on a grand tour of the world."

"Not this time."

So, he was neither without means nor lacking in worldly understanding.

"Oh?" she said, leaning forward with a mischievous grin. "You're here to buy our incomparable thoroughbreds?"

A hint of a smile curved his lips. "Hardly."

She tilted her head. "You're smuggling contraband?"

"Do I look like a smuggler to you?" he shot back.

She laughed. "Not really, but then, how would I know what smugglers look like?"

"I'm glad that you don't know." He paused thoughtfully.

"Good, right?" He nodded slowly.

"Very." He took another, larger sip.

"Do you really want to know why I'm here?"

"No. I'm enjoying your mystery."

He froze, shrub in hand, before narrowing his gaze on her. "You're impossible, you know that?"

"Thank you," Sera said sweetly, unable to stop her lips from stretching into a wide grin. "I do try." She eyed him. "I still can't believe it's your first time in a tavern."

"And I still can't believe you're a regular."

"What else is an English lass to do?" she teased.

"Your customs are certainly different from ours."

"Not much. I'm just more adventurous than most."

"You mean mischievous."

"That, too." She lifted her glass to him. "To freedom, spontaneity, and breaking all the rules."

He chuckled, shaking his head as he clinked his glass against hers. "And more."

"And more," Sera echoed.

"Whatever more may be." And could she have it with this man?

"Well, well, well," a man suddenly said, stumbling to their table. "What do we have here?"

ALEX CURSED WHEN someone crashed into their table a moment later. The impact nearly toppled their tankards. He caught his just in time to prevent it from spilling, but Sera wasn't so lucky. Her glass shattered on the floor, and she jumped up to avoid most of the mess.

The entire tavern fell silent.

The man laughed but showed no foresight to apologize. He cast a glance at Sera and leaned in close, slurring, "Well, hello, little bird. Aren't you a pretty thing? How 'bout you come 'ere and warm me up?"

She grinned back at him. "Hello." Then she stepped forward and kneed him where no man wants to be kneed. The man fell to the ground, clutching his groin. "Now goodbye."

Alex stared at Sera in shock, the woman he both admired and, maddeningly, could not have. She hadn't even touched him, but he felt the pain, too. He'd never witnessed such a scene. The dim light of the tavern illuminated her, making her appear like an avenging angel sent to punish the gutters of an inferno. Yet, she also seemed completely at ease.

The man let out a loud curse and stumbled to his feet again, pointing a finger at Sera. "You... You..."

"I, what?" Sera shot back.

Alex lurched from his seat to block the man as he lunged toward Sera. "Watch yourself, sir."

"She...!"

"I know," Alex said. "And if you don't want to lose it entirely,

I'd step aside if I were you."

"You dare threaten me? Do you know who I am?"

"Of course I don't," Alex replied, bored. "But if I had to wager a guess, I'd say you're rubbish."

"Bastard!" The man swung his fist toward Alex, who sidestepped. What he didn't expect was the man's first opponent's fist, which hit him square in the jaw, sending him into the wall and then to the ground.

"Alex!"

But he couldn't appease her. Not when facing two tipsy thugs. He jumped to his feet, and from the corner of his eye, he noticed Sera walking over to the wall. He blew a lock of hair from his eye, narrowing his gaze on the two men, assuming a fighting stance.

Before he could make his move, a sharp glint caught his eye, and Alex's jaw nearly dropped. Sera stood there, sword in hand, expertly aimed at the two men. "Leave, or die today, gentlemen."

"Madam, enough," the barman's voice cut through the silence, his calm footsteps approaching as if it were a mere afternoon tea. He caught the two men by their collars and yanked them away. "I'll handle them. Fresh shrub is on the way."

Sera lowered the sword. "Much obliged."

Alex dusted off his pants as she returned the sword to the wall. Had he entered some sort of dream? Their table was quickly cleaned, the shrub replaced, and the light chatter of the tavern resumed. "Shouldn't they hang that thing somewhere safer?"

"The sword? Oh, that thing can't slice through a fresh loaf of bread, but it can hit rather hard."

Alex suddenly laughed. "You bluffed?"

"They were too drunk to think, so of course."

"I could have handled them."

"But you don't need to," she quipped easily.

He didn't need to… What oddly comforting words. "Just who are you, Sera?"

She laughed, picking up her fresh glass of shrub and taking a generous sip. "Wouldn't you like to know?"

"I would."

"But I'm enjoying being just a girl."

"Just a girl?" Alex shook his head, fingers circling his tankard. "There's nothing just about you. You're taking me completely and unfairly off guard."

"No." She grinned at him. "There's nothing just when it comes to me."

Draci. This woman. "So, is there a husband in your near future?"

She cocked her head. "More like a pesky suitor who's been attached to me since birth."

"That sounds rather… interesting."

"Well, this is England, isn't it? Our parents decide our lives for us here."

He took another swig of shrub. "Isn't it like that everywhere?"

"You, too?"

Alex sighed. "It's the world we live in."

She nodded thoughtfully. "The world we live in… I'd very much like to change that world."

"Change? I suppose one could try to advocate for change."

"Ah, there's that word. Try. Trying means a chance of failure."

"Failure is part of life. Failure is… a companion to success."

"I suppose. However, when it comes to matrimony, failure is not an option. There's only one chance to change your future. The moment you say I do, no matter who arranged it, you're stuck for life." Her eyes met his. "How would that be for a world where we don't have to be stuck for life?"

"That would be quite the world." He certainly wouldn't mind living in that world.

"You know what, Alex?"

Alex eyed her with skepticism. "We should aim for such a world. And we should try, no, we should succeed in taking our life back into our own hands. For me, it's ridding myself of that pesky suitor promise."

"If you need my help, I'm all ears."

"*Your* help?"

"I'm a man. I can be your best aid to rid yourself of this pesky suitor of yours."

"Will you give me advice, or…" Her smile suddenly blinded him. "Kiss me."

Chapter Eight

S ERA STEPPED OUT of the tavern, with Alex following closely behind. Was the man worried she might be accosted? He practically loomed over her! Sera's cheeks tingled from the heat, though she wasn't sure if it came from the shrub or Alex's chest nearly brushing her back. Either way, her head was buzzing, influenced by either the alcohol or his protectiveness. Or both. It was flattering beyond measure.

She didn't want to leave him just yet.

She wanted to stay by his side a bit longer.

"That was quite the adventure," Alex said, finally stepping up beside her, but now leaving her back a bit chilly. His tone was light, yet there was a smile in his voice that made her pulse skip.

This man…

Just who was he? Why did she feel like she'd rather not know? She needed to jot down a few lines on how effectively mysterious he was! If women could master this as a skill, the only spinsters that would exist would be women like her sister—who didn't want to marry. Ever.

"No need to thank me." She smiled at him. "After all, you were the one who fell and ended up all dusty."

He waved her comment aside. "It's nothing."

Nothing? It was just a little push and a fall. It wasn't much, but it could have been! Sera stopped abruptly, forcing him to halt as well. She glanced at Alex, and for a moment, she simply looked at him. He was so tall, and his features were exceptional. Striking. Even a bit rumpled, he looked entirely out of place in this modest little street. Yet here he was, letting her lead him wherever she pleased. Keeping her safe.

He'd been this way since she met him on the beach.

It made her want to lead him to an even humbler place.

Sera didn't think. She merely grabbed his hand, her fingers curling around his and tugged him into a smaller side alley. An abandoned cart leaned against the wall, its wood splintered and its wheels crooked.

Perfect.

"What are you doing now?" he asked softly, uncertainty evident, but allowing her to lead.

She turned to face him. Her heart pounded as she took a step closer, the air between them charged with something she didn't want to name. Not yet. Not now. "Don't ask questions. But you should be very concerned."

"Then…" He suddenly chuckled. "What if I'm not?"

"Nothing." She stepped up to him, her front nearly brushing against his. She reached up to adjust his hat. "You just stand there."

"And?" His voice dropped. "I'm standing here, still."

Still.

Everything inside her came to a halt at that one small word.

Still.

Frozen.

Sera kept the thought of the prince—her fiancé—at the very edge of her mind, as if ignoring it might make it less real. Whenever her guard slipped and the reality of him crept in, it froze her. She couldn't return to the life she once had, not now. But moving forward felt impossible, too. There was only this in-between space, this endless pause where nothing belonged to her—not her choices, not her future.

Even the idea of their "royal destiny," as her parents had called it, made her teeth clench. What destiny? What future? Royal nonsense was more like it. A suffocating, glittering trap dressed up as something worth having. And the worst part was that it wasn't just fear holding her in place—it was him. Always him. Always this looming presence she hadn't asked for but couldn't seem to escape.

She didn't want to marry the Hohenzollern-Sigmaringen prince. She couldn't even pronounce his name!

"Sera?"

She looked up at Alex. "Promise me." She inhaled deeply and exhaled softly. "Promise me you won't change from the person you are right now. Promise me."

"Ehm…" She gave a hysterical laugh. "Please don't."

"So many words." His gaze dropped to her lips. "Why did you drag me here?"

She placed her hands on his chest, her fingers twitching at the steady beat of his heart beneath her palms.

"To say goodbye."

His head lowered slightly. "Must we…"

Sera nodded, tilting her head up to meet his eyes. "Unfortunately, as it stands, if I don't go home, my mother will send out the cavalry. So, let's part here."

And then she kissed him.

It wasn't any sort of hesitant kiss. Nor was it a shy one, despite her limited experience. It was bold, unrestrained, and completely Sera. She poured all her confusion, her frustration, and her reckless dreams into it, hoping to find some clarity in the chaos. If that were even possible.

Perhaps not.

But she could savor this kiss.

His lips were perfect against hers, and for a heartbeat, he didn't move. Neither did she. Then, as if the ocean roared, he kissed her back.

Yes.

His hand cupped her face, and she felt herself pressed against him, the solid strength of his body sending all sorts of alarming sparks through her. This wasn't new this time, but it felt stronger. More alive. More intoxicating.

He slowly pulled away, resting his forehead against hers, his hands still framing her face. "Sera," he murmured, his voice rough, "what are you doing to me?"

"I could ask the same of you."

He groaned. "You're impossible."

"And yet here you are, following me into an alley," she teased. "Pray tell, why is that?"

"You know why."

Sera's smile faltered, his words stealing the breath from her lungs. She did know. She'd felt it since they met. In every glance, every word, every stolen moment between them. But knowing didn't make it any less terrifying.

"This can't be real," she said softly, more to herself than to him. "It's too… complicated." And thrilling all at the same time, even with the shadow of her engagement looming over her.

He brushed his thumb over her cheek. "That doesn't make this any less real."

"Also, not less complicated. However, for once in my life, I want to stop thinking about what I should do and think about what I want to do."

"And what is that?"

She grinned at him.

Without another word, she pulled him down into another kiss. This one more urgent than before. His arms wrapped around her, pulling her up against him, as though a storm had erupted inside him.

ALEX DIDN'T KNOW what had possessed him. His back pressed

against the rough stone wall, but he didn't care. His attention was consumed entirely by the woman in his arms. She was close, so close. Her scent—like cherry blossoms and sea breeze—clouding every single judgment that cautioned him against going further.

He couldn't think when she was this close.

This wasn't just passion. It was a storm of emotions he'd worked hard to control, to perfect over the years. He'd built the right number of walls, set rules for himself as a prince—and yet, here he was, breaking every one of them with her.

What's one more?

His hand slid to the curve of her waist, pulling her closer until there was no space left between them. The heat of her body seeped into his, making him itch to burrow himself in her completely. He'd never had this impulse before in all the years of his life. And it wasn't just pure attraction. He could tell. He could *feel* it. It was more, something he didn't want to name because naming it would make it dangerous.

He broke the kiss, gasping for air, for control, for anything that would make sense of his pounding heart. "Sera." A mutter. A plea.

She smiled. "Alex."

He opened his mouth to speak, but words failed him. What could he say? That this was madness? That he had an engagement, a duty, a life planned out that didn't include her—couldn't include her? No, he couldn't do that. Instead, he kissed her again, harder this time, as if he could lose himself in her and forget everything else.

Her hands slid up to his neck, her fingers tangling in his hair. It was utterly unladylike and completely intoxicating. But then, everything she did was unladylike and intoxicating and he couldn't get enough of her. He'd never imagined a woman could be so bold, so free in her actions. And he never thought he'd crave it as much as he did.

She tilted her head, giving him better access, and his lips moved from hers to her jaw, then lower, tracing a line down her neck. His lips found the soft skin at the curve of her neck, and he kissed it, gently at first, then with more insistence. He sucked lightly, unable to stop himself. He wanted, no, needed to taste her.

Her breath hitched, and he felt her fingers tighten in his hair. That small sound brought forth a dark, possessive part of him that he never imagined existed.

"This…" she said, barely more than a gasp.

Some distant, rational part of his mind screamed at him to stop. This wasn't fair to her. It wasn't fair to anyone. But the rest of him—the part that was hopelessly lost to her—didn't care. He didn't want to stop. Not now. Not ever.

But he had to.

Alex pulled back; there was a faint mark on her neck. He stared at it, his chest tightening with a mix of pride and guilt. What the devil was he doing?

Sera's fingers brushed the spot, her lips curving into a small, breathless smile. "Are you hungry? Should we have bought a meal in the tavern?"

"Sera, I—"

She placed a finger on his lips, silencing him. "Don't ruin it," she said softly.

Alex sighed. How could one woman defeat him so effortlessly every time?

She stepped back, putting some distance between them, and he instantly felt the loss. She adjusted her dress, smoothing it down, and then looked up at him with a playful glint in her eyes. "Be honest. My mother won't be able to tell we kissed, right?"

Alex blinked at her. What? "I cannot believe you just asked me that."

"Why?"

"I don't know. It just feels wrong in so many ways."

She laughed. "Let's part ways here. I'm afraid if I stay away any longer, I'll court death by a reticule."

"Wait," Alex said as she began to leave. "When will I see you again?"

She grinned at him. "Are we not leaving it up to fate once more?"

"I don't want to leave it up to that fickle thing."

She laughed. "When do you want to see me again? And let's not do it in public again. Too many eyes and ears."

He hesitated. He shouldn't. He knew he shouldn't. But the thought of not seeing her again because he left it up to fate was unthinkable. Almost unbearable. "The beach. Tomorrow. At dawn."

"Very well." She turned to leave, but not before glancing back over her shoulder. "I shall meet you on the beach at dawn." And then she was gone, leaving him behind with brisk steps. Alex stood there for a long moment, staring off into space. He touched his lips, still alive from the kiss, and let out a deep breath.

What in the world was he doing? He had an engagement, a duty to his family, a life that had been planned for as long as he could remember. Yet, no matter how often he repeated this thought, these practiced lines, he still couldn't shake her off.

Sera had entered his world like a whirlwind, throwing everything into chaos. She made him experience feelings he hadn't thought possible—feelings he hadn't wanted to face. How was he supposed to carry on with a marriage he never asked for after feeling such desire for another woman?

This was their second kiss, but it was so much more.

It represented a line crossed, a boundary shattered. And he had no idea how to put it back together. Alex dragged a hand across his face and adjusted his coat. He needed to clear his head. Perhaps a long walk would help, though he doubted it. Sera was in his thoughts, in his blood, and he wasn't sure he'd ever be able to shake her.

And the truth was, he wasn't certain he wanted to.

Chapter Nine

"HOW COULD YOU slip away like that?"

Sera flinched at her mother's demand, her sharp voice cutting through the carriage as they made their way home. She adjusted the folds of her gown, smoothing the muslin over her lap, and braced herself for the impending scolding.

Isabella, seated beside her, offered no support, only sending her a smile that seemed to shout, "This is what you get for slipping away."

"Do you have no concern for your safety?" her mother insisted.

Sera sighed. "Mama, this is Cornwall. What should I be afraid of?"

Her expression could have shaken the heavens. "Don't give me that! No matter where you are, a woman alone and without a chaperone is in danger! If you are not physically harmed, what about your reputation? Besides, you've been acting strangely lately."

Sera straightened in her seat, her fingers smoothing the folds of her gown. "I simply needed a moment to myself," she said, her voice calm but brittle. "Shopping for things I'll never choose, for a life I didn't ask for, is hardly entertainment, Mother."

Her mother's gloved hand landed sharply against her lap.

"And what exactly do you think your life would be if it weren't for our sacrifices? You're destined for dignity and comfort—you'll be a princess, Sera." Though her tone was laced with frustration, there was something more beneath it: a crack of doubt, quickly hidden. "Do you even realize how fortunate you are to escape the marriage mart? To not be paraded around Almack's as a commodity like so many other girls?"

"Fortunate," Sera echoed, her lips pressed together as she stared out the window. The crowded streets outside blurred together. "And what exactly am I fortunate to gain? A title? A man I've never even met? Do you know anything about him except for the glitter of his crown?" She paused, then turned to meet her mother's gaze, her voice steady even as her chest tightened with each word. "Do you even know if he's kind? If he cares? Or is that too much to ask?"

"Naïve, as always," her mother replied, her tone heavy with reproach. "Men and kindness rarely coexist, darling. Don't judge others based on your father. Marriage isn't about love or dreams—it's about permanence. Stability. Do you understand what safety that brings?"

Sera felt her sister Isabella's gaze shift to her, a flicker of discomfort crossing her face. But Isabella said nothing, the usual amusement she found in these exchanges absent.

"You speak of safety as if it's a gift wrapped with a bow," Sera said, her voice softening. "But safety isn't chains. It isn't a gilded box I'm shoved into because it's easier for everyone else. You expect me to be grateful and not question any of it, but how can I feel grateful when every choice is made for me? When I don't even have the right to say 'no'?"

"This is supposed to be better than Almack's, not worse." Isabella's laughter briefly broke the tension, light yet uneasy. "Always so dramatic, Sera," she teased, though it lacked her usual warmth and sharpness.

"Don't encourage her, Isabella!" her mother snapped, visibly rattled as she turned back to Sera. "And we will not burden your father with these tantrums. Do you think we did this lightly? That we didn't think of your future?"

Sera's jaw tightened, her voice dangerously even as she pulled her hand free from her mother's pointed grasp. "You thought about my future only in the way it benefits the family. You didn't ask what I wanted. You never bothered to ask."

"It will benefit you. Then your sister. And it gives us all stability. Is that such a bad thing?" Her mother's expression faltered, if only for a second, but she quickly recovered. "And what would you have us ask, Sera? What fairy tale would you like to live in? This is real life. You have responsibilities, just as we all do. And every family member has to contribute in their capacity."

Sera leaned back, her head resting against the cushioned seat. She had no strength left to argue, to press against walls that would never move. "I don't want a fairy tale, Mother. I only want the chance to choose. Is that too much to ask?"

For a moment, silence filled the carriage, tension pressing harder against the fragile truce between them. Isabella shifted uncomfortably, glancing between their mother and Sera, seemingly unsure where her loyalties should lie. Her mother sat stiffly, her lips pursed as she stared straight ahead, but she didn't answer.

Sera's mood darkened at the mention of her upcoming marriage, her lips pressing into a thin line. "Why should Father be anxious? I'm the one marrying the prince, not him."

"Yes, but you are the one worrying him with your lack of interest! Not to mention giving me heart palpitations with your reckless behavior. You put everything on the line when you disappear as you did today."

Sera snorted softly, earning herself another glare. "I never asked to be betrothed to a prince, Mama. I'd be happy to marry a pauper if only he loved me."

"Do not say such blasphemous things! It's nonsense!" Her mother clutched at her pearls as if her daughter's words had physically struck her, and Sera sighed.

"What else am I supposed to do when I'm being forced into a marriage I don't want?"

"This is your duty, Seraphina. Your marriage will elevate the entire family." And plunge her into a lifetime of misery.

"Do not sugarcoat the truth, Mother. I am a sacrifice for a greater cause—and that's business."

"Seraphina!"

"It's no use feigning affront at the truth." A moot notion, but hypocrisy was ever so useful in discussing matters of Society. Her mother's sharp eyes suddenly fixed on Sera's chin. Then lower.

"What is that mark on your neck?"

Sera's brows furrowed as she reached up to touch her throat. "I don't know," she replied, though her heart had begun a steady gallop in her chest as her memory sparked.

Isabella, always too curious for her own good, leaned closer and gasped. "What a curious shape!" She fished a small pocket mirror from her reticule and thrust it toward Sera.

Taking it reluctantly, Sera tilted the mirror to get a better look. There, just below her jawline, off to the side, was the faint shadow of what could only be described as a scandal! Her pulse quickened as she recalled the way Alex left a trail of kisses to that spot, burrowing his face and lips there.

Sera applauded her calm as she said, "I must have been bitten by a bug." A very large, handsome bug.

"A bug?" Isabella pulled a face. "What kind of bug leaves that sort of mark?"

"A gnat," Sera quipped, forcing herself to sound bored rather than flustered. "And an overzealous one, it seems." She handed the mirror back to her sister.

"What an unfortunate place to be bitten," her mother said with a deep scowl. "You should cover your neck for a few days. It's a rather unsightly mark."

Sera didn't share that opinion. She quite liked the mark from Alex. It made her feel claimed by him for the world to see, as if she belonged to him in a way that was uniquely hers.

"It's just a small mark, Mama. Bug bites aren't contagious," Sera reassured her. "It will disappear in a day or so."

But her mother would have none of it. "A day or two is too long! What if someone else saw it and misunderstood?"

Sera wanted to ask her mother why anyone would misunderstand, but she held back. Such topics shouldn't be discussed in front of Isabella anyway, even if she only wanted to tease her mother.

"No one saw me... ahem... it... the bug biting me," Sera winced at her own incredulity about the explanation. "And if they did, they probably didn't care. I'm not some precious jewel to be locked away."

Her mother's lips thinned. "You are a jewel, Sera, whether you care to admit it or not. You are betrothed to a prince, and every move you make reflects on his household—and ours. You are my daughter, and you will always be precious. You and Isabella are my most valued jewels."

"If this is about reputation, I suggest we worry more about folks talking about my cold feet than my gnat bite."

Her mother gasped again, clutching her chest as though she might faint. "Cold feet? What on earth are you talking about?"

"Do you really think I'm excited about marrying a man I've scarcely met? Anyone who looks at me properly could tell." She shook her head. "This is no fairy tale, Mama. It's a contract. A transaction. I'm being sold."

"Sold? Don't be ridiculous. You're being secured a prosperous future. I don't want to hear any more about cold feet or reluctance. And if you can't muster excitement, at least manage decorum. You're marrying the prince, and that's final."

Sera bit back the retort bubbling on her tongue, her gaze darting to Isabella, who was watching them with wide eyes. Her sister squeezed her hand.

Sera returned the squeeze. At least she had her sister on her side, so she didn't feel entirely alone. "Whatever Mama wishes."

Her mother huffed but said nothing further, and the carriage fell into a tense silence.

Sera's thoughts drifted back to the encounter that had put her in this predicament: his blond hair curling against his neck, soft lips sending shivers racing down her spine. She shouldn't have let him get so close.

It was dangerous.

She certainly shouldn't have allowed him to kiss her neck. But she was the one who instigated that encounter. And yet… her fingers brushed the mark once more, and a small, secret smile curved her lips… She couldn't quite bring herself to regret it.

But one question remained startlingly clear in her mind: could a merchant's daughter betrothed to a prince truly change her fate?

"WHAT HAPPENED TO you?" The valet's skepticism echoed in the hotel room. "Was there a storm that swept through Cornwall that I didn't hear about?"

Alex exhaled, his body sinking into a cold bath. He swore he could hear the water hiss against his skin. Ever since their kiss in the alley, his body had been burning hot, and he couldn't shake off the heat simmering beneath the surface, as if Sera's touch had ignited a fire only she could extinguish.

"Why?" He glanced at the valet, scrutinizing his clothing with hawkish eyes. He winced; some spots on his jacket and trousers were smeared with dust from their tavern escapade. "A minor scuffle. Nothing noteworthy."

He didn't want to elaborate on the details.

The valet simply snorted.

Alex clenched his teeth as the water rose to his collarbone, his body cooling quickly. He sighed with relief.

"But I must say, Your Highness, Cornwall doesn't seem to suit you. Every day you return more disheveled than the last."

On the contrary, he thought Cornwall suited him quite well. In fact, he couldn't recall why he wasn't staying in Cornwall to spend more time with Sera. Perhaps he could inform his brother, Stan, that he needed more time for Cornish affairs? One particular matter of the heart, to be precise…

"And before I forget, Your Royal Highness, a letter arrived for you today."

Alex turned his gaze to the man, curiosity piqued. "A letter?" There were only a few people who knew where he was.

"Yes, Your Highness. From London."

Alex straightened slightly in the tub, extending a wet hand. The valet hesitated, then retrieved the letter from a nearby desk and handed it over, careful to avoid the dripping water.

Alex broke the seal, his eyes scanning the neat handwriting.

Dear Alex,

First of all, I apologize for disappearing and not reaching out sooner despite your enquiries. Now, however, I write to you with an urgent request that weighs heavily on my heart. The situation in our realm has become precarious, and I fear for the stability of our alliances.

You know as well as I do the importance of the upcoming formal introductions with Miss Lyndon's family; it is crucial for our political strategy. But it is also vital that you join me in London at the earliest opportunity. We need to consolidate our position and ensure that our allies remain steadfast in their support.

The stakes are high, and I need your strength and wisdom by my side.

Awaiting your swift reply.

Yours,
Stan

The cold water clung to Alex's skin, seeping into every inch of him, but it was the letter resting on the edge of the tub that chilled him deeper—a slow, creeping frost that wrapped around his lungs and squeezed, turning his breath into shallow, uneven gasps. He understood the stakes all too well… a certain Prussian baron with a vendetta against his family.

Baron von List had inflicted chronic pain in the region around Braşov, but judging by the urgency in Stan's words, it was worsening. A brotherly plea to return to London clashed with the need to see Sera. A bloody double-edged sword that could cut not only his throat but also his family's if he didn't respond to the threats posed by von List.

The paper trembled in Alex's hand, its words seeming to seep into his skin. But the weight of duty was immense, crushing his chest like an iron plate. A vague image of Miss Lyndon, with her refined upbringing and undeniable fortune, loomed in his mind as a symbol of his expected life. It was a life he could picture vividly—the measured steps, the polite smiles, the unyielding rhythm of obligation. Yet, with that clarity came suffocating stillness.

Sera, in contrast, was chaos incarnate. Every thought of her crackled through him like lightning, alive and uncontrollable, throwing his pristine world into disarray. She hadn't asked for him; she had demanded nothing. Yet, she had planted herself so firmly in his mind that leaving felt as unnatural as severing a part of himself.

The idea of Cornwall without her was a hollow ache he couldn't bear to dwell on. But what was he to do? Swap the certainty of a kingdom for the tenuous heat of a handful of stolen moments? Trade the promise of stability for the reckless pull of the unknown?

He'd been raised to choose honor, always honor.

But in the face of her, of everything she was, honor felt like a half-empty word if it meant betraying not only his heart but also his convictions—and he was becoming more and more convinced that Sera deserved his heart and loyalty as much as his family.

Whoever Miss Lyndon was, she'd have to find herself another prince… He flung the letter aside, its corner catching the sunlight before it fluttered to the floor, a thing so light for the crushing burden it carried. For a moment, he pressed the heels of his hands against his eyes, as if he could scrub away the images, the war waging between duty and desire that clawed at his chest. When he drew his hands down and looked at the discarded letter, all he felt was dread—centered around one consuming question.

Could he live with himself if he walked away?

Could he live with himself if he stayed?

A Hohenzollern-Sigmaringen prince didn't marry for love. No, marriage was a tool—a strategy. Alex knew that well enough. The union with Miss Lyndon wasn't about desire or choice; it was about necessity. Her family practically controlled the fleets on the Black Sea, a lifeline for trade and defense.

A single vow, a simple "I do," and he'd secure an alliance that could bolster his entire principality.

Peace. Prosperity. Stability.

Words his advisers hammered into him like a mantra. It wasn't just his future they discussed—it was their future, their power, their survival. And yet, all that weight, all that responsibility, didn't make it easier to swallow.

This marriage wouldn't just shape alliances; it would cement his legacy. A bridge to peace, they called it, but it felt more like a chain binding his choices to the will of others.

Draci! Could he ignore his duty?

Could he dismiss what had been drilled into him since birth? The answer whispered back to him, cold and unwavering.

No. He couldn't.

His principality needed this; his family needed this. But why, then, did the thought sit like a stone in his chest? Why did the shadow of someone else—someone who made him feel alive— refuse to leave him in peace?

And he was ready to topple it.

Which nearly scared him to death. But this country girl… She had taken hold of him in a way that caught him off guard. There was no coy hesitation, no demure retreat. She met him earnestly, and yes, with a hunger that matched his own.

But he felt her inexperience in her kiss.

This connection with Sera was real affection, not merely a summer fling. Even the second kiss in the alley. It had been a mistake and a revelation. She wasn't just a distraction; she was a threat to everything he had meticulously planned.

And he craved her so.

Longed for her.

Alex pushed himself upright, droplets streaming down his chest as he rose from the bath. He reached for a towel, his movements brisk and decisive.

"I need you to arrange a few things for me," he said to the valet, who was still fussing over the discarded clothes.

"Anything, Your Highness."

"A boat," Alex began, wrapping the towel around his waist. "And a picnic."

The valet blinked. "A picnic?"

"Yes." Alex's voice was firm, though his mind churned. He would leave Cornwall soon—there was no escaping that. But before he left, he had to see Sera one last time. "I have an urgent matter."

"If I may, Your Highness, you seem troubled. I am at your disposal if you require any assistance."

"I am a prince," Alex muttered. "I am always wrestling with something. There's just something I'm not entirely clear about, that is all." The valet inclined his head. "Of course. But might I remind you that even princes are allowed moments of clarity? May I inquire as to the nature of your uncertainty?"

No! Alex huffed a laugh, though it held little humor. "Clarity is a luxury I can afford but would regret."

Curiously, the valet said nothing for a moment. "But it seems to me that Cornwall has offered you something—or someone— worth considering."

His brows furrowed as he contemplated this obligation. Yet, his heart tugged in another direction. He was loath to leave. But the neatly penned words were clear: Stan needed him in London for a matter of grave importance, and Alex would never turn his back on his family. He couldn't delay his return anymore.

Yes, she was worth considering.

But that was all he could do.

Consider.

He would leave the day after the next.

Not without a goodbye.

Chapter Ten

A LEX WAS AS excited as a young boy.

It was morning, and after some convincing... *ahem...* kissing, she finally agreed to join him on the cutter that Charles had arranged.

"I can't believe you would take me on a boat after my near-drowning experience in this very ocean!"

Alex grinned at Sera. "It's a big ocean."

"The Atlantic... hmpf!" Her grip on the bench was so tight that the cutter could topple, and the ocean couldn't pry her away. The wind tugged at his shirt as he adjusted the mainsail, the cutter slicing through the waves with practiced ease. Water stretched endlessly around them, and with Sera in the backdrop, he could scarcely take his eyes off her.

He leaned against the gunwale, the faint salt spray cooling his cheek as he turned to her with a wry smile. "Think of it, if you must, as your most agreeable abduction."

Her eyes narrowed, the wind catching loose strands of her hair as she squared her shoulders. "Agreeable? How are you going to make it more agreeable than we did on land?"

His chuckle was low, an amused rumble beneath the rush of the waves. "Do you trust me to surprise you?"

Her lips parted, ready with another sharp retort, but the

ocean breeze stole it away before she could speak. For a moment, neither spoke, the untamed vastness of the sea mirroring the uncertainty sparking between them.

"So, you planned to abduct me and then..." She drew circles in the air with one hand, then quickly fastened her grip.

Alex chuckled. "Only if you threaten to outwit me," he replied, glancing at her again. Outwit my heart.

She sent him a hot look. "Abduction is a rather extreme method for dealing with your lack of confidence, don't you think?"

He laughed outright. "Well, be that as it may, it is certainly the best way to regain your perspective about the ocean."

"Don't be so sure about that."

"Seduce with a glance, confuse with a word, refuse with a smile—then watch as the game truly begins." He grinned as he skilfully adjusted the rigging. The boat tilted slightly, and the pristine white sails billowed gracefully, perfectly harnessing the wind's pull. "See, Sera, it's all about feeling the rhythm of the boat," Alex said with a grin as he leaned effortlessly into the motion. "You move with it, letting your body flow instinctively."

"Flow instinctively? It's a test of my survival instincts!"

"You're surviving quite admirably," he said, his gaze flicking to her white-knuckled grip on the bench. "Relax a bit, and you'll get the hang of it," he encouraged. "Admire the beauty of the ocean. Or just the cutter if you prefer. After all, every inch of the vessel speaks of craftsmanship and power. A regal beast in a disguise of elegance."

"Sure. Very regal." Calling her tone unconvinced would mean that Alex had mastered the art of the English understatement.

His gaze caught her other hand lifting to press against her stomach, while her eyes darted between him and the horizon, her usually bright complexion several shades too pale.

"Are you well?" he asked, glancing at her between tying a knot and adjusting the mainsail. The sea required his attention for the moment, though he couldn't resist stealing a glance at the woman perched in his boat like an uncomfortable bird. He itched to crouch before her and take her hands in his.

"Fine," she said tightly, her eyes darting to the horizon. "Just… acclimating."

"You look like you're plotting my untimely demise," Alex remarked, his lips twitching. Amidst the ebb and flow of the boat, he couldn't help but admire her. Despite her unease, she remained resilient.

Sera released her grip just enough to shoot him a pointed look. "Perhaps I am. Just keep the boat from tipping. That won't win you any favors."

Alex leaned against the mast, finished with the knots. "I thought I'd already won your favor. Or was I mistaken?"

"Why do you look so utterly unrepentant asking that question?"

"Why are you blushing asking yours?" Her eyes widened, and her cheeks flushed, though whether from indignation or the wind's kiss, he couldn't tell.

"You're too smart for a skipper or whatever term one uses for the crew," she muttered, looking out at the waves with a touch of irritation and amusement.

"How about Captain?" he asked, his tone teasing.

"Too young."

"But you have to admit, this is quite something, isn't it?" He gestured expansively to the endless blue surrounding them.

Her gaze tilted toward the horizon, where the sun was beginning to rise. "I'll admit… It is a bit breathtaking. As long as I don't have to hold my breath underwater."

Alex grinned. "Good. I wanted to share this view with you. Because it is the perspective from where I love to see the world."

And you.

She blinked, her lips parting in surprise. For a moment, she seemed at a loss for words, a rare occurrence that Alex drank in greedily. But she quickly recovered. The sea breeze tangled through her hair, scattering dark strands across her cheek, and he couldn't help but stare, transfixed by the way the sun gilded her skin. He wanted to know her—truly—and that desire filled the air between them like a silent demand.

He wanted to understand her essence.

Circumstances seemed unimportant against the vastness of the sea, as he was flooded with a more fundamental need to know her deeply and completely.

"They say Proteus, the old sea god, could take on any shape to guard his secrets," Alex mused, his gaze lingering on her. "What form would you choose, if you could?" It was an unrefined question, one he hadn't meant to ask, but when her gaze flicked to him—startled yet intrigued—he didn't regret it.

Sera tilted her head, a slow, contemplative smile curling her lips. "A tigress," she replied at last. "Then no one would dare tell me what to do."

"And yet, even tigresses can be coaxed closer," he said softly, a smirk playing against her playful defiance. "Though I suspect it takes a clever hand and an endless supply of patience."

Her laugh carried over the waves, light yet edged. "And I suspect you think you're clever enough to try?"

It wasn't a question so much as a challenge, and Alex accepted it with a slight tilt of his head. He leaned lazily against the mast, though his eyes tracked her every movement like a hawk. "Perhaps. But fair's fair, Sera. Your turn."

Her eyebrow arched, but she didn't hesitate. "If you weren't bound to the sea, what life would you choose?"

Alex blinked, the question catching him off-guard, and in that moment, her smile deepened, as if she had scored a small victory. Where to begin? Bran Castle was set aside for his oldest brother. London didn't hold the same allure for him as Stan. The only calling he had at this moment were her lush pink lips. And yet, she mustn't know who he was—not until he was free to ask her what had become the inevitable question on his mind. Not yet. "You ask as if the sea is all that binds me," he countered, buying himself a moment.

The wind tugged at her skirts as she leaned casually against the gunwale. "Isn't it?" she asked, her voice softer now, curious.

For a moment, all he could hear was the rush of water against the hull. "Almost," he admitted. "But there's something freeing in the chaos. No maps to follow, just the horizon ahead." He paused, eyes gleaming. "What about you, Tigress? Would you choose the forest over a ballroom?"

"Without question," she said quickly, and then, "Though there is a certain power in a well-played waltz." Interesting. Odd, actually, for he hadn't expected Sera to be familiar with the formality of ballrooms and waltzes.

"And a tiger paces just as gracefully as any lady," he murmured, his tone charged, though the smile tugging at his lips betrayed him. "Come now, I believe it's my turn."

Sera's chin tipped, almost daring him. "Ask away," she said lightly, though the flicker of her lashes revealed a spark of anticipation.

"If you could grant one wish to anyone, who would you give it to—and what would it be?" His gaze held hers steady, curious but not prying, and he knew, somehow, that her answer would carry weight.

Her smile faded slightly as she glanced toward the horizon, quiet for a long moment. The silence stretched, though he didn't dare interrupt it, not when he saw flickers of something untold moving across her countenance. Finally, she replied, "I would grant it to my younger self… a wish for freedom."

His chest tightened unexpectedly at the soft honesty of her tone. "I find it hard to believe that you've lacked freedom here in Cornwall."

She turned back to him, her mask of confidence slipping back into place. "I have been free in some ways, but not in the way that matters. Not free to fight for what you wish to keep, even when it hurts." Her eyes sparkled. "But I don't think we're playing honestly. That was two of my questions answered for one of yours."

Alex barked out a laugh, the tension easing as he took her obvious bait. "Caught me," he admitted, responding to her light-heartedness with ease. "Then here's a simpler one to even the score—what's your least favorite word?"

She straightened, crossing her arms with theatrical solemnity as if preparing for a duel. "Obedience," she said flatly, the word sharply emphasized.

His lips twitched as he tried to suppress a laugh. "Figures. I'll have to remember never to say it within earshot."

"Your turn," Sera said quickly, fixing him with a pointed look. "Spill it—what's your greatest flaw?"

Alex pretended to ponder, rubbing his jaw as if sorting through a laundry list. "I suspect my fatal flaw is this very habit of questioning bright, sharp-tongued women who seem to enjoy making me work for every inch of conversation."

"Good." Her grin widened. "A man ought to work for what he gets. Don't you agree?"

"I find I do," he replied casually, though his voice dropped, soft and unguarded. "Especially when the prize carries such… rare allure."

Her eyes searched his, and for a brief, suspended second, the game stilled; their words softened, their barriers slipping into something unspoken but deeply felt. Until she inhaled, breaking the moment and tilting her head, mock-seriousness painting her features.

"Your move, Captain."

The flirtation resumed its rhythm, yet now, an undercurrent of shared truth threaded between the laughs, something fragile yet undeniable. The horizon blurred into evening light, but Alex barely noticed. For all his efforts to explore the vast ocean, it seemed the one mystery worth solving stood merely feet before him, more untamed than the sea itself.

A smile tugged at his lips. "My tigress," he said.

She was fierce, that much was clear. It spoke of independence, of strength, and perhaps a hint of something more delicate beneath. Tigers, for all their ferocity, were solitary creatures, which granted, she had been since they met. They roamed alone. That same solitude, he thought, might echo in her answer. Was her defiance a shield against the loneliness that came with refusing to let others in? Or did it reflect how fiercely she protected herself, unwilling to risk the kind of weakness that came from depending on anyone else?

Interesting.

"You certainly are fierce," he murmured. "And you don't like the water, just like a big cat."

"And you?" she asked, a spark of curiosity lighting her eyes. "What animal would you be? A fish, perhaps? Since you seem so at home in the water."

He pretended to look wounded. "A fish? I'm offended. Can't you tell? I'd be an eagle."

Her brow arched. "An eagle? How very noble."

"Not noble," he corrected. "Just practical. They soar above it all, seeing everything from above. It's always in control."

She nodded thoughtfully. "Then you enjoy being in control."

"Always."

It wasn't just the majesty of the eagle that appealed to him—it was the way it moved through the world with an innate sovereignty, effortlessly commanding respect. But perhaps, deep down, his choice stemmed from a yearning to rise above all that constrained him, to seek the freedom he had long accepted as lost.

She studied him for a moment, clearly assessing his words. "Well, I suppose I can see it, though you seem more like a carp than an eagle in my eyes."

He chuckled softly. "Perhaps I do have a touch of carp in me."

Perhaps a bit of love, too.

As if hearing his thoughts, a gust of wind blew into the sails.

Sera's stomach tightened.

"Don't worry."

She wasn't going to, but he must have glimpsed the ashen look on her face.

"I'm fine. Entirely fine," she replied in a high, strained voice that felt anything but fine. A sharp gust of wind filled the sails, and the boat tilted gently to one side, creaking as it sliced through the waves. A muffled groan escaped her lips.

"What's so funny about this? The rocking of the boat or that I almost fell out?"

He burst out laughing but felt a pinch of guilt. He'd brought her here to share the sunrise over the sea and, hopefully, to help her overcome any fear lingering in her heart. He didn't mean to traumatize her. "You didn't almost fall out at all."

"How would you know?"

"First of all, I wouldn't allow it. Second, you're about three feet from the bulwark."

Her fingers clutched the smooth curve of the bulwark, its polished wood a cool, solid anchor against the jarring sensation of the wind ripping at the sails. To her, it wasn't just a part of the cutter's structure; it was a lifeline. She glanced at Alex—oh, so confident and capable, his focus flitting between the sails and her—as if he'd notice the slightest tremor in her small finger. A flicker of warmth curled through her chest.

If she slipped, if the sea claimed her balance, he would save her again. She knew it as surely as she feared the water beneath them.

Her gaze lingered longer than it should on the clean, deliberate set of his shoulders, the seemingly effortless strength in how he moved. Everything about him—the precision of his stride as they walked the uneven path, or how his arm extended to steady her over a slippery rock—spoke of power wrapped in grace. He didn't lumber or stomp; no, Alex was made of control. Every movement was aligned, smooth, and swift, as though nothing in the world could weigh him down. Yet his eyes told a different story, and that contradiction opened something within her.

There was a heaviness to his gaze, a shadow that flitted there even in moments of laughter. For all his easy, almost careless physicality, that look had struck her—deep and painfully familiar, like the loneliness of a half-forgotten dream. She didn't need to know what burden he bore; all she knew was the aching wish to share it. To take on some of that hidden weight if only she could. And yet, when his eyes landed on hers, the darkness in them shifted. It softened, just for her.

Was that wishful thinking?

She didn't believe so.

She trusted him more than she thought she could trust anyone. It hadn't started with him saving her life—though that day had etched itself into her memory. The raw strength in his hands as he pulled her from that perilous depth. The steadiness of his voice as he whispered reassurances, words that wrapped her trembling body in a calm she hadn't known she could feel while so close to danger. It wasn't just that Alex had saved her; it was how he had done so. Not as a prince or protector, not because it was his duty—but because he simply couldn't choose otherwise.

She'd felt it like an unshakable truth.

And since then, being near him felt like safety itself.

But it wasn't just safety Sera craved. Oh no, her heart didn't flutter for simple comfort. The maddening part of Alex was how he left her completely unsettled. It was his hair, always slightly unruly at the edges, at odds with the precision of his tone and the rigid posture that seemed to be carved into him. She'd wanted to reach out and brush that errant strand from his brow.

But reassurance didn't erase unease.

The shoreline in the distance felt impossibly far, and the ocean seemed both magnificent and threatening. Awe warred with trepidation, her earlier courage cracking under the immensity of it all. Only he gave her comfort, and she drew strength from the way he moved, his practiced ease. Even so, her heart whispered for the steady embrace of arms.

You are hopeless, Sera!

"We're awfully far from shore," she said.

"Not all hope is lost far." Then he winked at her.

Her heart fluttered.

Oh no, that made it even worse because her stomach seemed to twist. Sera glanced back toward the shore. Cornwall was a small, jagged line against the pale blue horizon now, growing fainter as they sailed farther out. The open sea stretched endlessly before them, and she swallowed her fear.

I am in charge.

Alex tightened a line and tested its pull, the movement smooth from what seemed like years of practice, even though he was so young. She inwardly snorted. Right. He must be a man of the sea. Probably a smuggler!

And if she could be his pirate bride, she'd rather live a life on the run with him than be locked in an ivory tower with a prince she didn't want.

I want you, Alex.

"An interesting plan for an outing."

"I'll have you know, this entire excursion is part of a very well-thought-out plan," Alex said, his grin widening.

"Enlighten me."

"Step one: take you out on the water. Step two: charm you with my undeniable wit. Step three…" He trailed off, his gaze locking with hers. For a moment, the playful banter gave way to something more flirtatious.

"Step three better involve getting me back to shore in one piece," she muttered.

He chuckled, his grip tightening on the tiller. "Consider it done."

The cutter dipped slightly as the wind shifted, and Sera's hand shot out instinctively, her fingers curling around the edge of the bench. But he steadied the boat with ease, his movements confident. His hand tightened on the tiller, coaxing it with a precise adjustment, while his booted foot pressed against the deck to counterbalance the shift. The muscles in his shoulders and forearms flexed with practiced control, every motion instinctive, as though the cutter were simply an extension of his body. The creak of the wood beneath him and the snap of the sails above were familiar notes in a symphony he'd mastered long ago.

"You're safe with me," he said, his voice low and reassuring.

She glanced at him. "I suppose I don't have much of a choice."

"No," he agreed. "But I like to think you'd choose to trust me anyway."

She rolled her eyes, but the hint of a smile on her lips betrayed her. "You're impossible."

"And you're unforgettable," he replied, his gaze lingering on her for just a moment too long before he turned his attention back to the sea. A hint of sadness bubbled up in her chest because she never wanted to be away from him, locked in some castle where she would have to forget this. Him. She willed the thoughts away.

"I am terrified." In more ways than one.

"Terrified?" He feigned shock. "You, the tigress?"

She tilted her head toward him. "If I were a tigress, I'd be pacing the deck, demanding you turn this thing around. I don't think tigers like being on boats. Besides, I've yet to find my sea legs. They seem to be lagging behind."

The boat pitched again, a larger wave sending a spray of saltwater across the deck. Sera startled, gripping the bench, gasping.

"Easy," he said. "The cutter moves with the waves. You have to trust it."

"And if I don't trust the waves? They can be rather vicious."

"Then trust yourself," he said simply. "You got onto the boat, didn't you? Trust my experience at least."

That she did. "Speaking of experience, how old are you?" she asked, changing the subject. Such a wise old man in such a handsome young body.

"How old do I look?" he asked, his grin still in place, even though she could just see half of it.

Hmm, she considered that for a moment. He was built like a man, muscular with broad shoulders, veins popping out of his lower arms when he held that mast or whatever it was called. And yet, there was boyish mischief to his expression that made him seem so much younger than the experience and skill he showed with anything related to boats, water, and—Sera gulped—the open sea.

"Five-and—thirty?" she guessed but instantly knew it was too much.

"What? Really? You think I look eleven years older than I am?"

She laughed, enjoying the stunned look on his face. "So, you are four-and-twenty?"

"Cunning minx."

Cunning… But then, she was, wasn't she? Like the tiger she claimed she'd be if she were an animal, ready to carve her own path no matter what the consequences to her family. If she couldn't, in the future, she'd be on a larger boat than this. "That's me, all nineteen years of age," she muttered almost bitterly. "Cunning."

Suddenly, he was there, crouching before her on one knee, the wind tousling his hair. "Why do you look as though I've sent you to your doom?"

She hesitated, then shook her head. She couldn't lay bare her internal struggles to this man—not when he was offering her the gift of a sunrise shared with him. "I've never been this far from England. That's all. It doesn't feel… safe."

His brow furrowed, and then he laughed, the sound a warm burst of humor against all the turmoil she fought in her heart. "Safe? Sera, if you think this is far, I must tell you—I've crossed the Atlantic, the Mediterranean, and I've sailed around the Aegean Seas. Boston is leagues farther, and believe me, the sea carried me right back again, safe and sound."

Because you, Alex, are so very capable.

She tried to laugh, a weak attempt that turned into a grimace as the boat pitched slightly to one side. "Well, I've never been farther than Bath, so forgive me if the sea and I aren't on intimate terms. I've never been unchaperoned for this long either."

There's so much you don't know about me.

And yet, somehow, it felt as though he knew everything about her that mattered.

He smiled, steadying himself as the boat rocked. "I'll make a sailor out of you yet."

"I should think not," she countered quickly, her voice breathy as the nausea threatened again. "The rocking... It doesn't feel like Earth. It's as if we're floating nowhere at all. Or about to sink. It doesn't make any sense now that I say it aloud—it's just all too... unsteady. Like I don't belong in it."

"Then don't think of the boat or the water beneath us," he murmured. "Think of the horizon. The wide-open space of it all—not just Cornwall behind us but all the places beyond it. You stand at the edge of something vast, Sera. It's magnificent."

She glanced sideways at him, her nausea momentarily eclipsed by how he spoke about the sea, as if he and it shared old stories she couldn't understand. "Why are your words suddenly so charming?"

He laughed. "Weren't they always?"

She scoffed, but despite the queasiness in her stomach, her heart filled with a different kind of ache, one born of love and the impending separation she dreaded. It made her feel even more out of place, as though he belonged to something she could never claim. Her affection—or was it love? Whatever it was, what she felt for Alex was a deep, swelling tide, and the thought of leaving him felt like a storm brewing inside her. "And yet," she said, her voice quiet and laced with emotion, "it only makes me realize I don't fit in your world."

He pinched the bridge of her nose. "The smuggling world? Sailing the seas?"

She slapped at his hand. "Exactly! However, I won't deny it sounds thoroughly intriguing. I just… Don't know where I belong."

His fingers tightened around hers, pulling her focus sharply back to him. "My world is a bit different than you may imagine. And trust me, you fit," he said firmly. "Anywhere you decide to fit. The sea may not be for you, but I—" he hesitated, glancing toward the distant shore, "I'll be in London soon. Duty calls me there."

Sera's lips parted in a small gasp. "London? I—our family will be in London, too. Perhaps not tomorrow, but soon. Within the next week." The words tumbled out quickly, as though she wanted to catch this lifeline before the rift between them widened any further. *What are you even thinking, Sera!*

A spark lit in his eyes, and a small smile tilted his lips. "Then, shall we meet there?"

She blinked, caught between surprise and relief. "Perhaps. Where?"

He cocked his head, considering. "I've never been, so I wouldn't know."

Never. Been. To London.

How smuggler of him!

And yet, how was it possible that Alex was so worldly and yet had never been to London? The man was as mysterious as ever!

"Vauxhall, let's meet at Vauxhall."

The nausea threatened again, but it didn't matter quite as much anymore. For the first time since stepping aboard the vessel, she reached for the horizon and saw possibility instead of dread.

There was hope, right?

Chapter Eleven

S ERA INHALED DEEPLY as the salty ocean breeze filled her lungs. Then Alex brought them back to shore with the skill of an entire ship's crew.

Finally.

Land.

Her bare feet sank slightly into the cool, damp sand with each step, her slippers dangling from her fingers. The beach stretched endlessly before her, as if it were at odds with time. With her life. She enjoyed the boat ride, but she loved strolling along the beach with Alex much more. Mostly because it felt safer.

Safer for her life.

But admittedly, more dangerous in other ways. Like claiming all her awareness.

Sera cast a sidelong glance at the man who'd so easily convinced her to join him on a boat. A boat! But she realized there wasn't anything she wouldn't do for him. The wind tousled his blond hair.

So handsome.

It was remarkable how comfortable he seemed in any environment, as if the sea and sand bowed to his presence rather than challenged it.

"Where are we going?" Sera asked, her curiosity getting the

better of her.

"You'll see soon enough," he replied, a maddeningly vague smile tugging at his lips. He, too, carried his boots in his hand, swinging them lightly, as if they were out for a casual countryside stroll rather than wandering toward some mysterious destination.

Alone. Together. Again.

"You're pampering me with mystery."

He chuckled. "So patient."

"Should I be impatient, then?" Sera quipped.

"No," he murmured. "But it is rather refreshing."

How interesting. "Are you usually surrounded by impatient women?"

"I cannot in good consciousness say yet. The most outspoken women in my life are my mother and my sister."

She laughed. "But you can't say no either." After a brief pause, she wondered, "Where is your family?"

"Well, my mother is at home with my father, but it turns out my sister is in England. Let's not talk about things that give me shivers," he said, visibly shuddering. "I'd rather not think about the trouble she's in."

Before she could say anything more, they arrived at a… cave? No. An alcove? How had she never noticed this before in all her years? He led her into the alcove, and she blinked at the sight before her. A blanket was spread in the center with a basket.

"What is this?"

"A picnic."

"Who arranged this?" Sera asked, unable to tear her gaze away. There was even a candelabra with candles! "Who set this up?"

"Someone who knows the area better than I do," he said, leading her over. "Sit. And don't worry. He is very discreet. Plus," he grinned at her. "I don't even know your full name, remember?"

"I don't know if I should rejoice or be alarmed by that."

Sera lowered herself onto the blanket, watching as he knelt

and unpacked the basket one item at a time, spreading it between them. Sandwiches. Eclairs. Grapes. Wine. Then he quickly lit the candles.

"This is quite romantic," Sera couldn't help but remark.

"It's dinner."

Sera chuckled. "What a typical male thing to say." She pointed at the spread. "Did your friend arrange this?"

"Of course."

"You must trust him a lot."

"He has his strengths."

Her eye caught something, and Sera leaned closer, her gaze narrowing. Her hand darted out to pluck a napkin from the basket, and she froze when she saw the emblem embroidered in its corner—the unmistakable crest of her father's hotel!

Her suspicious gaze turned to Alex. "Where did you really get this?" she asked, holding up the napkin as evidence.

He hesitated for only a moment before answering, "From the hotel."

Her eyes widened. "Did your friend steal it for you?"

"No!"

"Then you are a guest?"

"Must I be a guest to receive favors?" he replied smoothly, a glint of amusement in his eyes.

"You don't have to be that mysterious!" She flicked the napkin at him. "Besides, you've been found out. Tell me. Did a hotel servant give you this? Or the cook?"

Come to think of it, fishermen or smugglers didn't have connections with hotels; they supplied smuggled goods. She glanced at the bottle of wine, which was from a winery she didn't recognize. French. Either he smuggled the contraband, or he could afford to purchase very expensive wines. Well, if he were rich, she supposed, he would do things differently than Father. She glanced at his polished boots.

All the signs were there already.

This man wasn't from simple means.

Sera crossed her arms, studying him as if trying to solve a puzzle. "How nice of your friend to package these so thoughtfully."

Alex chuckled. "He had a great many questions."

She lowered to the blanket and plucked a grape. "About what?"

"About whom I was meeting. What I would be doing. Why…"

Sera couldn't suppress a laugh. "I hope you didn't scandalize the poor man."

He grinned. "If I did, only a little."

She shook her head. The soft glow of the candle made the alcove feel strangely intimate; everything did, really. From the tiny sandwiches to the big man himself. She leaned back on her hand and tilted her head toward him.

"Thank you. This is quite unexpected." She slipped the grape between her lips, squinting as a burst of sourness filled her mouth.

"Are the grapes not sweet?" Alex asked.

Sera shook her head. "No."

Alex handed her a sandwich. "Here, try this."

Sera accepted it and took a careful bite. It was delicious, of course—her father's hotel wouldn't serve anything less. She chewed thoughtfully, watching him as he poured them each a drink from a flask before also enjoying a sandwich. The man just became more mysterious with each passing minute!

She lifted her glass and sniffed. "What's in this? Madeira?"

"Just so."

She arched a brow. "I can't have so much liquor on an empty stomach."

"Then eat what you like. There is tea also if you don't want wine."

"This is fine." She took a sip, studying him. "You should have given me this before we went on the boat."

Her mind couldn't stop turning over the mystery of his connection to the hotel. He didn't look like a guest, but then again, what did a guest look like? There was an ease about him, a lack of formality that set him apart from the usual posh that graced the establishment. "Is it possible to like someone you don't know?"

"Is that a question or a compliment?"

Sera shook her head, her gaze meeting his. "It's a question for you and me."

"I like you."

"You don't know me."

"And yet," he murmured. "You don't know me, but you like me."

Could she even deny that? But this was the "thing" between them, wasn't it? Mystery. Purposefully not allowing a hole to be poked through the veil. "You surprise me at every turn."

"So do you."

She nodded thoughtfully.

This man was unlike anyone she'd ever met—charming yet perplexing, confident yet utterly unpretentious. She wanted to ask him a thousand questions, but for now, she was content to sit with him in this alcove and enjoy the moment.

And yet…

Her eyes caught on a piece of paper that stuck out from the basket. Curious, she took a closer peek. "Reading material?" she said, nodding toward the papers. "Is this for when you get bored with our conversation?"

Alex scoffed. "I could never get bored in your presence."

She leaned closer, picking up one of the sheets. It was a language she didn't recognize, but she could spot the German words, thanks to her governess's incessant lectures. Curiosity burned in her chest. Her eyes caught on a small, intricate map sketched in the corner, the markings suspiciously similar to the route maps her father used for his shipping ventures—only smaller.

Had she been wrong?

This man wasn't a fisherman or smuggler but perhaps a pirate? A sudden question popped into her mind… "Why are you going to London?"

Alex stiffened, his gaze dropping to the paper she held in her hand. He had seen them earlier but hadn't thought much of them, too nervous. They were covered in neat German script, and he let out a breath.

Why the devil had the valet included this?

She wouldn't be able to read German, right? If she could read, this would probably just reinforce the belief that he was a rogue seaman.

Clearing his throat, Alex fought the urge to snatch the paper from her fingers. That would only make him look guilty. At least not guilty about any of her wild imaginings. Of course, he didn't plan on hiding his identity forever, but for now, it was best—for her safety, if not for any of his selfish reasons to keep the moment of having her all to himself. Especially since he was leaving tomorrow, and danger loomed.

"I have urgent business that can't wait, unfortunately."

She tilted her head, studying him with far too much interest. "Well, what do you know? I do too."

His brow shot up. "You do?"

She nodded, her lips curving into a slow smile. "Though I'm not sure when. It should be soon. You know, I have urgent business that can't wait."

Alex chuckled at her tease, though inwardly, his mind raced.

Sera in London?

The thought filled him with both excitement and trepidation. If their paths crossed there, it might complicate things.

Could he risk being near her? Could he not?

No, it might put her in danger. And she could go anywhere, from shops to restaurants, hotels, and ballrooms—where did she belong? But the thought of her in London, so near yet out of reach, would dig under his skin like a splinter he couldn't remove. It would itch and fester, threading through his every thought, until even the simplest tasks felt unbearable. He'd pace and brood, his chest tight with the weight of wanting, until the city itself seemed to mock him with her absence. But he still wanted her there, close.

"What's this?" she asked, interrupting his thoughts, her brow furrowing as she traced a finger over the paper.

"Just a commentary for a draft of a law," Alex said hesitantly, watching her closely.

"A law?" Her eyes lit up, and she looked at him like she'd just uncovered a particularly intriguing secret. "Why are you reading about laws?"

"To ensure others don't break them." He might be giving too much away, but he wanted to share something more about himself—just a tiny bit.

"Oh? What sort of law?"

"The kind that keeps trade balances," he replied, finally plucking the paper from her hands and setting it aside. "A boring conversation," he added, his pulse quickening under her unwavering gaze.

"Tell me, are you preventing smugglers or pirates, then? Or..." Her eyes narrowed on him. "Are you one of them?"

Alex stared at her, his lips twitching with amusement. "A pirate?" he repeated, leaning back on his hands. "Do I look like a pirate to you?"

She shrugged, her gaze sweeping over him. "I don't know. You seem awfully comfortable around the sea, and that map..." She cocked her head. "They're not typical reading material for someone enjoying a holiday."

"We all have our pastimes," Alex said with a smile. "I like maps."

"You also read German."

So, she recognized the language. "I do," he admitted, his grin widening. He couldn't deny it.

"Such grand skills," she said, arching an eyebrow.

He laughed again, shaking his head. "Let's just say I have an interest in ensuring the laws of the land—and sea—are upheld. I also have a love for language."

She shook her head with a small scoff. "We couldn't be more… opposite."

"And yet, here we are, opposites like man woman. Complementary," he said, his voice dipping lower. "I think that's a good thing. Keeps things interesting"

Her gaze flicked to his, her expression unreadable. "I kissed and followed the devil, didn't I?"

Alex's laughter rumbled deep in his chest. "I'm not the devil, nor am I a pirate. If you must know, my brother and sister are in London, and they need me there for an urgent business matter. Nothing illegal."

She leaned back, her curiosity undiminished. "So, you have a brother and sister?"

"Yes," Alex admitted. "How about you?"

"Just a younger sister."

"Is she just as fearless as you?"

She laughed. "More than you could imagine." She reached for one of the sandwiches from the box. "You are a puzzle, you know that, Alex?"

"Am I?"

"Yes," she replied, meeting his gaze. "And I don't think you're going to give me the pieces I need to solve you."

He grinned. "Maybe some puzzles are better left unsolved."

"Only a rogue would say that."

How he wanted to be a rogue at that moment!

He thought back to when they strolled to the cave, and Sera's footprints followed alongside his. It was almost symbolic, wasn't it? Every step they took, every footprint they left would be washed away by the inevitability of the tides.

Alex's chest tightened.

This woman sitting across from him, sipping on wine and enjoying their sandwiches meant so much to him. More than she could ever imagine. More than he had ever imagined. She wasn't an inconsequential acquaintance, and he just didn't want to imagine a life without her.

The realization struck him directly in the gut.

His time with Sera, whatever it had become, was lacking in permanence.

This can't be over yet. Not now. Not ever.

"Sera."

Her eyes lifted to meet his. It was impossible to build a future with her. He was duty-bound to Miss Lyndon who was waiting in London for his arrival. He had to do something about that situation, but there was another situation before him. Entirely different. His gaze caught on the soft tumble of her dark hair, rich as midnight and stirring gently in the sea breeze, as if beckoning him closer. Her green eyes held him captive, their depths shifting with light and shadow, like dappled sunlight through forest leaves. There was a warmth in them, a quiet intelligence that seemed to see right through him, undeterred by walls he hadn't realized he'd built. She was magnetic, a force pulling him in with a quiet ferocity that left him unmoored, and for a moment, he could hardly remember how to speak.

"I'm not ready to let you go," he rasped.

"Shouldn't you be holding on to me before you say something like that?" She grinned. She held out her hand. "Do you want to be held?"

Something surged within Alex, and it was stronger than ever before: the need to claim her. So beautiful and so precious. *Draci,* did she even know how he was clinging to her?

He was never the first son, the tallest, the best, but he was the only one here now and Sera was undoubtedly the most beautiful and intelligent woman he'd ever met.

Could she be mine? Wholly? Forever?

Alex swallowed hard and took her hand in his. "I just don't want this day to end." He wanted to hold onto this moment, to find a way to make their time together last. How could he freeze time? The idea of losing her was unbearable. His hand tightened around hers searching for the right words to describe his feelings, to tell her how much she meant to him.

"Then don't let it."

"It's not in my power to keep the sun from setting. Everything will be different tomorrow."

As a third son, he may have a title and responsibilities but hardly any political sway. He had no way to fight his future unless he rebelled outright.

Turned a true rogue.

Except that nobody had taught him how to not follow rules. Uphold honor, laws, even draft and pass new ones—yes. But his heart led him another way now.

"But you can control what happens right here, right now," she said, shifting her body closer to him.

"Sera, surely you don't mean—" his sentence cut off when he caught the glint in her eyes. But then she gently kissed the tip of his nose and lingered. It would have been the most innocent show of affection if she didn't linger so close to his mouth. A reflection of his own longing. Alex knew he had to do something, anything, to bridge the gap that the dawn would bring.

His future had been pre-written for him and signed with ink on paper. But how could anything matter if he was there in the moment with the beauty that plucked on the strings of his heart as though she owned them?

The breeze swept into the alcove carrying the scent of the ocean—a scent of freedom that he'd only ever experienced with Sera.

Draci! If he didn't kiss her now, he might perish!

Alex leaned in slowly, his lips touching hers with a feather-light contact that sent a jolt of sparks through his.

This only ever happens with you.

Sera's lips parted to welcome him. Her fingers found their way to the nape of his neck, threading through his hair. The heat of her body enveloped him, a flicker of fire amidst the cool air. The sound of the waves faded, leaving only the thunderous beat of his heart and the soft sigh that escaped her. He pulled her onto his lap. If he could have drawn her body into his, he would have.

"Alex," she mumbled onto his mouth.

"I never want this to end, Sera," he repeated once more, this time with more conviction.

"Just don't let it." She stared up at him and every point of contact between them thrummed with a startling energy.

The idea of her absence left a hollow ache he couldn't ignore. The realization filled him with determination so profound it seemed to echo across the walls of the cave. She was his, and he was irrevocably hers.

All he had to do was move the heavens, the mountains, and the oceans if he acted on it.

Alex's resolve to take a gentle goodbye from Sera faded. It just wasn't enough. It was time to tip his royal world upside down.

Consequences be damned.

Chapter Twelve

HE DIDN'T WANT *to let her go.*

Sera studied him, her puzzle. She was missing a key piece of this man to complete it, and she wasn't sure she would ever find that piece. There had been something about his tone when she'd asked him about the map—too even, too smooth—that made her suspect he wasn't being entirely truthful.

It mattered, but not enough.

Not at this moment.

He was a risk she wanted to take. But if she dared… So many things could go wrong, and yet so many things might go right.

Both included her heart.

On the bright side, she knew a little more about this mystery man now than she had an hour ago. He had a family waiting for him in London. But what kind of man was he really? The pirate theory had crossed her mind—he seemed too at ease with the sea to be anything else—but then there were the law and those maps. Was he too gentle for an outlaw? Perhaps he was involved in something more illicit, or perhaps she was letting her imagination run away with her again. No matter what, there was something thrilling about not knowing where the night—or Alex—would take her. The hard, heated truth was that he'd burrowed into her heart.

"Have you been with many women like this?" Sera asked, suddenly curious.

"Like this? No," he said. "I've never… not with anyone, actually."

"Really?" That surprised her. "No time for such things?"

He chuckled. "Something like that. Not the right time, nor the right woman."

She exhaled, her heart pounding. Could he feel her pulse? Despite the layers of mystery that seemed to cling to him, he looked undeniably handsome. Irresistibly so. But then, he must think the same about her, right? The mystery part. And perhaps the irresistible part as well. They were opposites, but she couldn't help but be drawn to him.

I really must update that little book—Matters of the Heart.

Oh, the book! Which reminded her *she* had a prince to rid herself of. But now was not the time to think about that. She would sort out that engagement with him when she arrived in London. For now, she had another prince before her who held all her attention. He might even be the dark Prince of the Sea. Even if he was, it didn't matter to her.

This is the moment. Take charge.

Yes.

Because she didn't want to let go of him, either.

"Well, I don't know whether I'm the right woman or whether this is the right time, but if you don't let go…" She took in his unreadable yet achingly intense face. He was likely at war with something within him. The same as her. She grinned at him. "Neither will I."

"Do you promise?" he asked, his voice low.

Her breath caught. There was a teasing note in his voice, but beneath it, something serious lingered. "I promise."

"This isn't a promise that you can break or take lightly." He stared at her unflinchingly, his words weighted with meaning. "It would mean the world to me but turn mine upside down entirely."

Same here. "I never give a promise lightly," Sera reassured, her voice steady despite the storm brewing within her. She wouldn't. Even if she had to run away, she would make sure she stayed at Alex's side. "So, I will keep you to this."

"Sweeter words have never been spoken to me, love." He smiled, then added, "You're quite good at making promises."

"That is because I don't make promises unless I am prepared to do everything in my power to keep them." She lowered her voice, but she couldn't help but laugh, too. "Alex, what does this mean? Promises exchanged, terms yet to be negotiated?"

Alex laughed softly. "I wasn't aware we were drafting a contract."

"Everything in life is a negotiation," she said with a shrug. This she had learned. "Even affection."

His smile didn't waver. "Not the usual process, is it? Business transactions?"

"No, it's not," she bristled. That was exactly what she was trying to escape. "But I suppose given how we met each time, there was no other process than this. Than ours."

"Ours," he said softly. "I like that." His grin widened, slow and teasing. "Then I hope I'm getting a fair deal?"

How could he still be so charming and yet so annoyingly male? "That depends on what you bring to the table," she paused, her green eyes gleaming, "or should I say picnic?"

His head bent closer to hers. "What would you consider a worthy offer?"

"Oh, I don't know," she said, pretending to think. "Loyalty, charm, a certain level of handsomeness—"

"A certain level?" he interrupted, brow arched.

"Well, I wouldn't want to inflate your male arrogance," she quipped, her lips twitching with a barely contained smile.

"Have I ever shown you any arrogance?"

"Just because you haven't doesn't mean it isn't there."

"Generous of you," he said, his tone wry. "And here I thought I had it all."

"You might," she conceded, "but that remains to be seen. Explored even…" She let her hand trail up his arm.

He studied her for a moment before saying simply, "I'll do my best, then."

"Then I suppose," she said, poking his chest, "you'll have to prove it."

Alex smiled, slow and infuriatingly charming. Then his lips captured hers again. Sera didn't hold back. Her heart spoke a language older than words, urging him onward. His fingers skimmed down her waist, leaving trails of warmth that tingled in the cool alcove. As his hands reached her bottom, she drew a sharp breath, a sound swallowed by the sea breeze. Her body reacted instinctively, leaning into his touch. The thrill of his closeness unfurled like the sails of their cutter catching a fresh wind.

The cool air brushed against her skin, but his presence banished any chill. Here, in this cave, beneath the vast expanse of the sky, Sera felt an overwhelming sense of belonging.

With him.

And she wanted more than she'd intended to take. She wanted more than just her engagement null and void. She wanted to be Alex's. She wanted to hold on to him.

Forever.

She wanted him with a fierceness akin to the need for air, as if every moment had been leading to this singular encounter. The beach, this night, the man before her—all conspired in a dance of fate that had brought them together. How else? What else?

No, she believed it was the only way her soul would allow, now that it was intertwined with his.

The universe had indeed carried him to her, and she could do nothing else but embrace the truth that had become as essential as the air she breathed. Here, in this sacred space, she was his, and he was hers, as if their fates had willed it so.

Now, all she had to do was grab hold of it and never let go.

COULD A FEW kisses truly sway the path of one's fate?

Alex didn't know.

But what he did know was that he wanted to risk it all. It wasn't a calculated risk, nor was it smart. But it was as necessary and vital for his being as the air he breathed. He needed Sera to the very core of his existence.

He brushed a thumb along her jawline, still baffled at how she made him feel both invincible and undone. "You know," he murmured. "Didn't your Shakespeare write that a kiss is 'a seal of love'?"

"That would be problematic for our first kiss, wouldn't it?"

He shrugged. "Unless it was love at first sight."

"Was it love at first sight?"

He blinked at her, then grinned. "No, it was more of a rescue at first sight."

"Also, a seal implies finality, and I think love—real, true love—is anything but final. It's endless, unpredictable. Ever-changing."

"Shakespeare underestimated love, it seems."

"Perhaps he merely oversimplified it," she said, in thought. "A kiss isn't a seal; it's a spark. One that can lead to an inferno—or burn out entirely."

"Speaking about kisses after a kiss," Alex mused. "Makes me want to kiss some more."

"You started it!"

"That I did." He dropped his voice. "Then let me offer you another line—'A woman would run through fire and water for such a kind heart.'"

Her look turned flat. "Are you implying that your own heart is worth such dedication?"

"Would you run through fire for it?" He placed a quick peck on her lips. "I would run through fire for yours."

She would, too. "Does it have to be fire? Why not fly to the moon?"

"I'll do that, too," he said, bemused. "In fact, that might be better?"

"Why?"

"Well, the moon is only one of the heavenly orbs and it controls the tides. Imagine life without the sun. It's the force that makes this life not only liveable but wondrous. If the cosmos fashioned a sanctuary for love to flourish, then surely it has mirrored that design in us and shows just how small we are." He cradled her face, his gaze falling to her lips. "Except within your gaze, I find the same quiet perfection that sustains worlds, and in your heart, the power to make life itself a marvel beyond comprehension."

Sera laughed softly, the sound like a melody against the backdrop of the night. "Such a charming tongue in your possession! But then, if I painted the Milky Way in watercolor, and that is if I could paint, I'd probably pat the paper dry and remove the inky blues to create that effect."

Alex shook his head gently, deep in thought. "The Milky Way isn't about removing darkness; it's about adding light, don't you think? Each star contributes to that brilliance, turning the night into something breathtaking."

She looked at him, and he swore her eyes reflected the starlight. "You always see the world in such a different light. I'm simpler, I suppose. It's one of the reasons I will never be an artist."

Alex took her hands in his. "You make everything around you more beautiful just by being yourself. You don't just see the world; you transform it with your presence. Just like the stars in the Milky Way, you add light to my life."

Her cheeks turned bright red. "You make me sound like some kind of enchantress."

"To me, you are," Alex said sincerely. "You have the power to turn the darkest night into something magical, just like the stars do."

"Thank you, Alex," Sera whispered, her voice barely audible above the sound of the waves. "For seeing me in such a way. It means more to me than you know. Fisherman, smuggler, or pirate—whatever your station or whether you have none at all—I've yet to meet a man who can match your sincerity."

Alex felt an unexpected warmth rise within him. For the first time, he wasn't just the third son, the prince relegated to the shadows, the spare of the spare heir. With Sera, titles didn't matter. If being a pirate didn't matter, neither would being a prince. She saw beyond all that—to the person beneath. Something he never thought he'd find. And for that, he was profoundly grateful.

Alex lifted her hands to his lips, pressing a gentle kiss to her knuckles. "I mean every word, Sera. You're a bright guiding star of what's right in this world."

Sera's eyes shimmered. "And you are mine, Alex. In every possible way."

"How long can I stay yours?"

"What do you mean?" Sera asked, her heart stuttering despite the smile on his face.

"Your family? Won't they be worried? Should I take you home?"

Sera shook her head, grinning. "Oh, that? Do not fret, kind sir, between my maid and my sister, there shouldn't be any worries. We at least have until breakfast tomorrow."

He pulled her closer, fully wrapping his arms around her. "Let's make another promise," he said softly. "No matter what the future holds, we'll always be each other's light. Agreed?"

"Agreed." Her voice rang with conviction. "Always."

Always.

And yet, in the back of his mind, the devil on his shoulder laughed. Just how could he keep her safe with danger looming overhead?

Chapter Thirteen

A LEX BANISHED THE thought from his mind.

He inhaled deeply, the cool night air filling his lungs and calming his racing heart, directing all his thoughts to Sera. She wasn't merely lovely; she was radiant—a vision that made the air in his lungs hitch and stumble, refusing to move under the weight of his awe. And she was all his.

For the whole night.

His gaze traced her body, the gentle curve of her shoulders, the delicate line of her collarbone vanishing beneath the whisper of lace. She appeared like a dream barely tethered to the mortal world, and he, a man made of earth and gravity, felt powerless in her presence. Something within him shifted, tipped, as if the steady ground he'd always known had been stolen away by the soft gleam of her bare skin and the way she looked at him—shy yet burning. The moment felt almost surreal.

He couldn't speak, didn't trust himself to do so. The words tangled in his throat, replaced by a tightness that bloomed and spread through his chest, across his ribs. He had to leave for London tomorrow, and she had her own journey to begin. It felt like an ending, yet he yearned for it to mark the start of something more. She was everything he had ever wanted, and the thought of saying goodbye, even if only temporarily, tore at his soul.

He couldn't accept the word final.

Right now, I'm here.

Yet, Alex could focus solely on Sera, every detail of her filling his memory. He gathered her closer onto his lap. She burrowed in without hesitation. The intimacy was intoxicating. What had this woman done to him? It seemed unfathomable that he could feel so much for someone he knew so little about. But it was the little he did know that mattered.

The quiet of the alcove felt impossibly loud, every rustle of fabric and breath between them charged with a heavy, delicious tension. Alex traced the curve of Sera's cheek with his thumb, his hand trembling slightly as if her skin might vanish beneath his touch. Her gaze met his, wide and earnest, but beneath her shimmering beauty, there was a slight hesitation—a flicker of worry he couldn't ignore.

"You are so dangerous, you know." Her voice, her laugh, her words chased away so many things that troubled him.

"*You* are dangerous," she countered. "Everything about you."

He gave her a slow, teasing smile. "Only to you."

"Only in a good way, I hope," she whispered, playfully.

Alex tilted his head, his forehead brushing hers. "The very best way," he promised. And in that moment, with her smile so close he could feel it and her breath mingling with his, every risk, every potential consequence faded into the background. All that mattered was her—wild, radiant Sera, the one thing in his life he hadn't been prepared for but couldn't imagine giving up.

But the edges of the forbidden still nipped at him, sharp and exhilarating. He knew the barriers he was breaking, the invisible rules he dared defy, yet he wouldn't stop. Instead, Alex traced the arch of her back, his touch light but lingering, and Sera leaned in closer, her fingers curling into his shirt.

"This is the most freedom I've ever tasted."

"Freedom," he murmured, smiling, happy, "still has its own constraints. It's a complicated set of luxuries."

"Perhaps. I still want to be free, like the seagulls," she said, her eyes locking with his.

Alex searched her expression. The flicker of the picnic candles battled against the encroaching darkness, their soft amber light dancing over the rough stone walls of the alcove. The air was thick with salt and the lingering scent of crushed lavender from Sera's hair, blending with the sweet, smoky aroma of melting wax as the flames burned lower. Each breath, each touch, each second felt stolen, stretched taut between them as though the stars above had slowed time itself, wrapping the moment in eternity. "And what would you do if you were that free? Free like a seagull?"

"For one," she wiggled, "free to sit on your lap like this. And for the second…" She trailed off, falling silent for a moment as if weighing her thoughts. Then, without warning, she leaned in and pressed her lips to his.

The kiss was bold, decisive—a clear answer to his question, spoken not with words but with the press of her lips against his.

This was what she would do.

Kiss him. Touch him. *Claim* him.

Everything else fell away. What remained was the wild desire to stay right here, in this fleeting, stolen piece of forever.

His hands moved to cradle her face, his fingers tracing her jaw. He could feel the rapid beat of her heart under his touch, mirroring his own. She pulled away, and he rested his forehead against hers, catching his breath.

"I don't want this to end," he murmured, his voice raw with emotion.

"You said that already." She smiled. "But neither do I," she replied, her eyes shining. "I want more of this. So much more of you."

"You can have all of me." Alex shifted her body and pushed her into the blanket beneath her, hovering over her. He leaned in, capturing her lips in another kiss, this one more urgent, more demanding. His hands roamed over her body, memorizing every curve, every dip of her form. She responded in kind, her fingers threading through his hair, pulling him closer.

Too many clothes.

"I want you."

She suddenly laughed, eyes sparkling. "Take me."

Her words made him rock hard. Alex could feel every breath, every heartbeat, every shiver that ran through Sera's body. It was as if the world had narrowed down to just the two of them, and nothing, no one else existed.

The air between them buzzed with a tension so thick it felt tangible, like a silk thread binding Alex to her. Slowly, deliberately, he reached for the ties of her dress, his fingers brushing the fine fabric as he peeled it away. Each inch revealed beneath the dim glow of candlelight was like a revelation, her skin so fair it gleamed with an otherworldly beauty. He leaned in, his lips seeking the warmth of her shoulder, trailing kisses down the curve of her collarbone with a tenderness that made her shiver. The sound of her quickened breath filled the otherwise silent alcove, and he grinned against her skin.

"More," she murmured, her voice soft but edged with longing as she sank into his touch. "I want to see and touch you, too."

The words sparked something electric in him. He rose to his knees, brushed some sand off his breeches. His movements seemed predatory yet restrained, and in one quick motion he stripped off his shirt and tossed it aside. Her breath hitched as her eyes roamed over the sharp planes of his torso, each muscle carved with an artistry that seemed almost unfair. The shadow-play of candlelight against his skin was both mesmerizing and maddening, but it was his gaze—the smoldering in his eyes—that unraveled her, leaving her cheeks flushed and her heart hammering as though he had touched her without lifting a hand.

"Is this what you were looking for?" he teased, his voice a low growl that made her swallow hard.

"Yes," she whispered, with no hesitation. Her hands were on him instantly, her fingertips trailing up the hard planes of his chest, exploring the ridges and valleys of his build as if committing him to memory. Every brush of her fingers sent jolts of fire through his body. Her touch—it was intoxicating.

But Alex wasn't one to be completely undone just yet. His lips curved into a wicked smile. Speaking of touches… "I want to take you out of this dress," he said, his voice rough yet steady, revealing the need coiling tightly inside him.

She tilted her head back and grinned up at him with a spark in her gaze. "Your wish… your task," she teased.

Alex chuckled, shaking his head. "My beauty. My love."

She was going to be the end of him.

MY BEAUTY. MY love.

Their eyes met and Sera's throat constricted. All of this was irrevocable, and she had put her heart and future in the hands of this man she knew so little about. Her mind was somewhat alarmed, but every fiber of her body and soul wanted to be his. It couldn't be wrong; it just mustn't be wrong.

"Make me all yours." The challenge, if it was one, only spurred him on. The intricate workings of her dress were no match for his deft hands as he stripped her of it in a matter of moments. He dispensed with the fabric, letting it pool to the floor like draped moonlight, and then he froze.

The world around her dissolved into shadow and candlelight, the quiet crash of waves beyond barely registering as she drank in the sight of him. His body was a masterpiece, every curve of muscle and line of strength illuminated in flickering amber hues. Sera's breath caught, her pulse quickening as her fingers traced over the planes of his chest, the warmth of his skin beneath her touch sending a delicious shiver spiraling through her. He looked impossibly strong, yet the way he gazed at her—like she was something fragile, precious—made her heart ache as much as her body burned.

"Alex," she whispered, the name trembling on her lips, a plea wrapped in wonder. The way his fingers skimmed her sides, feather-light but deliberate, made her entire frame come alive, like the night itself conspired to amplify every sensation. He lowered her gently onto the makeshift bed of borrowed clothes, his movements slow, reverent, as though he was laying an entire kingdom with castles at her feet. With him, she felt like a princess in fairy tales, free to love and feel. The moment demanded nothing less than unspoken devotion. Every brush of his lips against her skin felt like a vow, the steady rhythm of his breath against her collarbone like a promise only they could share.

She arched under him, her body answering his touch instinctively, offering itself to the pull of something far greater than them both. And yet, in Alex's hands, she felt safe, cherished—as though he was not merely unraveling her, but stitching together every piece that had longed to be seen. "You're perfect," he murmured, his voice rough, laden with awe, and it sent a flush rolling over her skin.

Her hand reached up, tangling in his hair to pull him closer, the tenderness mingling with a hunger that felt as inevitable as the tide. A soft laugh escaped her, breathless and light, as her lips traced along the curve of his jaw. "You keep looking at me like that," she whispered, "and you'll ruin me."

Alex's answering smile was soft but laced with fire, his gaze holding hers as though he'd never look away again. "Ruin you?" he echoed, the words rumbling in his chest as his hands slid lower, memorizing her, worshiping her. "Sera..." His voice dipped, his lips brushing over her ear until she shivered beneath him, warm and undone. "I only want to make you whole."

Her legs wrapped around him as if to pull him closer, deeper. "Please, Alex," she whispered, her voice trembling but unyielding. "Do it."

"I'll make you mine."

"And we will find a way to be together in London."

"In London."

He stood up. The whisper of fabric sliding to the ground sent a ripple through the air, a quiet sound that roared like thunder in Sera's chest. She watched Alex stand before her, his movements unhurried, deliberate, as his hands worked to untie his breeches. The flickering candlelight cast shadows along his frame, emphasizing the taut strength of his body and the quiet grace that seemed woven into him. When the last barrier fell away and for a moment, she forgot to exhale. He was raw and beautiful, his every muscle carved with precision, as if sculpted by the sea and wind itself. But it wasn't just his form—it was him, Alex, standing there vulnerable, bold, and impossibly hers. And then he climbed back over her.

Her hands moved before her thoughts caught up, drawn to him as if by instinct. Her fingers trembled as they brushed over his chest, tracing the ridges of muscle with reverence, as though he were something sacred. His warmth seeped into her palms, a living heat that tethered her to the moment, grounding her even as it set her alight. She explored the powerful lines of his arms, the curve of his shoulders, the sturdy breadth of his chest—mapping him with a sense of wonder she'd never known she could feel. When her touch skimmed lower, down the ridges of his abdomen, his breath shuddered beneath her fingertips, and the sound sent a thrill racing down her spine. She looked up, meeting his gaze, and her heart stuttered. His eyes, those stormy, unrelenting eyes, pinned her in place—not with demand, but with a depth of care so profound it made her ache.

"You're… perfect, too," she whispered, her voice breaking with emotion, as if the words themselves couldn't fully capture what she was seeing, feeling. Alex's lips curled into the faintest smile, soft and private, only for her. Then he knelt, his hands brushing her sides, steadying her as though she was something to be cradled even in her fierceness.

She held his arms, anchoring herself as his lips found hers, tender and deliberate, stealing her breath while giving it back all at once. Time stretched impossibly thin, and when Alex finally shifted, positioning himself over her, the world contracted until it was just the two of them. Her senses sharpened—the sound of his breath mingling with hers, the feel of his fingertips brushing her cheek, the weight of his body so near to hers it felt as natural as breathing.

Then, he moved, slowly and deliberately, and her body welcomed him like a tide rising to the moon. A tremble rippled through her, an aching, searing pleasure that felt both foreign and inevitable, like it had always been waiting for this moment. She stilled.

"Does it hurt?"

She narrowed her brows but didn't have the words to answer. He was pressing inside her and she wanted to take him. "I've never…"

"Me neither."

Their bodies were truly one and the world became a symphony of sensations—the heat of his skin, the subtle musk of salt and firelight, the way his every breath seemed to reverberate through her. Soon, he moved, and she moved with him, finding a rhythm as timeless as the waves beyond. Each touch, each sound, was a wordless conversation, an exchange of promises neither of them could ever take back. Sera arched into him, her body singing with unrestrained want, but more than that—with trust, with love.

She held him tighter, her hands tangling in his hair, her lips brushing along his jaw between breaths. "Don't stop," she whispered, even though every thrust only became harder. His touch was steady and unyielding, yet also gentle at the same time. It wasn't just passion; it was care, devotion wrapped in every motion. She closed her eyes, surrendering to the storm, letting herself become part of something infinitely bigger and brighter than herself.

In Alex's arms, as they moved as one, she felt whole in a way she hadn't known was possible.

There was no going back to Sera from before.

Chapter Fourteen

A LEX HAD ASCENDED to heaven.

Every inch of Sera's body was a revelation under his fingertips, a masterpiece etched with grace and strength, matching each of his thrusts. He couldn't help the shaky exhale that escaped him as his hands spanned the curve of her waist, her skin warm and impossibly smooth against his palms while their bodies moved together. She wasn't just beautiful; she was everything—light and shadow, fire and water, chaos and calm—all colliding in the slender frame beneath him. Her trust in him, the way her body moved to meet his, was something that humbled him even as it ignited life itself coursing through his veins.

She was breathtaking, her lips parted on a soft moan that sent a jolt down his spine. Alex lowered his head, his mouth finding her throat, the delicate pulse there thrumming against his lips like an unspoken promise. He couldn't stop himself from murmuring words against her skin, raw affection he couldn't hold back.

It wasn't just about the way her body responded to him, though that was enough to drive him mad. It was the way she looked at him, the way her fingers curled into his shoulders, grounding him in this moment, this now. She undid him—not just his control, but the careful walls he'd built around the parts of himself he never thought he'd trust anyone to see. And Sera? She saw it all, and somehow, she still wanted him.

The sensation of her nails skimming his back made him groan. This was about her—about making sure her every touch, every breath, every impossible sound she made was pure pleasure. Her body fit against his like they'd been designed for this, for each other, and the realization hit him harder than he'd thought possible.

She gasped his name, her voice raw, filled with a need that seemed to echo his own, and he felt his restraint fray. But even in the rawness of this connection, Alex was careful, deliberate, his movements attuned to every response she gave him.

She pressed her hips up beneath him, her head tilting back as a string of soft, breathless cries pushed past her lips. Alex groaned again, deep and low, the sound echoing through him as he pressed closer, then pulled out a bit and came back—deeper inside her with every thrust.

The way she moved with him, the way her body welcomed him, was exquisite and maddening all at once. Every inch of him was connected to her, to the way she felt, the way she tasted, the way her voice trembled when she whispered his name like a benediction. And as the tension between them built, surging to a breaking point that felt as though it might shatter the world, Alex understood something that stole his breath entirely.

He was hers.

Entirely, irreversibly hers.

Every movement, every breath he took, only deepened that certainty. Alex pressed his forehead to hers, rooting himself in her touch, her scent, her presence. This wasn't just passion; it was more. Far, far more than he could find words for.

Desire. Pleasure. Wonder. Being inside her. Claiming her and being taken in so fully. Becoming one, her skin against his, the taste of her lips, the sound of her breathy moans, was not something there were words for. He could feel her tremble beneath him, her body arching into his. He was lost in her, consumed by her, every nerve ending alight with breathtaking sensation.

Sera was his life now.

"I never want to lose you," Alex whispered into her ear as he thrust, repeating it over and over again.

Fallen.

He had fallen so deeply.

He wanted to tell her everything about him and his life. It hovered on his tongue like a cloud gathering water and might burst at any moment.

Just a little longer.

He would tell her everything.

Soon.

EVERY NERVE IN her body burned, alive with a sensation that was both pleasure and torment, too much and not enough. There was no air, no thought—only the ripple of tension and release, the steady rhythm of him moving within her.

So deep inside her.

Sera clawed at his shoulders, her nails biting into his skin, desperate to anchor herself as she spiraled farther into the unknown. Each thrust sent a shudder through her, a sharp, searing ache that melted into unbearable heat, building higher and higher until she thought she might break apart from it.

Her breath fractured, a short series of gasps that she couldn't quite catch, couldn't seem to hold. His name left her lips in a frantic cry, her voice trembling on the edge of something she couldn't name. It wasn't just her body—it was her soul, reaching out, clinging to the one person who had completely undone her.

"Alex…" A whisper this time. A plea. Perhaps a prayer.

There was nothing in the world but him, the way his hands gripped her hips, firm but reverent, his lips brushing over her neck as though he were worshipping her. Every touch—his fingers gliding over her skin, his breath hot against her ear—wove pleasure tighter around her, pulling her deeper under.

Alex.

Her body tightened, the ache intensifying as though some invisible thread were winding tighter with every stroke, every movement, until it threatened to snap. The initial pain had turned to something beautiful, something transcending anything she'd ever felt. She just knew she needed more. More of his touch, more of his voice, low and husky when he murmured her name. Her thighs trembled as he pushed deeper, the heat of him enveloping her, overwhelming but perfect. The tension coiled inside her, impossibly sharp, impossibly sweet, hurtling her closer to something she both feared and craved.

He groaned and she felt the vibration inside her.

"I—" The word broke apart, lost in a hitch of her breath as she arched against him, her body entirely beyond her control. The world around her shattered into a blazing constellation of sensation, a compound of pleasure so profound it drove tears to the corners of her eyes. She cried out again, her body clenching, trembling, as wave after wave spilled through her, powerful and relentless, leaving her utterly wrecked.

Sera clung to Alex, her fingers tangling in his hair, pulling him closer as though she could fuse them together and make this feeling last forever. Her heart thundered in her chest, her body still rippling with aftershocks as she whispered his name, each syllable thick with awe and unyielding love.

And he gave it.

Every touch, every kiss had felt like a declaration of love, a rebellion against the world that sought to keep them apart. She came undone in a way that shook the very foundation of her life. Her future.

It was forever changed.

He seemed to reach his own release, for he grunted, her name breathing from his lips before his head fell into the crook of her shoulder. "Sera," he murmured again, his voice even hoarser.

I know. She was feeling the same.

For a long moment, she simply held him, and he her, the reality of what had just happened sinking in. The night was silent except for the gentle lapping of the waves and her own heart pounding in her ear.

That little book knew nothing!

The thought was so sudden, she laughed.

"What's so funny?" he asked, rubbing his forehead against her neckline before slumping down beside her, limbs tangled together.

Sera tried to contain her grin but failed. "I just had a thought that the book I got from my friend never once mentioned anything like this."

His brow arched. "That is probably a good thing," he said, and added, "Does it have anything about how to hold onto the woman of your life?"

His comment about not wanting to lose her filled her mind. "No," Sera replied, her voice equally soft but filled with a quiet determination. "We'll find a way."

Not just a way, but the *way.*

Her plans were no longer vague. She knew what she wanted for her future.

Alex. Alex. Alex.

No compromise.

Reality faded into nothing—only the overwhelming presence of inside her, atop, around—everything became Alex.

He was everything.

Chapter Fifteen

THE MORNING ARRIVED with a whisper Sera didn't want to hear, the sky bleeding softly from purple to pink to golden hues that painted the world anew. She stirred in the cocoon of warmth they'd created together, her cheek pressed to Alex's chest, listening to the quiet, steady pulse of his heartbeat. Each beat soothed the chaos that had once lived within her, each rise and fall of his chest a reminder of the night they had just shared. The chill of the early morning air nipped at her where his shirt had slipped from her shoulders, but his arms tightened instinctively around her, chasing the cold away. She smiled softly against his skin, her fingers brushing idle circles over his side.

I'm ruined.

I'm in love.

The world outside seemed unrecognizable, brighter somehow, as though the universe had tilted just enough to cast new light on everything. Sera felt it in her stomach—in the peace that hummed where uncertainty once resided, in the quiet contentment that lingered beneath the storm of her emotions. They had found something precious in each other, a connection that felt sacred, unshakable, as though it had always existed, waiting for them to discover it. She tilted her head, her gaze locking onto Alex's sleeping face, his features softened in repose. He looked almost boyish in the sunlight, and the sight struck her with such tender longing that her breath caught. He had seen her, truly seen her, and in doing so, he had uncovered something in her that felt irrevocably changed.

But the morning wasn't just a beginning; it was also a reckoning.

Her chest tightened with the clutch of truth that daylight brought. She couldn't linger endlessly in this new world they had created under the cover of night; choices waited for her in the biting light of reality. She untangled herself from Alex slowly, carefully, not wanting to wake him just yet, though the thought of leaving the comfort of his arms sent a throb of resistance through her. Rising to sit at the edge of the makeshift bed, she gazed out at the horizon outside the alcove, the colors melting together like watercolors on wet paper.

She had to return.

Her sister, along with her maid, wouldn't be able to hold suspicion at bay once breakfast arrived and she was still absent. Luncheon and dinner she missed often enough once in the countryside, but never breakfast. It was a long-winded ruse, and Sera didn't want to lie about something—someone—as wonderful as Alex.

My Alex.

She closed her eyes, inhaling deeply, letting the intoxicating mix of sea air and Alex's presence wash over her. She had made her decision. London called to her with promises she could no longer honor. There were vows to break, doors to close, and truths to face. She needed to end the engagement that had hung around her like a gilded cage, a bond that had never been real. Somehow, she had to confess to her parents that she could no longer be the daughter they'd wished her to be.

The burden of *that* conversation pressed on her like an ancient artifact needing to be buried. Yet beneath that weight was a spark of hope—new, fragile, but glowing fiercely. For once, the future didn't terrify her. She turned back to Alex, her heart swelling as the early light kissed his skin. No matter what awaited them, she knew deep in her bones they would face it together.

Her heart raced, not just from the handsomeness of him, well, that, too, but more so from the daring plan that she concocted in her mind. She would simply inform the prince of her chastity.

He would never marry her then, right?

The hardest truth was sometimes the simplest answer.

She glanced back at the horizon. She couldn't bear the thought of marrying the prince in the first place, a man she had never met, and it was even more impossible now when her heart belonged to the man beside her. If being compromised with Alex meant escaping that fate, then so be it. The risk was immense, but losing Alex would be even greater.

"Sera."

Her name. A good morning. Simple. Sera chuckled.

"We can't stay here forever, you know," she murmured, even though she wished otherwise.

A rustle, then, "Why not?" Alex's voice was muffled against her hair, a lazy, contented drawl that made her smile despite feeling reluctant to leave his embrace. This alcove.

"All right. So, the pianoforte will go on that ledge." She pointed over her head. "The bed chamber will be upstairs, no wait… there isn't an upstairs. How about over there?"

He pretended to squint. "No, I think the pianoforte should be in the parlor. So, we can listen to the children practicing while we read at night."

Sera gulped when she saw his smile.

Children.

Plans.

"That sounds wonderful." As soon as I get out of the betrothal with a stranger. "So, the bed chamber shouldn't be just above the drawing room, it would be loud." She jested but then it wasn't funny. This dream could become their future, but she certainly didn't want it to be in a cave.

"I don't care where I'll sleep as long as I have you in my arms."

She sighed and cradled his gorgeous face. He looked sleepy and so disheveled that she was proud to see the effect she had on him. There was a raw, boyish vulnerability about him that left her concerned about his heart, which she didn't want to break if she couldn't get out of the betrothal. But she would if she was so thoroughly ruined, wouldn't she?

Sera bit her lip. "I don't want to steal some moments with you; I want a lifetime."

"Why can't we stay here a moment longer?" A complaint.

"Only a moment. Because the world will notice if we go missing." She tilted her head to meet his gaze. "And eventually, they'll come looking."

"We could run away." He propped himself up on one elbow. "I hear the Americas are lovely this time of year."

Sera raised an eyebrow. "Do I strike you as a woman who would survive a single day without tea and a proper bath?"

"They have luxurious baths. And lovely mountains. The oceans. I've been to Boston and farther north."

"Would you truly be able to do that to your family?" She couldn't. She might be willful, rebellious, and even reckless, but she loved her family.

A sigh. "No." Those dark eyes met hers. "Now that I've—" He cleared his throat. "Now that I've found you, Sera. With you… I hope you can meet them."

This wasn't going to be simpler than the betrothal, just different. "Let's go to Boston after all. It will be hard but—"

"You'd adapt," he teased. "I'd ensure your survival, of course. Hunt, gather, protect you from wild bears."

"Because wild bears are absolutely the first thing I think of when imagining the American wilderness."

Alex laughed, low and infectious, but the glint in his eyes turned serious. "If I decided I could leave my family, if I said I meant it—running away together—would you come with me?"

Her breath hitched. Run away with him? It sounded perfect. But it wouldn't solve problems. And she could never cut ties with her family in such a definite way. "Don't ask me that," she whispered, poking his chest.

He grinned. "Why not? Scared of your answer?"

"Yes, because I might just say yes." The temptation... It didn't whisper how easy it would be; it practically hollered.

"I know."

Sera nodded. "We can't run, Alex. We both have obligations—messy, inconvenient obligations. But that doesn't mean..." She hesitated, searching for the right words. "That doesn't mean the choices we make won't be worth it."

His grin returned. "Agreed. It will only make our reunion sweeter."

"I like that. Reunion."

"Promise that we meet in London," he pressed on.

Her eyes widened. Yes! "Promise."

"Very well, love. Vauxhall Gardens. Midnight. One week from now, the 30th."

"We'll have to be careful," Sera murmured. "If anyone sees us..." She might be dragged off by her parents to who knew where.

"We will be," he assured her, his hand brushing hers. "And even if something happens, I won't let anything happen to you."

Her heart twisted. This man... She loved him. By some miracle, in such a short time, she loved him. The thought terrified her as much as it thrilled her. "Then Vauxhall Gardens. Beneath the oak tree filled with lanterns—there is only one. Midnight. Eight days from now."

"I'll be there," he promised, his eyes locking onto hers.

"And if you're not," she warned, trying to keep her tone light, "I'll hunt you down and make you regret it."

"I wouldn't dream of missing it, my love."

Sera nodded. It was time to say goodbye until they reunited in London.

Eight days.

Just eight days, and they would be together again.

Nothing could go wrong anymore.

Two days later

THE DRAWING ROOM of Charlene's townhouse in Mayfair smelled faintly of roses and beeswax polish. A comforting, familiar scent. Sera sat perched on a delicate cream satin stool, her spine too straight to be natural, her fingers twisting restlessly in her lap.

Almost as if her judgment day had arrived.

Across the room, Charlene sprawled like a cat on the chaise, one bare foot poking out from beneath her lavender muslin gown, the hem scandalously undone, but Sera felt rather tight-chested to point it out. Maddie and Ashley, seated on the overstuffed settee, leaned in close, their faces alight with conspiratorial energy.

"So, he's coming to London? The prince?" Ashley asked. "Why didn't you tell us?"

"He was always so far away; I never truly worried about it," Sera replied.

"But now that he's coming…" Maddie curled her lips, adjusting the embroidered ribbon in her hair. "That is rather big news!"

Sera sighed. It wasn't the only big news. "I know. I'm sorry."

"You're truly engaged to him then?" Charlene asked dryly. "Our very own princess-to-be. I knew there was a good reason I was on good terms with you."

Sera offered an unconvincing smile, a tight thing that didn't reach her eyes. "It isn't as if I had much choice. You know how these things are decided among our parents the moment we first toddle about the ballroom."

If I had a choice, it certainly wouldn't be some unknown man from somewhere! It would be an unknown man from somewhere else!

Yes, the irony wasn't lost on her.

Maddie raised an eyebrow. "Oh no, you can't say it like that, Sera. Prince von Hohenzollern-Sigmaringen is every girl's dream! Isn't he? Just think of his connections to every royal family in Europe! You could live at a different castle each season." She turned to Charlene and Ashley. "He'd probably arrive at Almack's looking like a proper storybook hero—armor shining, sweeping Sera onto his perfectly white steed. You'd have no choice but to swoon."

Ashley snorted. "If only he'd had a rose clenched between his teeth, right? You'd have convinced the entire ton that a fairy tale could come to life."

Sera shifted, warmth spreading along her neck. "He's a prince, not a romantic fantasy," she said. "Which, I should remind you, means no fairy godmother will be coming along to fix my life when it all falls apart." She still prayed that wouldn't happen. She still had Alex. And she believed in him.

Charlene waved a languid hand. "Oh, don't be so dramatic. He may not have a fairy godmother, but he probably has Europe's most charming manners and more crowns than you'll know what to do with. Married to him, you'll have the world at your fingertips—and a wardrobe far lovelier than mine, I imagine."

Ashley smirked. "For once."

Sera snorted. Not everything was about glitter. She imagined the prince stiff and harsh, eager to clip her wings and make her an accessory to his overripe life.

The very opposite of Alex.

Maddie leaned forward conspiratorially, her fan forgotten in her lap. "He does sound appealing to the ear, doesn't he? We shall have to see for ourselves if this is the case with the eyes. Be that as it may, don't be too hard on your family. I don't believe they are conspiring to make a bad match."

Her throat tightened. "I know," she murmured, though inside her chest, her heart jack-knifed. A prince certainly was polished, regal, neatly checkered into the pre-approved plans of her parents. But he wasn't *him*. Initially, having a prince—any man— was not her dream. But now, Sera wanted Alex as much as she needed the air she breathed. Each imagined image of her future smudged, like spoiled ink, and then filled instead with a man with untamed blond hair and sun-warmed skin who had walked barefoot with her on the beach.

Alex. Simple, maddening, impossible Alex. "You're terribly distracted," Charlene prodded, inspecting Sera with narrowed eyes. "That's not like you."

Time to come clean. "I've decided I want to dissolve the engagement," Sera blurted, more abruptly than she intended. The words burned as they spilled out, but once free, they carved a surprising relief.

Her friends froze. Ashley's hand paused mid-air, her cup of honeyed tea forgotten. Charlene sat up straighter, her expression losing its lazy amusement. Maddie spoke first, blinking quickly. "I beg your pardon?"

"You heard me," Sera stated, her voice steadier now. "I will not marry the prince, so I intend to lose him."

"How," Maddie began, clearly flabbergasted, "do you expect to lose a prince this summer, in time before the formal an- nouncement of your engagement and wedding?"

Charlene leaned in, gleaming with interest. "Just asking out of curiosity, my dear, why would you wish to? He's rumored to be absurdly handsome, well-versed in European politics, and did I mention the crowns?"

"I find crowns unsettling," Sera shot back, exhaling slowly. "And I wish to… extricate myself because I can't, in good conscience, wed someone I don't—"

"Love?" Ashley cut in with a slight grin. "Is this the start of some grand romantic rebellion?"

Sera opened her mouth, then closed it.

Could she admit the truth aloud? Confess her discretion? *I love someone who isn't him, someone I met with the salty taste* of sea air on my lips. Someone who doesn't fit into cream-colored drawing rooms or balance Society's endless rules. Possibly a pirate.

Instead, she shook her head cautiously. "I don't feel it's right… for either of us. I don't care about those things. You ought to understand." It was Ashley, after all, who ended up engaged and madly in love with her nemesis, the Earl of Linsey. "Your husband certainly doesn't like being stuck in bland drawing rooms sipping on tiny cups of tea. Doesn't he have a brewery of his own?"

"Yes, he does, Sera. But one doesn't exclude the other. You know he cuts a fine figure in tailcoats and runs the estate with a firm hand. He doesn't like stuffy Society but that's not because he doesn't fit in—he certainly commands the room when he has to attend such gatherings—he merely prefers the honesty of the countryside over the hypocrisy in Society."

Charlene tilted her head, her golden curls shimmering in the late London sun streaming through the window. "Do you truly think it's that easy to lose a prince?"

Sera blinked. "Why wouldn't it be?"

"Because," Charlene smirked, her tone half-mocking, half-serious, "if you're seen as rejecting him, you'll become instantly fascinating. And sadly, utterly scandalous. He's a prince, dear. They don't make it easy to slip away unnoticed."

Sera sighed, heat creeping into her face again.

Maddie crossed her arms, the picture of mock skepticism. "Well then, do tell. How exactly do you plan to back out of this most advantageous match?"

A light laugh floated up from somewhere she couldn't pinpoint, though whether it was tension breaking or nerves fraying, she didn't quite care. "One step at a time," she replied with a rueful smile, her heart still oddly tangled and heavy. But as her imagination wandered, as it always did when her mind was untethered, it arrived, per usual, at him. Alex.

"Is there anything in our handbook about how to repel a

prince then?" Maddie asked.

"He's not a moth," Ashley said. "She'd have to completely ruin her chances—"

Sera held her breath and then pinched her lips. Maddie and Charlene seemed oblivious, but Ashley gave her a hard stare. "Sera?" her friend whispered. "What have you done?"

Heat crept up Sera's face and she felt caught like a cat that spilled the milk. She shrugged.

"No!" Ashley put both hands on her mouth. "You have?"

Now, even Maddie and Charlene set their cups down. "Have what?"

Sera fanned herself. *Why was it suddenly so hot in here?*

"Sera?" Maddie pressed on with a tone that left no secrets unshared.

"Perhaps I have," she offered vaguely. "A little bit." Sera looked to Ashley for help for she had, too…

"When?" Ashley asked, understanding lacing her voice and a tinge of concern.

Charlene and Maddie's heads flicked from Sera to Ashley and back again.

"In Cornwall." Sera wrung her hands.

"Where? At home?" Maddie asked, enlightenment dawning on her face. Charlene seemed frozen, slack-jawed and wide-eyed as well.

"No, at the beach," Sera mumbled. "In a cave."

"At the beach?" Maddie stood abruptly. "In public?"

Ashley seemed to suppress a grin and put a hand on Sera's. "Now, slowly, from the beginning. There's another reason you don't want to marry this prince, and I understand it now. Tell me how I can help."

Sera nodded. "Is your friendly support all I need?" But truth be told, she could use some help.

"Did it hurt?" Charlene asked, curiosity evident in her voice.

Ashley and Sera exchanged simultaneous deadpan looks.

"I mean, did it?" Charlene pressed.

"Well, no, maybe a little," Sera began, searching Ashley's face for support. Her friend, however, blushed furiously, making her blonde hair stand out even more. "It was actually quite wonderful."

"So, you love him then?" Maddie inquired.

"You can do this without being in love," Ashley attempted to explain, as if she were an expert on the subject. "Not that I would know, though."

"Me neither," Sera admitted. The confession came easier than she expected.

All eyes turned to her, and her friends seemed to hold their breaths.

That softened Sera, and she shrugged. "It just happened, I guess. Love crept up on us, and now… now I can't imagine life without him."

Ashley nodded solemnly. "We need to lose the prince this summer."

"That's what I said," Sera replied.

"Who's this again?" Maddie asked, but Sera only raised an eyebrow. *I'm not telling.*

"So, first things first. What do we know about him?" Ashley began with renewed enthusiasm.

"He's coming to London," Sera said. "That's all I know. And the engagement ball. But I have to break it off before the announcement."

"Well, finding the prince in Society shouldn't be too difficult. Leave it to me to uncover more about him—his whereabouts and so on."

"Then, I'll let him know," Sera said, feeling a sense of hope with the plan.

"But what if he doesn't let you out of the engagement?" Maddie asked, but the others' death stares silenced her.

Well, then, she would reconsider her plans to run away.

Cloverdale House on Abbotsberry Road, London

ALEX COULDN'T SHAKE the feeling of chains tightening around his chest during the entire carriage ride to London. The farther he traveled from Cornwall, the more constricted his heart felt. Being away from Sera felt like diving deep into the ocean—going deeper and deeper, unsure when the buoyancy would shift his descent to an ascent. Until he saw her again, he wouldn't breathe freely.

"Ceva nu e în regulă cu tine." Something's the matter with you. His sister, Thea, said in their native Romanian when he arrived at the rehabilitation center where she and their brother, Stan, had found a temporary home.

Alex bit his lip. "I'm fine; it's him I'm worried about." Stan had a large bandage on his shoulder and was suffering from an infection that had led to a fever. "How did this even happen?" Alex asked once they were alone, and the servants, along with Stan's nurse, left them in a small parlor with a lovely window overlooking the gardens.

"I'll be all right," Stan said, rubbing his shoulder. "I'm in capable hands."

"Yes, about that..." Thea's eyes met Alex's as she gave a meaningful nod. "This nurse of his is the one in good hands, I believe."

Alex furrowed his brow. "A nurse?"

Thea nodded, but Stan looked rather defeated. It was the first time he'd seen his brother wear such a look.

I know how you feel, brother.

"You fancy the nurse? Is it mutual? Is that even allowed? A nurse and her patient?" Alex asked. He never thought he'd ask his brother such a question. Then again, he never imagined losing his heart in Cornwall. The world was truly changing.

"Ask her. She wants to marry the orthopedist," Stan said, almost begrudgingly.

"Wait, what?" Alex's gaze shot to Thea. What was happening here?

"Well, he's not my doctor but yours. So, I'm not technically his patient," Thea crossed her arms.

"He looked after your ankle when he saved you from the kidnappers," Stan retorted.

Alex was confused. "Stop! Kidnapped? When were you kidnapped?"

"It has to do with Baron von List," Thea said with a sigh.

"The Prussian?" Alex deflated. It hadn't been clear from Stan's letter in Cornwall—only the danger. But he didn't want to think about it. Baron Wolfgang von List had been exploiting the gold mines in their region in Brașov for so long that it was worth it for Father to send Stan to England to confront him.

"What have you learned about von List?" Alex asked.

"It's a long story, Alex. We're going to have tea with my new friend, the Earl of Langley. He has some documents we ought to see."

Alex nodded. Of course, he'd help with anything that would ensure their home's prosperity. But he had the sinking feeling that he didn't quite know what he was facing in London.

The valet knocked on the door and motioned to Alex, who excused himself and strode over to the man who had followed him back from Cornwall. He'd ordered him to find him after he settled his belongings.

They retreated to his room.

He had one question that had been holding most of the space in his head. He didn't know the maps of London, the neighborhoods, but he knew the night sky and how to navigate to Cornwall—he just had to follow his heart. But first things, first. "How far is Vauxhall Gardens from here?"

"Three miles, Your Highness."

Alex walked over to the window, peering outside. "You think I'm incapable of navigating three miles on my own?" For her, he would navigate the whole world.

"I think," the valet replied slowly, "that London streets are not precisely the open fields of Cornwall. You might find unexpected dangers lurking here."

"Unexpected dangers lurked there as well." And he encountered the biggest one. But he understood the man's point. He glanced at his valet. "Also, it's not the streets I'm worried about, but the timing. Midnight."

The valet's second eyebrow joined the first. "Midnight. Vauxhall Gardens. Might I ask why?"

"No, you may not," Alex replied simply. He needed to protect Sera no matter what. It was already dangerous enough with his sister's kidnapping and his brother's injury.

The man sighed. "Very well. Though I should mention that midnight at Vauxhall Gardens is precisely when one is most likely to encounter all sorts of ne'er-do-wells."

Alex frowned. Did Sera know that? She was the one who had suggested the place. The tree with the lanterns. Oh no! He hadn't thought it through when they decided to meet. "I have no way to change the meeting."

The valet muttered something under his breath, something Alex suspected wasn't entirely complimentary. Fine. He was in the wrong here. Or rather, he was the one who was uninformed. But he couldn't change what had already been set in motion.

"What about the other matter?" Alex shifted the topic. "What have you discovered about Lyndon?"

"They arrived in town this morning, Your Highness."

Good. Then he could break this engagement without any trouble. "I need to see him as soon as possible."

The man nodded. "When is your meeting at Vauxhall? I'll prepare your attire for the occasion, something dark so you can blend into the night and match the clandestine nature of your escapade."

Alex grinned. "Thank you, that will be perfect. You know me too well."

"And yet, not well enough to stop you," the man muttered,

though there was no malice in his tone.

Six days.

Just six more days, and he'd see her again.

And if the stars aligned, perhaps this time, he wouldn't have to let her go.

Chapter Sixteen

T HE LYNDONS' DRAWING room, so often a place of easy conversation and gentle laughter, felt oppressive this morning. Though unchanged, everything seemed suddenly foreign, as though it pressed in on Sera's dissatisfaction. She wasn't content to be here, or anywhere else for that matter, not knowing where Alex was.

She simply missed him.

Delicate porcelain vases lined the mantel, and the scent of lavender polish clung to the air, yet none of Lyndon House's usual charm soothed her. It was as if the room itself anticipated something, echoing the quiet restlessness that had pulled her from sleep too early. Sera's gaze flitted to the clock on the mantel—a fragile thing adorned with gilded cherubs—and watched the hand tick past another moment. Waiting for the reunion at Vauxhall had never felt so interminable.

And to make matters even worse, she had to dress for a ball she didn't even want to attend.

"Silk or cotton, Miss Lyndon?" the modiste, Madame Duchon asked, her voice crisp but polite as she adjusted a pin on the hem. Off to the corner, her mother and sister were looking over some muted fabrics the modiste had brought along with her for Isabella, who insisted she didn't want a dress, but her mother insisted otherwise.

"Cotton," Sera replied firmly, stepping carefully onto the wooden stool, her slippers making no sound. The air in the room smelled faintly of lavender sachets tucked into drawers, mixed with the bite of freshly pressed fabric. Sera sighed as she stood still, letting the modiste bustle around her like a bee attending to a flower.

Cotton. It was practical, comfortable—her Cornwall wrapped in every stitch. She thought of those carefree days along the Cornish shore, the sea breeze knotting her hair, her toes digging into cool, damp sand. Even though it was only a few days ago, it had been too long since she'd walked barefoot, without anyone fussing about what she'd wear or how she was to behave. Now, she was to be Miss Seraphina again, polished and proper, when she'd rather just be Sera.

Sera and Alex.

Short and sweet.

Seraphina and Alex.

Urgh.

No. Just Sera and Alex.

The modiste gave her a nudge. "Hold still, Miss Lyndon, nearly done," she said, her fingers working deftly with a needle near Sera's sleeve. It seemed like lace atop sarcenet atop muslin—perfect to keep its shape—or to force her into a shape and life she didn't want. The gown's pale-blue fabric layers were stiff and cool against her arms, a far cry from the simple flowing cotton dresses she longed for.

Her gaze drifted to the large bay window.

She squinted at the bright sunlight until her eyes adjusted, and that's when she saw it. A grand carriage, drawn by four sleek horses with coats that gleamed under the afternoon sun, rolled to a stop just beyond the garden wall.

Sera leaned slightly to the side, curiosity tugging her closer to the view.

"Lady Seraphina, please keep still," the modiste said as she tugged at the hem, but Sera's gaze was fixed to the goings on outside. The man who stepped down first wore dark tails, his posture erect and manner deliberate. His hair was blond, short and—Sera swallowed hard when the memory of that night flooded back. It was mere days ago and yet seemed as if it had been in another lifetime. How she'd gripped Alex's hair, feeling the silky softness of his golden locks between her fingers. He'd held her, supported her, given her strength to face the earth-shattering sensations he'd sent through her body. It had been an awakening that fueled her appetite for more.

For him.

As her mind drifted, Sera couldn't take her eyes off the tall man outside. He paused, slipping on a top hat with a flick of his gloved hands. Sera caught her breath. If he weren't so polished, she'd have thought it was Alex. His broad shoulders filled his coat perfectly, and the natural ease of his movement awakened a memory she hadn't buried deeply enough—or not at all. But the stranger wasn't Alex.

It couldn't be Alex.

This man assisted an elegantly dressed woman stepping from the carriage—a woman whose shining blonde hair, elegantly tucked beneath an elaborate bonnet, resembled someone from a royal portrait.

The woman who stepped out of the carriage placed her hand on his arm as if they belonged together—as if they'd never been apart. She moved with practiced grace, her slender frame draped in a gown of soft lilac silk that shimmered faintly in the sunlight. Her hair was swept into an intricate chignon, delicate strands catching the light like threads of fine gold. Perched atop her head was a wide-brimmed hat adorned with clusters of pale pink and ivory flowers, each petal so perfectly arranged it looked as if it had just bloomed there. Her posture was regal, her chin held high, and her gloved hands rested lightly against the gentleman's offered arm. Though she carried herself with quiet authority, there was a warmth in the slight turn of her lips, a reserved calm that heightened her elegance.

This was what her mother aspired for Sera to be. But it was in vain, wasn't it?

Her gaze caught the man again.

Not. Alex.

Stop. Looking.

Miss Seraphina fit in with people like these—not Sera from the beach. Her throat tightened as she wondered what Alex would think if he saw her now in this lovely yet rigid gown. Would he laugh? Or would he nod politely, as if she were a stranger he had never met? Would he stalk up to her, grab her shoulders, and demand to know what was going on?

She'd wager on the last.

Her fingers twitched at her sides, a longing she couldn't shake, forcing her to hold her breath. And then, just when she thought the scene couldn't twist her heart further, another man descended from the carriage. His hair was dark, not fair like Alex's, but everything else—the cut of his jaw, his height, his deliberate stride—made her falter. Although Sera willed him to look her way, all she received was his side profile.

Did everyone look like Alex to her these days?

"Miss Lyndon, you're leaning too much," scolded the modiste, tugging at her skirts. Sera straightened, but her eyes stayed fixed on the figures outside. And that man. Who were they? She craned her neck for another glimpse as the trio stepped away into the driveway, their faces turned just far enough from her view, leaving her with nothing but silhouettes and endless questions.

Oh no! "Do you know who they are, Madame Duchon?" Sera asked, her voice soft but slightly hurried.

The modiste chuckled, but the older woman had her back to the window and didn't lift her gaze from the needles. She didn't even glance up. "I haven't the faintest idea, but if they're heading to the Linsey estate next door, they're likely royalty or close enough." Of course, they were.

People like that weren't ordinary, not with carriages and

clothes that seemed to belong in a storybook. Sera swallowed hard, trying to stifle her feelings, and looked down at her own reflection in the long mirror to her left. The pale-blue gown billowed gracefully around her. Every pin and stitch made her more of Miss Seraphina and less of the girl Alex would recognize. Who did she want to be for the rest of her life?

Her mind drifted back to Cornwall.

To him.

She could still hear his easy laughter over the rush of the tide, still see the way he'd kicked off his boots without hesitation, that lopsided grin and confidence as they strolled down the beach. His presence had been warm and steady then, his voice rich and teasing. She closed her eyes for a moment and tried to summon that feeling—the sun on her shoulders, the wind cradling her hair, and Alex beside her, bare feet and all.

"Miss Lyndon?" Madame Duchon's voice pulled her back. "You're leaning again."

"Oh! I'm sorry!" Sera blinked, her gaze retreating from the empty street outside the window. The carriage was gone now; the figures had vanished like a dream she hadn't quite held onto.

"We'll need another fitting." The modiste didn't wait for a reply, already packing up her tools. "I shall fit your sister then too."

Sera nodded absently. She couldn't shake the ache in her chest. Miss Seraphina was someone these elegant strangers might recognize. But Alex? Alex would only know Sera, the girl on the beach—and worse, he might prefer her that way.

But she was both, she supposed.

Oh, why didn't I tell him my real identity? Why didn't she formally introduce herself in a witty informal manner? She wanted to do so at Vauxhall; however, she had thought that might have dragged it out too long.

Across the room, her sister pulled a face and shot her an expectant look. How could she quickly get out of this engagement?

She needed to confront the prince.

Soon.

THE INSTANT ALEX stepped off the carriage and his boots landed firmly on the cobblestones, the hairs on the back of his neck stood up. It was a strange sensation, sharp and insistent, like the gaze of unseen eyes. He adjusted his top hat, squared his shoulders, and scanned the street. Nothing. Just the quiet sway of trees lining the lane and the occasional flicker of movement behind the thick-paned glass of the houses. He absentmindedly reached out to help his sister off the carriage.

"You really seem odd these days," Thea remarked, throwing him a quick glance. His sister had always been attuned to his feelings, but he wondered if she could understand him now.

I fell in love, and now I don't feel complete without her.

"Come on, pull yourself together," Stan said as he climbed off the carriage, wincing before pressing against his shoulder.

"Be careful. Should you have left the rehabilitation center?" Alex asked.

"I'm trained for worse, brother. You should know." Two years of naval training had honed his senses. Unfortunately, it seemed that a few days with Sera had undone most of it. His brother was right. He needed to pull himself together.

Still, the feeling lingered.

He turned his head slightly, his sharp gaze sweeping over the row of houses. Was someone there? Watching? A faint silhouette shifted behind a curtain, and Alex narrowed his eyes, but moments later it was gone.

He'd only ever felt such acute awareness in her presence, a tension crackling down his spine like a static charge.

Alex reached a gloved hand to lightly adjust his cravat and exhaled. Foolish.

Sera wasn't here.

She couldn't be.

That life—those days—they belonged far from this finely dressed, proper corner of the world. And yet, his chest felt heavy, as if she were nearby, like the scent of the sea clinging to the edges of memory. He shook the thought away, tightening his jaw. He wasn't the boy who had strolled through orchards by her side. Not anymore. She wasn't the girl in bare feet, wandering through the sand as if the world were hers to conquer. And besides, this world wasn't hers—not here.

His brother came up the stairs just ahead. "This is the residence of the Earl and Countess of Langley," Stan noted, waving a hand at the grand house before them.

"The earl and I have been working on the problem with Baron von List for a while. He's eager to hear your thoughts on a few documents," Stan added.

"Hm-hm." Alex tilted his head, glancing toward the house again before shifting his focus to the neighboring property, a quieter presence with delicate hedges and a far less imposing façade. "Do you know the neighbors there?" His hand lingered at the edge of his coat, unsure why he felt drawn to that house, just knowing that the unease under his skin grew.

Stan stopped halfway to the door "Just some wealthy people, I'd wager." came a soft, matter-of-fact voice from behind him. Thea descended after them, her silk skirts brushing the step lightly. She adjusted her gloves, her tone light yet firmly dismissive.

Alex turned his gaze back to the quiet house across the lane, surveying it once more. Just some wealthy people... but something didn't sit right. He couldn't explain it, even to himself.

Something about this place unsettled him.

The odd prickle on his skin persisted as if it knew better than he did. At last, he shook the thought away, his fingers curling into a fist before unclenching.

The heavy oak door of the Langley residence suddenly swung open, revealing the straight-backed butler waiting within.

Without a word, Stan took the lead, ascending the steps to the entrance. Thea offered Alex a faint smile as she followed, completely unbothered, her steps precise and light.

Alex cast one last glance over his shoulder toward the quiet houses. Then, shifting his coat slightly, he turned and climbed the stairs, his boots firm against the stone. Whatever nagging feeling gnawed at him would have to wait. For now, they had business inside. Once they were ushered in with all the pomp and circumstance due two princes and a princess, Alex noticed that the Langleys' parlor was bright and spacious, draped in elegance without tipping into ostentation. A patterned rug softened the polished floors, while the golden light of the afternoon sun streamed through tall windows dressed in cream-colored draperies. A faint aroma of roses lingered in the air, blending with the sharper scent of lemon polish on the furnishings. Alex stepped into the room behind Stan and Thea, where two couples were already waiting.

The Earl of Langley stood near the settee, his posture straight despite a streak of gray in his well-kept hair. Age seemed to have tempered his movements, but there was no mistaking the sharpness in his eyes or the authority in his bearing. He hovered near his wife, Violet, the Countess of Langley, glancing toward her with an attentiveness that bordered on protective. She sat gracefully, one hand resting lightly on the curve of her swollen belly, her cheeks flushed in a way that spoke more of contentment than discomfort. Beside them were two more people, a young man and woman.

"Welcome," the earl said after the usual formal introductions, his voice warm. He extended his hand to Stan and then to Alex, the grip firm but quick. "We're glad you could make time to visit before the ball. My wife is especially grateful for the chance to rest before the festivities begin."

"Congratulations," Alex said with a curt glance at her round belly. Thea and Stan seemed to know these people, but they were strangers to Alex—regardless of Stan's trust in the Langleys.

The countess smiled at that, her gaze sincere as it swept over the siblings. "Quite right," she said, her hands folded in her lap. "But how lovely it is to have such fine company already. Please, make yourselves comfortable."

Stan and Thea obliged with ease, each choosing a seat. Alex, however, took the closest chair. His unease hadn't completely left him; nerves still prickled at the edge of his awareness like an elusive shadow in the corner of his mind—his every thought circling back to Sera.

Before he could dwell on it, a cheerful voice broke through the hum of polite conversation.

"And here we are," Thomas continued, leaning slightly toward his companion, "remiss for not having come together sooner."

The blonde young woman at his side turned her head graciously, her features smooth and bright with expression. Her hair framed her face perfectly, styled to invite admiration, though she seemed utterly unbothered by it.

"Allow me," she said, rising in a single fluid motion. Her smile reached Alex even before her words. "Lady Ashley, and this, of course, is my fiancé, Thomas, the Earl of Linsey. We do hope you will remain in England long enough to attend our wedding?"

Alex stood as manners dictated, bowing slightly in recognition, and placed a quick kiss on her knuckles. "A pleasure, Lady Ashley. Linsey," he added with a nod toward Thomas. He smiled back warmly, and Alex thought that these were people he could befriend. Perhaps they were the sort of nobles who'd even accept Sera if he could introduce her to Society. But if not, he'd either take her back to Bran Castle as his princess or purchase a manor in Cornwall, her favorite place in the world.

Alex felt heat rushing to his head and he tugged at his starched cravat. It had been so much easier to breathe on the boat with Sera, the wind in his hair and her gaze on him instead of the prying eyes.

The open windows lining the hallway offered scant relief.

He moved to stand near one of them.

He glanced to where his sister sat, her posture impossibly straight despite the oppressive warmth. Beside her, Lady Ashley perched on a sapphire settee, her fan moving briskly but doing little to combat the heat.

"Lady Anna's ball promises to be the grandest affair of the year," Ashley said, her voice crisp and bright, breaking above the hum of nearby chatter. "Truly, the very thought of it makes me giddy!"

Alex bit back an eye roll and made no effort to hide his disdain entirely. Balls were meant to be endured, not celebrated. They were glittering spectacles concealing the same well-worn ambitions and schemes in different gowns each season. Thea caught his reaction immediately, her sharp eyes narrowing briefly.

"This isn't just another ball, Alex," she said, her tone measured but resolute. "It's my introduction—a welcome of sorts. I have waited for this moment, and I intend to make it count."

He studied her, noting the determined tilt of her chin. A strand of blonde hair stuck rebelliously to her temple, but she didn't reach to fix it—either because she didn't notice or, more likely, refused to care. She really meant it, Alex thought. She wasn't here to fade into shy obscurity. She planned to step fully into the swirling currents of her new arrival in London, and society wouldn't miss the point.

That meant attention.

Attention felt no different from the threats posed by opponents in Alex's life. Yet, he didn't react. Instead, he leaned back enough to take in a long view of the hallway beyond. Beads of sweat pricked at the back of his neck beneath his cravat. Lady Ashley and Thea had already shifted the conversation, their voices dipping into topics that he refused to waste his thoughts on.

Grateful for the respite, Alex's attention turned to the pair of men standing near the fireplace. His brother Stan stood tall, his arms loosely crossed in a way that hid the tension Alex recognized. The earl rested one hand on the mantel, his expression grave as he leaned slightly toward Stan, their conversation clearly meant to remain hushed with occasional glances at the women. They didn't want to alarm the ladies, Alex guessed.

"Very dangerous," Stan muttered, his rich, steady voice unmistakable even in hushed tones.

The earl nodded, his brows knitting together. "Unpredictable," he added, his voice equally quiet.

Alex didn't need to guess who they were speaking of. The mention of danger and unpredictability could mean only one man—Baron von List. His name alone carried a weight that whispered of hidden schemes and new threats lurking on the horizon. *Or in this case, shimmering among glittering chandeliers,* Alex thought grimly. Balls like the one Lady Anna hosted offered the ideal stage for shadows to blend seamlessly into the light. He dreaded the ball for so many reasons.

"Lady Anna's event isn't just about the dancing," Ashley's voice spilled into his focus again. He turned his head just enough to glimpse her fan, fluttering as she smiled at Thea. "This is *the* ball of the summer, and the most important evening I can think of!"

Thea smiled, soft but pointed. Her voice, in stark contrast to Ashley's almost fevered excitement, was calm and deliberate. "I can't wait."

Alex lifted his glass to his lips without sipping. The thought of the ball twisted deep into his plans, feeding an urgency he rarely allowed to surface. He couldn't wait either, but only because the moment it ended, he intended to leave. The ball, its opulence, its guests—all of it blurred in his mind, unimportant next to a single purpose. He was going to find Sera. He just needed to free himself from the Lyndons—and the precarious arrangement surrounding their daughter—before anyone noticed.

Careful to sound unaffected, he finally asked, "Will Miss

Lyndon be in attendance with her parents?"

Thea's brows knit so briefly he might have missed it if he hadn't been watching her so closely. Her warning glance followed, sharp and almost imperceptible. But Alex ignored it, meeting Ashley's animated gaze instead.

"Yes, of course," Ashley replied, oblivious to Thea's subtle rebuff.

"Then I shall try to speak with Mr. Lyndon before the ball," Alex said mildly, pinching a wrinkle at the corner of his sleeve while his tone stayed even.

The earl turned toward him for the first time, his polite expression giving little away except formality. "Are congratulations in order?" His words held the undercurrent of something more, but his delivery was perfectly cordial.

Alex forced himself to meet the question with a steady nod. *Congratulations are simple enough,* he thought bitterly. *Unless they're given for the wrong reason.*

Miss Lyndon was wrong. Sera would be right.

"Your suggestion was simply perfect, Ashley," the countess soon said, her voice lilting. She straightened in her seat, her attention on her young friend. "It was so thoughtful of you to suggest that we introduce them all before the ball."

Ashley turned then, her eyes bright as they met Alex's as if she expected his reaction. She leaned toward him, her movement as smooth as her words. "It's not every day I meet someone who enters a room with such grace and looks as though he's assessing it rather than enjoying it," she remarked.

Alex resisted a slight retreat of his body. "I tend to find myself doing both since my naval training. It's a habit I suspect isn't easily broken."

"And here I thought habits like that belonged to the older generation," she countered. Her gaze searched his face, curiosity gleaming.

Something about the lightness of her tone stirred turmoil within him, though he wasn't quite sure why. The air in the room still felt too heavy, the kind of weight that only prompted more questions. Nevertheless, he met her glance steadily, offering a faint but polite curve of his lips.

"When did you arrive in London?" The Earl of Linsey, whom everyone seemed to address casually as Thomas, asked.

"Only yesterday," Alex murmured offhandedly. "I was in Cornwall for a while."

"Oh?" A spark flickered in Lady Ashley's eyes. "I see. I have a dear friend who adores the Cornish coast. So, have you enjoyed your time in England so far?"

"Thank you, yes." Mostly the English girl. *My girl.*

"That's good," the countess murmured, rubbing her swollen belly.

"And what about Cornwall's beaches?" Lady Ashley asked again. "It gets dreadfully windy toward the end of summer, doesn't it? Wild some might say."

It was wild but not because of the wind. "Wind is a sailor's friend. It puts wind in the sails," Alex replied politely. Not even his brother grilled him like this.

"Ashley," Thomas murmured. "Give the man some room to breathe."

"I'm just curious, that's all," she said with a smile. That smile took a turn that made Alex's skin crawl. "You are engaged to Miss Seraphina Lyndon, aren't you? She is a friend of mine, you see."

Alex's heart sank.

His gaze instinctively darted to every escape route in the room.

He cleared his throat. "What a small world."

"Quite small," Lady Ashley agreed.

Langley chuckled. "About the wind in the sails, I'm afraid I've somehow stolen yours," the Earl of Langley began, nodding toward the door. "Ladies, would you please excuse me for a moment while I share some documents with the princes?"

Alex shot up from his chair. "Let's."

This woman was dreadfully unsettling.

She kind of reminded him a little of Sera.

Just a little bit.

Chapter Seventeen

Later that afternoon

S ERA SAT ON the wide window seat, her bare toes brushing against the rug as she leaned her head against the cool pane of glass in the sitting room. A gentle breeze stirred the edges of the curtains, bringing with it the faint scent of black tea from the pot in front of her.

She took another sip from her cup, but nothing could warm her in London as much as Alex's touch had in Cornwall. Even though it wasn't windy, she didn't feel the same ability to breathe. She had abandoned time for the moment, wondering how she'd extricate herself from the ball and her family long enough to meet Alex at Vauxhall. Before that, however, she had to face the prince.

Sera felt a twinge of anxiety. Soon, summer would be over, and she hadn't made much progress in losing a prince—only her heart. Since leaving Cornwall, her mother had kept a hawkish eye on her. And when she couldn't, there were always maids hovering nearby. She hadn't been able to leave the house even once!

The sharp crack of the door opening drew her attention, and the butler announced her friend. Ashley swept in, her slightly flushed cheeks brightened by the ivory day dress she wore. She brought all the energy of someone bursting with news.

"You'll never guess who I met at the Langleys'," Ashley started, unpinning her wide-brimmed straw hat and flinging it onto a nearby chair.

Sera shifted, tucking her feet beneath her as her curiosity stirred. "Don't say? Please tell me the prince is awful."

"I met him, yes, and his brother and sister. They are quite lovely, by the way. So educated and accomplished. I mean, the way they speak and—" Ashley's smile deepened, a playful glint in her warm brown eyes as she plopped down in a chair, "and his smile." She fanned herself.

That had nothing to do with her.

However…

Her heart sank slightly at the announcement. If he was good, he might be "good" and forgive her. If he was heroic… Well, then he might not accept the broken engagement! She didn't want him to be *good*. She wanted him to be a bad man, extraordinarily picky.

She caught her friend's look. "What? Is he a toad?" she asked, her tone half-teasing but edged with hope.

"Why?" Ashley asked. "Would you marry him if he is handsome?"

Sera scoffed. "Of course not! I'm just afraid my mother might marry him off to Isabella after I break off the engagement. My mother melts at a beautiful face."

Ashley laughed and then said, "The man is no toad."

"Ah well, what about his intelligence? Is he empty-headed?" Sera pressed, leaning forward slightly, as though trying to will an unfavorable answer with her intensity. "Mama has a thing for beauty, and my Papa has a thing for brains."

"I'm afraid not even a little bit slow-witted," Ashley said with a shrug.

Very bothersome, indeed.

Sera crossed her arms, pouting. "Then he must be rude and haughty." Anything. Ammunition she could use to justify to her parents the reason beyond "I gave my heart and flower to someone else." She clung to this possibility, needing there to be some flaw in a man who had surely been bestowed every privilege imaginable. Ashley's reply came quickly, dispelling the notion with a shake of her head. "He's none of those things, I'm afraid. He's… well, young. Quite charming, actually. Some would even consider him perfect."

Very well, but still perfectly wrong for her. "And from what I heard, he's very capable. He'll be assisting the Langleys in resolving some diplomatic issue—something to do with a treaty, I believe. His sister, the princess, is apparently brilliant herself. She drafted some documents, a charter of sorts," Ashley admitted thoughtfully. Her friend waved a gloved hand in the air, laughing a little. "It all went completely over my head, but everyone seemed impressed." She pulled off her gloves and helped herself to a cup of tea.

But Sera had lost all ability to swallow.

Her fingers tightened around the hem of her skirt. Whoever this prince was—and his brilliant, impossibly perfect brother and sister—was undoubtedly the center of admiration for everyone present, lifting him higher while ensuring others remained firmly in his orbit, gazing up. She shifted on the window seat, her gaze flicking toward the lace-covered glass. She would be a pariah if she broke off the engagement.

"I suppose he has the favor of the entire ton now," Sera muttered after a moment of uncomfortable silence.

"I imagine so," Ashley replied, tilting her head slightly as she studied her friend. "What about this man you met in Cornwall?"

Sera grinned, thinking about Alex. "Where do I begin? He is the exact opposite of what you say about the prince."

"So, a peasant, then?"

Sera tossed a pillow at her friend. "What peasant? He is a man of the sea."

"A sailor?"

He probably could be. "I'd wager he's probably the captain."

Ashley's back shot straight. "Dear me, do you even know?"

"I know he's the one!"

"Sera! Are you telling me you slept with a man you don't know?"

Well, when Ashley put it that way… it did seem a bit reckless. But what in love isn't reckless? "His name is Alex."

"Ah, so it's Alex. What about his last name?"

"I imagine it's just as sweet as his kisses."

Ashley's eyes sparked with disbelief. "What do you really know about him?"

"I know everything I need to. He saved my life, Ashley. He could have died in the process. He is a good man. And I love him so."

"And where is he now?"

"He has business in London. We'll meet soon at Vauxhall. By then, my engagement should be broken."

"What if he's a deckhand with no home or land?"

Sera shrugged. "I have a house and land. If titles and riches were all I wanted, I could marry a prince, couldn't I? I don't love him for his fortune; I love him for who he is."

"So long as you know what you're doing." She suddenly leaned closer. "How was it? You know, that?"

"A lady never tells." The smirk tugged at her lips before she could stop it, like letting a secret slip for the fun of it. A spark of satisfaction flickered in her chest, brief and fleeting, before it gave way to something heavier. She exhaled softly, though the sigh pressed harder within her than what escaped. Even as she carried the lingering warmth of mischief, there was a knot curling low inside her, one she ignored with practiced ease. "Is this the part where I point out you're not a lady and you'll never be now?" Ashley arched a brow, but her smile was conspiratorial and playful as always.

Another pillow flew across the room. "I'm a lady at heart."

Ashley laughed. "And a hoyden in bed, right?"

"Ashley!"

"What? Prince and court versus sea man and beach. You

chose a sea man at the beach! It's scandalous!" Sera's breath hitched, because her friend was right; she had betrayed her station quite badly.

But then Ashley winked at her. "I, future countess of Linsey, will support you. The beach is far better, anyway."

That brought a genuine smile to Sera's lips. "You're right," she agreed, the words fitting like a secret just between them. "The beach is far better."

No prince, charming or not, could replace the feeling of sand beneath her feet or the sound of waves crashing in her ears. No prince could replace Alex. Her sea man. Poseidon, truly. He was built like the Greek ruler of the seas from mythology books and had the heart of a prince, even if he lacked the title. But as she reassured herself, a question lingered in her mind—would Alex have belonged in a world like that, among titles and treaties?

And if so, could she have fit by his side?

"This is what I propose: I'll arrange a little gathering and invite the Langleys, you, and a few other friends. The prince will be invited, and you'll have a chance to see him before you make up your mind." Ashley folded her hands primly on her lap and looked pleased with her idea.

"That's a terrible idea!" Sera sighed. "I don't need to make up my mind. I have a mind; it's made, thank you very much!"

"Perhaps you'd like to change it? Or at least give yourself the option?"

"Would you want to give yourself another option? An alternative to Thomas?"

"Of course not!" Ashley rose from her seat. "Never!"

"Aha! Then why should I?" The mere thought made her want to claw up the walls.

"I know. I just want you to be sure. If you meet the prince, at least you'd have a chance to pick the better man."

"First of all, Ashley, I don't need to choose a man; I choose love. And besides that—"

"Just think about it carefully, please. That's all I'm asking.

Because you don't know if your sea man will show up at Vauxhall. I'm just afraid you lost your man in Cornwall without even realizing it. Don't ruin your entire life on a gamble. But even if you do, I'll still be here for you."

"I didn't lose him in Cornwall; I left my heart safely with him, and I will only ever feel complete when he returns to me."

Ashley exhaled sharply and buried her face in both hands. "I hope you'll find him again. And until then, be there on Wednesday at four o'clock. Meet the prince."

"Very well." And then she would end it for good.

CLOVERDALE HOUSE ON Abbotsberry Road had many bedrooms and truly suited its purpose as a rehabilitation center for nobility splendidly. Except that Alex wished he and Thea didn't need to be there to keep their brother company because he was a patient. It reminded him of times he'd rather forget.

"I can't believe he injured you, Stan. It looks terrible," Alex tried not to flinch when the doctor carried a tray of bloodstained bandages out of Stan's room just as Alex entered.

"It'll heal. I'm in good hands with the doctors and nurses from Harley Street. You know they're all here—"

"Yes, but it's the Prussian pest of a baron who shouldn't be here. And yet, he got to you." Alex ran both hands through his hair. "When you wrote me, I expected some sort of diplomatic crisis, not a life-threatening infection you're battling while trying to keep up appearances."

"Why do you think I am pretending?"

"Oh please, Stan. You're my little brother. I can read you like an open book." Alex never hesitated to use the eleven-month age difference as if it were his trump card.

"Listen, von List is dangerous. That's why I'm here and I called you for help. We have to protect our family and what we stand for." Stan's tone revealed his concern.

But what Alex feared was bringing Sera into this family, always on the lookout for enemies.

The truth was, she was a part of his heart; it was inevitable. Then there was that dratted engagement to the other woman. They were meeting at Vauxhall in a few days, and this mess couldn't have come at a worse time. Untangling the knot of his engagement while keeping the family safe from the baron's relentless assaults gave him a severe stomach ache.

"Stan," Alex interjected, pushing away from the wall, "Langley said that von List has allies at St. James Palace?"

"Yes, the bailiff. Self-appointed from Vienna."

An international crisis. Alex sighed.

"That girl from Cornwall—can she protect herself from von List?" As soon as Stan spoke the words, Alex's heart plummeted to his knees. "You know, they caught Thea. They're trying to get to anyone we're close to."

"She's not part of this," Alex said, more forcefully than he intended. "And I'll make sure she stays out of it. There's no way he could find out."

Stan's expression softened slightly, but his voice remained firm. "If she matters to you, then she's already involved. You can't forever divide your life into neat little corners. Sooner or later, these worlds will collide."

His brother was right.

Alex's mind raced. Both the immediate threat of the baron and the meeting with Sera were impending. Breaking his engagement was non-negotiable. Sera deserved more than half-measures, and he couldn't move forward with her while bound to another. *Draci*, he couldn't go forward with life without her. And the baron and all the dangers surrounding the House of Hohenzollern-Sigmaringen were part of that life. At least for now.

But even if the baron weren't, there were always enemies lurking. He couldn't hide her from them or them from her.

"So," Alex said. "What's the plan? What do we do?"

"We remain alert and wait till he strikes," Stan said, his gaze flicking to Alex. "We're not going to attack him or else the German Emperor could come after us."

"But you're injured, Stan."

"I'll heal. Just make sure you're not spreading yourself too thin, brother. We can't afford to lose focus—on any front." In other words, don't let emotions cloud his judgment.

"I won't." *I already did.*

Perhaps it was a family thing—leaping toward their hearts' direction. And his pointed only one way.

Stan chuckled. "We are representing our entire family, Alex. If there's one thing we're good at, it's clawing our way out of impossible situations. Just remember what we're fighting for."

Love.

He was fighting for love.

For Sera.

For the chance to love without regret. And he wouldn't let anything—or anyone—stand in his way.

Chapter Eighteen

Wednesday, teatime at Ashley's father's house, London.

I T WAS INCREDIBLY kind of Ashley to organize a gathering.

Gathering.

Only sixty people, eighty at most.

Sera stood on the landing of the second floor and watched Ashley and Thomas greet guests alongside Ashley's parents, the Earl and Countess of Chaswick. Some guests congratulated them on their recent engagement and expressed their surprise at the match. She angled her parasol just enough to shield her from the fading direct sunlight, her wrist tilting awkwardly as though unsure of its proper place. The delicate lace edges trembled faintly in her grasp while, in her other hand, the fan wavered, moving not for cooling but simply for something to do. Her fingers brushed over its ribs, tracing the painted surface thoughtlessly, her movements more intentional in their distraction than their purpose.

Oh, how surprised everyone would be if they knew that Sera had tried to dissolve hers—with the prince, of course. Not Alex.

Speaking of the prince, Sera needed to confront him and yet feared the encounter.

Her fiancé.

A shiver of dread coursed down her spine.

And people probably thought she was a complete dimwit for

trading a man she'd spent a few days trailing barefoot along the beach for a lifetime with a prince, but yes, she much preferred Alex over anyone else. Ever! She didn't want to meet any prince, no matter how "capable" and "stunning" he might be.

The garden buzzed with conversations that drifted between the trimmed hedges and rose-covered arches. Thus, Sera stepped away from the crowd, her slippers scuffing the stones as she sought the shadows near a blooming jasmine bush. The air was heavy with the fragrance of flowers and the faint tang of overheated summer wine. It pressed against her, thick and unrelenting, much like the endless parade of smiles and expectations surrounding her tonight.

She clasped her hands together, her skin cool against the warmth radiating from her flushed cheeks and turned her face toward the darker edges of the garden. She exhaled carefully, her chest tight, her lungs heavy like they were fighting the weight of all the unspoken judgments around her.

It would probably soon come.

They would think her ridiculous, a girl who had traded the impossible dream of marrying some princely paragon for the quiet simplicity of a man who held none of their titles or powers.

But no one knew.

No one could know how she had learned the way Alex's laugh softened when it came unbidden, or how his voice dipped in kindness when he told her she could do anything to him. How could she explain to anyone that no title mattered when Alex looked at her as if she were the only person in the world who mattered?

Sera's fingers tightened around the grip of her parasol. She stood still, her eyes fixed on the maze of blooms stretching before her. Just another moment here, just one. Far from the polite smiles and endless guessing games until she could seek a formal introduction, speak to the prince, break the engagement, cause a scandal, a rift in her family, perhaps the collapse of *Lyndon Fleets and Transportation.*

Absolutely no pressure at all. Yet how terrible could it be to say those simple words to the prince? A *good* man?

"I will not marry you," Sera announced.

"I won't be your wife," Sera practiced again.

She cleared her throat. "I have lain with another man."

Yes, that was all she would need. It felt like a snowflake turning into an avalanche that not even the oppressive London heat could melt this summer.

Another moment to gather her courage.

The days without Alex hadn't been easy. She kept doubting, dwelling, and questioning whether their bond was truly strong enough for him to meet her at Vauxhall. Her heart said yes, but her mind wondered whether Alex might be too good to be true.

She didn't want these thoughts.

But they crept in again just as Sera walked deeper into the garden until she reached the end and came to the cobblestone path that led to the park.

How utterly miserable that he was here in London, just like her, and she had no way of finding him! No way to reassure herself that the heart truly grows fonder apart and doesn't turn indifferent.

She stepped onto the grass, wishing she could remove her slippers and toss them aside as she had on the beach. Yellow butterflies flitted lazily among the blooming rose bushes, and the soft breeze carried the earthy scent of freshly cut grass. Sera paused at the edge of the garden, her fingers lightly brushing the iron gate as she took in the scene from afar.

Ashley had truly outdone herself.

There, nestled between two rows of flowering rose arches, stood a white tent. Its light fabric billowed gently in the breeze, the edges tied back with ribbons that danced as if they understood the charm of the afternoon. Beneath the tent lay a row of tables, their white linens neatly arranged and topped with centerpieces of pale pink wildflowers. Each arrangement was effortlessly elegant, the kind of detail that could only come from Ashley's thoughtful touch.

How she loved her friend!

Everything looked perfect.

However, Sera felt like a spot of spilled ink in an otherwise idyllic afternoon tea garden party. Her mind certainly didn't match the decor! Even the weather appeared determined to align with Ashley's efforts, showcasing a sky stretched endlessly blue, unmarred by even a single wisp of cloud. The warmth of the sun sank into Sera's skin, gentle yet insistent, though the brim of her bonnet shielded her face. A soft chatter of voices carried faintly from the tent, punctuated by the chiming laughter of someone clearly reveling in the hospitality.

Someone who wasn't hiding like Sera, yet her feet moved farther away from the scene and over to the park.

"Sera!" a voice called out. "There you are! What are you doing? You should be in the thick of things, not lingering on the outskirts!"

Sera turned to see Ashley rushing over. "How did you find me?"

"I know you better than you think. What's wrong?"

Sera sighed. "I don't know. I just need a moment to breathe."

"You're not ready to meet the prince, are you?"

"Yes, no, I don't know."

Ashley arched a brow. "Having second thoughts?"

"Of course not!" Sera pinched the bridge of her nose. "I'm just apprehensive. What if he is dead set on this marriage no matter what? What if he tells my parents and I'm locked away until the wedding?" She had never felt more regretful about not telling Alex the whole truth about herself. Because if the worst happened, how could he help her escape? And would he even help if he knew?

"I understand," Ashley said, hooking her arm into Sera's. "Let's take a walk." Ashley led her toward the tree-lined path winding deeper into the garden. Her heartbeat matched her growing sense of restlessness, Ashley's earlier words nagging in her mind.

What if Alex didn't show up at their designated time and place?

What if she had lost her heart with no hope of getting it back?

She had to banish the thoughts. Somehow.

"The prince accepted the invitation," Ashley continued. "He should be arriving soon, if he hasn't already. It's best just to take a deep breath and face the situation head-on."

Sera's hands found the folds of her gown, smoothing them absently as she stole one more glance toward the tent. The roses framed it, creating a pretty picture. Perhaps Ashley had hoped Sera might bloom amidst all this well-crafted beauty, grasping her future with boldness. She almost laughed; she'd given her flower away already! All she could hope for now was that she wouldn't wilt away in London with a broken heart!

How long ago it seemed that he had saved her life. She could remember how his hands had steadied her—firm but not rough. Now, she could only feel the absence of him, a hollow space inside her chest.

"What if I lack the courage?" Sera asked as they approached a spot near the pond at the center of the garden and sat down alone.

"We all lack courage once or twice or maybe even seven times," Ashley replied. "I nearly lost the love of my life for lacking the courage to tell him the truth about why I approached him. Fortunately, courage comes when you think it has utterly forsaken you."

Sera smiled. "What if I believe that now?"

Ashley scoffed. "You are stalling, not lacking courage. There's a difference, you know. We all stall in the face of discomfort."

A bee droned too close to her ear, and she flinched, snapping the fan open with a sharp flick of her wrist. One of the eddies from the pond sent a fleeting burst of cool air her way, rustling the brim of her bonnet.

"You know," Ashley said, "you could just swat away the

prince like that."

The garden was alive with the gentle hum of conversation and the flicker of lantern light, yet Sera found herself oddly detached from the revelry. She laughed softly, glancing at her gloves—snow-white and fitted, a contrast to the muddier emotions knotting her stomach ahead of her meeting with the prince later that afternoon. Nerves had their place, surely, but this felt heavier, more insistent than mere anticipation.

Ashley leaned closer suddenly, her fan fluttering without purpose. "So," she began, too casually, "you mentioned you did… that with your sea man."

Heat rushed to Sera's face as she stiffened under the question. "Yes, what about it?" Her voice teetered between defiance and unease.

Ashley lowered her tone. "The only reason I ask whether you… you know… is because there's a certain risk—"

"Risk?" Sera interrupted sharply, both flustered and indignant. "You make it sound as though there's only one. There are many, I suppose, but no matter the risk, I shall face them all."

The words spilled out too quickly, a little too defensive. She could hardly voice it outright, but she felt the weight of Ashley's question settle in, igniting something unfamiliar, something that had been lingering. Was it possible? The very notion made her breath hitch slightly, though she managed to mask it behind her open fan.

Had she been reckless?

Or perhaps she'd been only truthful, acting with heart and body alike, refusing to deny herself even the smallest taste of happiness. But—Sera blinked, her thumb tracing the edge of her glove—if she was carrying Alex's child… could this not bring her the strength she needed? The prince's titles and fortune were naught; they would live with no secrets between them, not if Alex shared that future with her.

Before Ashley could respond, Thomas emerged from behind one of the hedgerows, his hair slightly disheveled and his grin as insufferable as always. "There you are!" he declared, with mock indignation. "I've been looking for you. How could the hostess vanish from her own party?"

Ashley spun on him with an exaggerated sigh. "I disappeared because the host was still there!" She slapped her forehead with her hand. "Now we have to return together, or else people will think…"

"Abandoning your fiancé so publicly only to return ruffled from the garden," he teased, laughter threading his words, "how indecent."

Ashley huffed. "It's not abandonment if it's for a friend, Thomas! We are having a think."

"You're having a think. Is that something one can have in this heat?" Thomas raised an eyebrow, entirely unoffended.

"Does it make you sweat if women gather to think?"

He cocked his head and then flattened his lips. "Sweating, you say?"

Sera found herself smiling despite her spinning thoughts. But as Ashley fired back another quip, Thomas pointedly turned his gaze toward her, mischief glinting in his eye. "And what about you two? Just the same? Sweating… Ahem… thinking here in the garden?"

That earned a laugh from the three of them, light and unburdened. Still, the shift in conversation gave Sera the space she needed to bow out, mentally if not physically. Ashley's earlier warning lingered like a shadow beneath the afternoon glow.

Risk? Oh, yes, there was risk. But as her fingers found her midsection and her chest rose and fell with steadier breaths, she knew one thing for certain. Courage would follow, as surely as desire had, and she would face anything for Alex. Even a prince.

Ashley scoffed. "Men perspire, while ladies merely glisten."

Sera laughed at that.

"Oh!" Ashley suddenly exclaimed, pointing to the pond where a boat glided around the bend. The oars caught the light as they sliced through the water, each stroke steady and unhurried.

The sight made her heart spike briefly—not out of joy, but closer to unfathomable anticipation, the kind that pressed against her ribs and made her want to fold in on herself.

Sera blinked.

What was this feeling? Because of a boat?

She must be losing her faculties!

Twisting her neck, she craned for a better view of the boatman steering the small craft, but the sun behind him blurred his figure. She drew the open fan up to her lips and allowed the parasol to tilt low, obscuring half her face. A quick glance at the tea tables confirmed that no one else had seen it. Was the boatman lingering?

"Who is that?"

"I'm not sure," Ashley murmured.

"It should be one of the guests," Thomas replied softly.

"Thank you for stating the obvious, darling," Ashley shot back.

Tucking her parasol under one arm, she squinted and smoothed her skirts before stepping deeper into the shade of the willow. The boat drifted closer, cutting a soft line through the glassy surface. She knew better than to entertain thoughts of who might be on board. And yet, her breath caught, and her gloved fingers curled into the fabric of her parasol.

For some reason, along with this peculiar anticipation, she wanted, no, needed to see who was on that boat.

"Come," she said to Ashley, making a quick decision. "Let's go to the tent."

⇶⟩⟨⟨⟨

THE CROWD PRESSED in too closely for Alex's liking, each murmured conversation skimming the edges of his attention, while his siblings gestured toward their target—a man standing smugly by the refreshment table. Baron Wilhelm von List, the

Prussian snake poised to wrap himself around a victim and suffocate them.

And as if that weren't enough, von List would break every bone or send his lackeys to do the damage—just as they had tried with Stan. It was easy to see why his brother and sister suspected him of duplicity—perhaps even crime like the Earl of Langley. They were probably all right. von List's smile didn't warm his eyes, and the aura of self-satisfaction hung around him like a fog. Why and how that man managed to infiltrate every special event in town was a mystery—but not one Alex cared to unravel.

And just who had invited him?

Was the Earl of Chaswick ignorant or an ally?

But then, it was his daughter he'd met at Langley's. Still, no one could be ruled out as an accomplice or mole.

Whatever the case, Alex held little hope that mingling among the garden guests would yield anything of value against von List. Finer espionage had been required of him during his years in the Navy, and now he found himself reduced to eavesdropping on a man pouring lemonade. He bit back the flicker of irritation and crossed the lawn, his polished boots brushing against the edge of a rosebush.

von List caught sight of him, a smirk twitching on his lip in mock friendliness. "Ah, Prince Alexander von Hohenzollern-Sigmaringen, *nicht wahr?" Isn't it?*

Ah, he tested his German.

Very well.

"Jawohl, Herr Baron. Doch leider wartet jemand auf mich." Indeed, baron. But unfortunately, I'm expected.

"Ach ein Tächtel-mächetel im geheimen Garten bevor man Ihnen die Braut ins Bett legt. Sehr gewitzt, Eure Hoheit." Ah, a tryst in the secret garden before your bride's put in your bed. Very clever, Your Royal Highness.

Alex tasted acid and couldn't extricate himself soon enough.

Apparently, von List didn't think much of women, fidelity, or any virtues except those that could enrich him. Stan had been right when he'd said that von List was the sort of aristocrat who gave all nobility a bad name.

Alex ignored the deliberate pause, maintaining his tone at a steady level. "Baron von List." He edged closer, forcing himself to embody every inch of the polished gentleman. "You seem to enjoy these gatherings. I suppose there's much to be said for good company."

von List chuckled like a hyena, though the sound was devoid of humor. "Good company, Your Royal Highness, is a rarity these days. Too many people are showing interest where their interest doesn't belong. Wouldn't you agree?"

Alex's jaw tightened. The implication was clear—von List had noticed his and Stan's careful scrutiny. But how like him to not practice what he preached.

"Some might argue that curiosity is best embraced," Alex countered, his voice deceptively light. "Especially when there's something worth uncovering."

For a moment, the corners of von List's mouth curled downward, his sharp gaze flaring with obvious discomfort. Then, just as quickly, his grin returned. "How bold of you. The Navy must have trained you well. I'll leave you to enjoy the afternoon. I prefer mine free of… distractions." He tipped his hat with a mocking air before sauntering off across the lawn.

Alex exhaled sharply, anger simmering beneath his skin. He hated when men like von List spoke in riddles, with veiled threats that left little room for retort without causing a scene. Thus, he turned away. The quaint garden party, with its pastel dresses, summer blooms, and polished elegance, had become entirely unbearable. He craved fresh air—no, open water. That was where he could think.

The path toward the pond stretched out before him, the chatter of the party fading behind the low hum of the breeze and insects. The surface of the pond mirrored the sky, a stretch of glass inviting him closer.

Close enough.

The wooden skiff at the water's edge waited, tethered to a post. Alex kicked off his boots, urgency to cast off replacing his earlier irritation. He shed his coat and waistcoat, unfastened his cuffs, and rolled his sleeves to his elbows. As he followed suit with his breeches, each movement liberating him from the constricting trappings of land, he stepped into the skiff, his bare feet rocking slightly with the boat's sway. The oar in his hand brought a familiar comfort, the kind only the rhythm of water against wood could offer. Setting the oars to the surface, Alex rowed, his strokes deliberate and steady. The tightness in his chest eased gradually as the boat glided farther into the pond's calm expanse.

For a while, it was enough to move—to feel the pull and plunge, the control in his hands as he maneuvered across the pond. But as he skimmed the edge of the tree line, something caught his eye.

A woman.

Distant and still, her silhouette partially obscured by a willow. She wore a bonnet, shadowing her features, but something about the tilt of her head and the curve of her shoulders beneath the parasol struck a chord deep inside. The fine hairs on the back of his neck prickled, an almost instinctual awareness that defied reason.

Sera.

It couldn't be her.

Yet, every fiber of every nerve insisted otherwise. He adjusted his grip on the oar, trying to guide the boat closer, but the woman shifted, vanishing behind the hanging branches of the willow. Just when he thought he could see her face, she turned and disappeared under a parasol. His frustration mounted, the possibility of her presence only fueling his need to confront the truth.

It wasn't her.

He was losing his head, apparently, seeing Sera in others. He missed her. This entire day had been a failure. He wanted to leave. He wanted to find Sera. If possible, before their meeting. Only then would he feel relieved. Alex rowed back, set the boat aside, and went to find his brother and sister. Striding back toward the gathered guests, his siblings waited near the pavilion, their eyes watchful. He ignored their questioning looks as he approached.

"I'm finished with von List," Alex declared curtly. "But I want answers about Sera." His gaze was fixed on the worn map spread across the table, but his thoughts were far from the inked lines of streets and alleyways.

Stan leaned back in his chair, arms crossed, his brow lifting. "I'll ask my contacts. What's her whole name and address?"

Alex stiffened slightly, his jaw tightening.

A name.

An address.

Details he didn't have. Not yet. He thought he'd known everything that mattered. The way her laugh sounded softer when she wasn't trying to impress him. How her eyes searched for meaning, or how her voice carried this unshakable undercurrent of strength, even when she doubted it herself. Wasn't that enough? He knew who she was—at least, the most important parts of her.

Thea arched an unimpressed eyebrow, her fan resting against the edge of the table. "Tell us everything you know about her," she said, her tone sharp enough to slice through Alex's silence.

The only words that tumbled out were, "I love her." Words he could no longer keep sealed away. He glanced at his sister, then at Stan, daring them to challenge him. "With all my heart. And I need to keep her safe."

Thea huffed softly, though her frown deepened. "You're awfully worried about a girl whose name you don't even know."

Stan laughed, leaning forward now. "That's rich, Alex. Didn't think you falling in love would make me hunt shadows."

Alex's grip tightened on the edge of the table, his knuckles pale against the dark wood. Their words stung, but only because he knew they were right. Yet, it didn't matter, not to him. All that mattered was that Sera was safe. von List's presence made him edgy. He didn't like it. The gnawing knot in his chest tightened further. If he couldn't find her, midnight at Vauxhall would truly be his only chance.

"What if von List finds her before we can?" he said finally, his voice breaking through the charged silence. "What if she's already in danger? I wouldn't even know where to look. If we can't act quickly enough—" His throat closed off, the thought too bitter to finish.

Neither Thea nor Stan interrupted. For all their teasing, they weren't blind to Alex's open plight. He shook his head and exhaled hard, steadying himself as the weight of his own words settled. "Make inquiries discreetly," he said firmly. "If she's anywhere near this mess, I won't—no, I can't—allow her to be pulled into it."

The siblings exchanged a glance, and Thea said, "Don't worry too much, brother. If you don't know her full name, neither would von List."

Alex didn't know whether to laugh or grit his teeth. Thea was right. But tell that to his heart.

"Don't worry," Stan said, too. "We'll keep von List occupied."

"Good, because what happens to her, happens to me."

Thea folded her fan, her frown deepening before she rose. Stan followed suit, giving Alex a faint grin that didn't reach his eyes. They understood the gravity of his words. When Alex spoke like this, with an unrelenting resolve that turned his voice into stone, there was no room for debate.

For Alex, the villain wasn't the greatest danger here. It was losing Sera—that she could fade from his life as easily as she'd slipped into it.

He would bow to duty in most things.

Some things, never.

This was one.

Chapter Nineteen

"To the Lyndon estate, Charles," Alex instructed as his valet held the carriage door open. He stepped in, settling stiffly against the leather seat, bracing himself for the task ahead. The horses jolted forward, and the carriage rolled on, its polished wheels gliding smoothly over the cobblestones.

Houses passed by, each more refined than the last, row upon row of symmetry and pristine show. He might have enjoyed the sight, but his mind was elsewhere—not along manicured streets, but back in a shadowed alley, where elegance had been forgotten completely.

This memory was exceptionally sharp today.

He could still feel Sera's hand tugging his, the way she'd pulled him into that narrow space, with scattered laundry above swaying between soot-darkened brick walls. Nothing about it had been proper or polished, yet it had felt breathtakingly real. She had kissed him first, her lips unhesitating, her boldness rendering him speechless. He hadn't just kissed her back; he'd claimed her, holding her as if the narrow walls around them were the only refuge they'd have.

The memory burned—raw and unmistakable.

And somehow, she had left a mark on him that went far deeper than anything physical. Sera had unlocked something in

177

him, unbidden and wild, that no one else had dared to reach. She hadn't just kissed him; she'd unraveled him. Alex clenched his jaw, looking past the passing streets, their elegance fading into insignificance against the memory of her.

Until then, his life had been perfectly ordered, much like the immaculate avenues of London. A carriage bound to stay within its narrow path, pressed between constraints and expectations. Safety, formality, order—it had all boxed him in. Yet, as the carriage swayed lightly, Alex realized how suffocating it all had been.

His soul wasn't made for these streets.

It craved open waters and boundless horizons. Sera had made him see that. She was like the schooner he had always longed for, untethered and wild, braving the Atlantic winds without a hint of hesitation.

He shifted, restless, as the estate loomed closer, its ivy-covered walls echoing tradition and expectation. The delicate bouquet in his hand felt absurd—utterly at odds with the turmoil churning in his chest. Miss Lyndon was another reminder of every confined obligation he'd allowed to steer him this far, and it was time to put an end to it. Guilt nipped at him, but he shoved it down with the resolve that had guided him through many battles—not just for himself, but now for his love.

He scowled at the flowers. They felt less like a thoughtful token and more like a misplaced prop in the drama he was about to unravel.

What he was about to say would require delicacy, perhaps even a pretense of tact. Ending the engagement would be a blow to Miss Lyndon.

He knew that much.

Yet, as the ivy-shrouded estate loomed closer, Alex reminded himself that he didn't owe her anything more than his honesty. Their agreement had been one born of convenience, after all—a union to strengthen ties, enhance fortunes, and provide titles where needed. There had only ever been an obligation, and would releasing her be a gift of freedom? And yet, breaking it wasn't so simple.

The Lyndon family controlled one of the most powerful shipping fleets in the region. *Lyndon Fleets and Transportation* had long served as a vital partner to Alex's family. Even as his pulse quickened with resolve, a shadow of doubt followed close behind. Would severing personal ties jeopardize the business entirely? Could the families remain civil, complications and all? Somehow, he thought, it had to work out. Somehow. It wasn't just his reputation on the line—it was his family's standing, their future partnerships, entire trade routes. The weight of it pressed on him like an iron mantle.

But none of that mattered as much as Sera.

How could it, when she had gripped him with a force he didn't think possible? His feelings for her burned with such intensity that they seared through every other priority, leaving nothing in their wake but one desperate truth. His love for her was something raw, untamed, and utterly at odds with the immaculate world Miss Lyndon represented.

Ferocious—that was the word for it.

And Cornwall. Well, the Cornish beach was where it happened—that wild, windswept corner of the country that had torn his predictable world asunder. He hadn't meant to fall in love there. And he'd never planned on stepping past the invisible boundary society had so carefully drawn around men of his rank. But with Sera, reason hadn't stood a chance. He'd taken her into his arms, claimed her willingly, and been claimed just as fiercely in return. A thousand rules shattered under the weight of their shared passion. That moment had changed him in more ways than one, not least of all because he had taken something from her that could never be undone. Her chastity. But he'd given his heart in return.

Plus, he'd promised Sera to come to Vauxhall.

By then, he needed to be free of Miss Lyndon.

The word echoed bitterly in his mind, filling him with something close to guilt, though he wasn't sure whom it was directed toward—himself, for having crossed the line, or the strictures of Society, which had drawn it in the first place. What mattered now was what it meant. He hadn't simply fallen for her; he had tied her to him forever in a way that neither of them could ignore, even if they wanted to.

And he didn't.

The horses slowed, and the carriage came to a halt outside the sprawling Lyndon estate. Alex's fingers tightened around the bouquet, but his thoughts were far from the delicate blossoms. He exhaled slowly, pushing his misgivings aside. Everything about what he was about to do might feel impossible, reckless even.

But what choice did he have?

Sera had made him see the truth of himself—one no title, fleet, or alliance could bury. He loved her. And now, it was time to face the reality that came with that love.

The butler, a man with a face as stiff and straight as his collar, received him with a raised brow, informed him that Miss Lyndon was indisposed, and requested—no, commanded—him to wait. Alex took a seat, then promptly rose again, too restless to pace the drawing room's length like a caged animal. A tapestry depicting some mythical conquest stared back at him, the embroidered knights looking vaguely accusatory. He tried not to feel judged by a swatch of fabric.

"Prince Alexander?" came a piping voice from the doorway.

Alex turned to find a girl standing there with an impish grin. Her pinafore was slightly askew, and her light brown hair tumbled in a torrent of disorder.

"Yes," he said cautiously, glancing behind her only to notice she was alone.

"I'm Isabella Lyndon, the younger sister," she said, almost proudly.

She looked all of twelve but carried herself with a confidence entirely unsuited to her years.

Trouble, he thought instinctively.

"A pleasure to meet you, Miss Isabella," he replied, bowing slightly while clutching the flowers tighter. Perhaps too tightly, for one of the stems audibly snapped.

She stepped into the room with a gravity that suggested she was deliberating over his worth as a candidate for public office. Her gaze dropped instantly to the bouquet in his hand. "Are those for my sister?"

"They are," Alex managed. Somehow, this felt even more humiliating to admit aloud.

"Have you finally come to court her?"

Alex blinked. "Ah… Not… Exactly, no."

"Right, I suppose chivalry dies when an engagement starts." Her eyes narrowed, darting from his face to the flowers and back again. "If you're not, then why bring flowers? They're nearly the same thing as a proposal, you know. But you are already betrothed, so this should be an apology, right?" She wrinkled her nose and tilted her head, eyeing him with the same discerning gaze as a matron four times her age.

Alex coughed. "They're a gesture."

"Of an apology. Otherwise, I can only assume it's a bride."

Vexing little brat. "Fine, it's a gesture of an apology."

Her eyes narrowed to slits. "Then you should have bought a garden."

He opened his mouth, but the words fell between his head and tongue. He was defeated in the face of this child. "Isn't there something young ladies your age ought to be doing right now? Such as playing with a hoop and stick?"

She wrinkled her nose. "That's dreadful. Besides, you've interrupted my pianoforte practice, so now I have nothing to do except examine your character."

Her spunk reminded him a little bit of Sera. "And you can't possibly return to the pianoforte now that I'm here?"

She shook her head. "Of course, not."

Alex sighed, glancing toward the door as though by some

divine intervention, the butler—anyone—might appear and rescue him. No such luck. "I simply wanted to speak to your sister about a mutual matter of importance."

The girl plopped herself into an armchair with all the grace of a seasoned dowager and rested her chin in her hands. "You'll have to wait a long time, then. She's out."

"I gathered that." Alex's pulse tightened. "Out where?"

She shrugged with deliberate vagueness. "Shopping, I suppose. Or visiting someone. She has many friends, you know. Now that we have returned to London, she has calls to make. Why do you need her so badly, anyway?"

He hesitated. That was hardly a question he could truthfully answer here. "It's too complicated to discuss with an eight-year-old girl."

"I'll have you know I'm twelve, and everything's complicated with grown-ups," she declared dramatically, leaning back until her head dangled upside-down over the arm of the chair. "Why has it taken you this long to fulfill the duties of your engagement? You know that my sister has been out in society for decades. The common lady would almost be considered firmly on the shelf."

"Decades?" Alex stifled a laugh. Miss Lyndon was three years his junior, so there weren't *decades* passing yet. "Are you supposed to know these things at your age?"

"What do you suppose they teach little girls if not all the things to catch husbands?"

"Catch?" Alex coughed. "I stand corrected." This conversation started to feel like a duel.

But having grown up with an impertinent sister like Thea, he knew his best course of action was to agree with whatever the girl said.

"Forgive my ignorance." Her expression turned suspicious. "Let me ask you, do you even know what my sister looks like? Have you ever seen her likeness? If you want, I can show you her miniature? Everyone always gawks when I do."

Alex blinked—a portrait. He'd never even thought to ask for

one. In his mind, it didn't matter what she looked like. The deal had been made and needed to be severed. Even now, it didn't matter. However, looking at this little brat, would she stop unless she got her way? It might save him from more of this absurd interrogation.

"Do you have one?"

She grinned. "Oh, we've got a little one. But why should I show it to you now? It's clear you haven't had any interest before." Clever girl.

"I only thought since you offered—" Before he could finish his sentence, the child dragged a small oval picture framed in gilded swirls, with a chain and tassel hanging from it, and thrust it under his nose. Alex glanced down at the face staring back at him and blinked. A slow scowl formed across his brow. Was she serious? He glanced back at the girl—she was—then back at the portrait. It was a delightful rendering of... a four-year-old child. Three, perhaps.

"Is this your sister?" he asked after a stunned silence, adding, "This isn't her current age, right?" He grimaced at his own foolish question.

"Mm-hmm. She was adorable, wasn't she? I looked the same at that age."

Alex leaned back slightly, staring at the sweet-faced child in the picture before nodding. "Certainly," he said slowly. Regardless of whether she was adorable, he still had to end things with Miss Lyndon.

Alex cleared his throat and cast a desperate glance toward the doorway. Waiting here was proving more perilous than any battlefield. "Is your father at home?"

"He isn't. Neither is my mother. I'm not sure when they will return."

Alex rose to his feet. "Well, then I won't take up any more of your time, Miss Lyndon."

It seemed he would have to hunt down his fiancée.

And before the ball.

SERA SLUMPED AGAINST the soft velvet pillows as her carriage rattled down the streets of London, listening to merchants calling from booths as they passed. She peeked out of the window. A flower girl darted between pedestrians, her basket bursting with blooms that she waved imploringly at a passerby.

She looks free.

Unblemished by any worry.

Her earlier conversation with Ashley replayed in her mind; Ashley's bluntness about everything—everything—set her cheeks aflame once more. Where had Ashley been in Cornwall? Some things had been thought-provoking, yes, but also… illuminating. Now, with the heat of London making the carriage stifling despite its fine design, the most persistent thought that came to her wasn't Ashley's advice but Alex.

Always Alex.

Sera clutched her stomach. What if there was more of Alex already within her than she'd thought?

She closed her eyes, allowing a soft sigh to escape as the carriage lurched over a pothole. Her eyes shot open as her head hit the glass.

Confound it!

If only she had something to anchor herself to him, some direction, some absurdly simple way to find him again. She'd thought—no, she hadn't thought clearly at all since that day, had she? Every detail of him was etched into her being, from his attentive gaze to the curve of his lips when he smiled. It had been just days, but they felt like an eternity of wondering. Still, her heart tugged at her, an invisible tether she couldn't sever. It whispered nonsense, like the ridiculous notion that he might somehow be within reach. She scolded herself for this silliness but found it hard to resist.

She wanted to see him.

But London was so vast, the largest city in Europe; how could she expect to find her Alex among millions of people?

The roar of London faded as the carriage turned onto a quieter lane, trees rising in orderly rows as they neared her family's townhouse. Sera shifted, her gaze fixed on the road ahead. Just as the carriage slowed to a halt, another vehicle caught her eye. A sleek black coach rolled away from her home, its wheels spinning lazily, as if it had all the leisure in the world.

She leaned slightly forward to look more closely. The crest on the door gleamed in the light, unfamiliar yet undeniably elegant. Her fingers brushed absently against the seat, curiosity flaring within her. It seemed to have come from her home. Who had just left? And why did something about its sudden departure tug at her in a way she couldn't quite explain?

Could it be…

The footman opened the door after they came to a stop, and Sera stepped down, her soft leather slippers meeting the pavement as the black carriage disappeared around the bend.

"You had a caller, Miss Lyndon," the butler announced flatly. She narrowed her eyes at him. Why did he make it sound like she had missed a chance of a lifetime—or was that merely her sinking heart? She shook off her unease and moved toward the entrance. Inside, the house was everything she expected—cool air, the faint scent of lavender, and the persistent hum of domestic life—but as she handed off her bonnet and gloves, her sister's voice rang out like an explosion of bubbling champagne.

"Sera!" Isabella nearly skidded into view, her skirts swirling from the effort. Her twelve-year-old enthusiasm filled the hall as completely as music. "You'll never guess! Your prince was here!"

Sera blinked, startled. "My what?"

"Your prince," Isabella repeated, already spinning back toward the drawing room. "He was here! Just a moment ago!"

"Explain this," Sera said, following her wildly excitable sister. She couldn't keep the faint touch of irritation from her tone, even though her chest had abruptly tightened. "Why was he here?"

Had he come to meet her? Had she just missed him at the tea party only to miss him here too? How unlucky! This must be the universe conspiring against her.

Isabella tilted her head as if considering whether Sera could grasp her brilliance. "A very handsome man," she declared finally, with the authority of one who had thoroughly assessed the whole matter. "Tall. Blond hair. He brought flowers. Didn't wear a crown as I had pictured."

"Aren't you supposed to be on my side?"

"Who said I'm not?" Isabella shot back.

Right.

"Did you—did he give his address, by chance?"

"Oh, no," Isabella said breezily, as though she hadn't committed a grave offense against curiosity. "But he was terribly sweet. Oh, and the best part," she added, beaming with delight, "he asked to see a portrait of you."

Sera's brow furrowed. "The miniature?"

"Well, I practically goaded him with it. But he said yes, so I showed him the one Mama had." Isabella clapped her hands together, her eyes sparkling. "From when you were four!" Isabella giggled triumphantly.

It took every scrap of dignity Sera possessed not to groan. She should have known. "And what," she asked, folding her arms, "did the prince think of that?"

"Oh, he didn't say, but he looked…" Isabella pursed her lips, miming consideration. "Utterly baffled. It was brilliant."

Sera closed her eyes briefly. The joke was completely lost on her, though Isabella's laughter soared unchecked through the room.

"And you're sure it was the prince and not another man?"

"Of course!" Her sister sent her a suspicious glance. "Who else could it be? The man introduced himself as such, too." Sera drew in a steadying breath, trying to quell the strange mixture of frustration and longing that formed a knot just beneath her ribs. It couldn't have been him. It could not. And yet, her fingers curled slightly, aching to hold the smallest thread of certainty. Well, she might be out of luck today, but so was he. She didn't want a prince; she wanted Alex. And yet her freedom remained just out of reach. Again.

Chapter Twenty

THE NIGHT OF the ball had come too soon, Sera thought when she stared at her reflection in the mirror as her sister helped pin the last of the pearls in her hair. Tonight, she wore a beautiful pale-blue gown that everyone believed marked her engagement. Only she knew this gown was for Alex, also meant to break off the engagement that had weighed on her body and soul since she met the only man she would love in this lifetime.

"Done," Isabella said, stepping back to admire her handiwork. "You look… like a proper lady about to create the biggest scandal in all of London. No, England."

Sera managed a weak smile, her fingers fidgeting with the lace of her gown. She certainly didn't feel the part. Tonight was her engagement ball, but all she could think about was how she would meet Alex at midnight.

The thought of him sent a jolt of nerves through her.

How many days had it been since she last saw him? Would his eyes light up when he saw her? Would he still look at her the same way? Or—her stomach twisted—what if he didn't come?

Isabella, oblivious to her turmoil, grinned. "I'm so very proud of you."

Sera arched a brow. "For causing a scandal?"

"For defying the rules and fighting for what you want, silly."

Sera glanced at her sister through the mirror. "Isabella, what flowers did the prince bring when he visited this morning?"

Her sister tilted her head, distracted as she reached for a strand of pearls to fasten around Sera's neck. "Does it matter?"

"Yes," Sera replied. She'd been too shocked to ask before. "Flowers have meaning."

"Well, I can't rightly recall. He took them with him when he left."

"How odd."

"Right? I guess he wanted to give them to you in person." Isabella wrinkled her nose. "Who brings flowers just to leave with them again?"

Sera nodded, though the prince's peculiar habits were the least of her concerns. Her mind raced ahead to the evening's true purpose: to end this engagement. She would enter the ballroom with her parents and then find an excuse to slip away. It shouldn't be too hard to find a prince unless he didn't want to be found.

A risk still lived and breathed. Breaking the engagement unilaterally would be one thing. But if he didn't want her either, she'd be shunned. She would be the subject of the greatest scandal of the season.

What if Alex cared about her reputation after all?

Isabella quickly fastened the pearls at the back of her neck. "Are you nervous?"

"Nervous?" Sera echoed. "Hardly. What is there to be nervous about?" A bold lie. But she was also excited.

Tonight, she claimed her freedom.

"Oh, I don't know," Isabella said with a mischievous grin. "You look rather terrified to me. I would be too if I were the one going against Mama's wishes."

"That's not what bothers me." Her parents would be furious, but they would forgive her. Besides, with Isabella on her side—and being the daughter they doted on the most—Sera was confident in this.

"Well, all in all, if you ask me, you're handling it all rather well," Isabella said. "I'd be a trembling mess if I were in your shoes."

Sera sighed. "Sometimes I wish I could trade places with you, just for a night. To be that age again."

"Oh, please," Isabella scoffed. "You'd have to listen to Mama lecture about posture and needlework."

"I suppose you're right," Sera replied.

At that moment, the door creaked open, and her mother breezed into the room. Her eyes lit up when they fell on Sera. "You're the most perfect blushing bride, dear."

Sera stiffened, her knuckles whitening as her grip tightened on the edge of the vanity. Her breath caught as she glanced at her reflection, a face framed by curls, lips pressed so tightly together they barely looked like hers.

I'm really not a bride.

Behind her, her mother's gentle humming filled the room, a familiar melody from Sera's childhood that now carried an unbearable weight. The rustle of fabric as her mother spread a gown across the bed sent a wave of unease prickling at the back of Sera's neck. She couldn't bring herself to turn around, not when she felt the joy radiating from her mother like sunlight on a summer morning, because this was the day she'd disappoint her mother the most.

Once her mother stopped fussing over her dress, she tenderly wrapped a strand of Sera's curls around her finger and sighed wistfully.

A knot twisted painfully in Sera's stomach as she caught a glimpse of her mother's smile reflected in the mirror.

It wasn't fair.

None of this was fair.

Her hands trembled on the vanity, and she forced herself to steady them, pressing down harder until she felt the faint indent of the carved edges against her skin. Her heart thudded, each beat heavier than the last. She couldn't do it, not yet. She couldn't shatter the hope so clearly written in her mother's expression without at least giving her time—time to adjust, time to understand.

Sera drew in a shallow breath, the faint scent of rose water drifting from the nearby pitcher. A scent she'd always found calming, but tonight, it only tightened the knot in her chest.

"Mama," Sera said slowly. "I'm not marrying the prince."

"What did you say?" her mother didn't seem to understand the idea. "I'm so proud of you," she said as if she'd overheard Sera's impossible declaration. "My oldest daughter will be a princess. A princess bride."

"No, I won't."

Her mother froze mid-step. "What are you talking about? That's madness, dear. Nothing could be worse than you rejecting the prince!"

Sera said more forcibly, "Mama, I will be neither blushing nor beautiful for the prince. I don't want to marry him."

Her mother's expression shattered into shock. "You cannot be serious!"

"I am very serious. I'm in love with another man."

Her mother's face darkened. "That's preposterous! You don't know any other men!"

"I do. And I want to be with him instead."

The older woman grimaced as if she'd burned her mouth on hot tea, then put her hands on her hips. "Come again?"

"I don't want to marry this prince. I don't know him. Nobody ever asked me what I wanted."

"So, before you ever met the prince, you wish to reject him? Honestly, Sera?"

"It's not the life I want." Sera remained firmed.

"The best kind of life? That of a princess, you mean?"

Sera cringed. Stupid, yes. But she was madly in love; what should she do?

A familiar tightness settled in her chest, the kind that always came when her mother's doting words bore down like a weight from which she couldn't escape. It wasn't her mother's happiness that made her shift uncomfortably; it was how completely assured she seemed of Sera's.

"My dear sweet girl, it's common to have cold feet," her mother said, her voice lilting like she'd rehearsed the words.

The phrase prickled at the edge of Sera's mind.

Cold feet?

Her mother continued, her enthusiasm rekindled, "But trust me, you're well-prepared for this life as a princess. He will take you to Bran Castle for your honeymoon and you'll see your—" she waved her hand with a theatrical flourish, "kingdom!"

The words grated against Sera's thoughts. It was all castles, kingdoms, princesses—the kind of fairy tale fragments that should have been thrilling. But instead of wonder, she felt something much colder wrapping around her. Her throat tightened. She stared hard at the mirror across the room, locking her gaze on her own strained reflection.

Then her mother's tone softened, affectionate now, but somehow sharper for it. "My sweet girl. We have done everything to ensure you have the best possible life! A princess! That is what we made possible for you! And you'll do well in this role, paving the way for Isabella, too."

She cast her little sister a look, but Isabella pretended to be immersed in curling a strand of pearls around her index finger fully absorbed in the task. Smart girl.

"You're going to accept the prince gracefully, become a princess, and that's all," her mother declared.

There it was—that word again.

Princess.

Spoken like a threat. Something that should make everything worth it, a sacrifice Sera wasn't willing to offer. A thousand tiny moments fell into place at once: her father's scheming, her mother's constant assurances, the pressure placed on her shoulders from the moment this match had been proposed all those years ago. It hit her all at once, the truth behind it, a truth she couldn't unsee no matter how hard she tried.

She straightened, the muscles in her back drawn tight like a string pulled to the breaking point. The guilt that had held her hostage began to fray and dissolve, replaced by heat that crept up her neck and into her face. Her mother's words spun in her head, her voice soft but cutting, weaving something beautiful from what Sera knew was nothing but a gilded chain. But Sera no longer listened.

How could she not have seen it? How could Mother not understand? Sera turned, her heart pounding like a drum in her chest.

"You did this for me?" The words tumbled out before she could stop them, her voice rising with disbelief. "How can you say that when it's Papa who stands to benefit from this marriage?"

"You will be a princess!" her mother snapped, as though that settled the matter.

"I never wanted to be a princess!" She never wanted any of this! From the very beginning, she had never been given a chance. No one ever asked her what she wanted. No one had cared. They believed they were doing the right thing for their business, not for their daughter.

"So, you'll ruin your sister's chances for a good match too?"

"I don't want to marry and move away like she will!" Isabella declared, stepping forward with a fiery defiance that matched Sera's.

"See what you've done?" her mother exclaimed, pointing at Isabella. "You've corrupted your sister!"

"I am merely following my heart, Mama," Sera countered. "Can you truly fault me for that?"

"Yes! It was never part of my plans."

"Well, then blame me all you want because I cannot do as you wish."

"Me too," Isabella said, moving to stand beside her sister. "Sera didn't corrupt me. I corrupted myself!"

Their mother's face turned red. "Ungrateful, both of you! Wretched, selfish girls! How dare you do this to me?" She stormed from the room, slamming the door behind her, shouting for Father in the halls. Sera and Isabella remained in heavy silence.

Isabella crossed her arms, her chin held high. "Well, that went well."

"It will get much worse," Sera said.

Sera stared at the door, her heart in her throat. "Yes."

This was only the beginning.

Seven o'clock at Cloverdale House

ALEX STARED AT his reflection in the mirror while Charles adjusted the lapels of his freshly pressed coat. That evening, he and Stan were getting ready for Lady Anna Ashford's ball. Thea had taken up residence with Lady Ashford in anticipation of her introduction to society, and it was supposed to be his engagement ball in the traditional Austrian way. He was to present Miss Lyndon with a bouquet of red roses and then invite her to waltz. If she accepted, they'd be married.

Alex nearly convulsed at the thought.

He had only hours to stop the charade before he could find Sera at Vauxhall.

Five hours only. The man gazing back looked every bit the part of a respectable fiancé preparing for his engagement ball, except for the dark circles beginning to form under his eyes.

He sighed.

He was tired.

This situation with von List had remained unresolved and it bothered Alex more than he wanted to show that Stan had been injured. It meant von List was dangerous. And if he, Thea, and Stan had been in danger, then Sera might be, too.

He glanced at the flowers he forgot to leave at the Lyndon residence. Come what may, tonight was the night he would break it off with Miss Lyndon. He owed her that much, didn't he? He wanted to follow his heart. And honesty, no matter how brutal, was better than a lie prolonged.

His sweet Sera.

The thought of her was both a balm and a torment. He missed her so fiercely it was as though his heart had been carved from his chest. But alongside the ache came doubts. What if she didn't feel the same any longer? What if absence hadn't made the heart grow fonder but had instead extinguished the flame?

The valet cleared his throat, interrupting Alex's spiraling thoughts. "You've been standing there like a statue, Your Highness. If you're planning to look brooding all evening, you might frighten away your ladylove."

Alex glanced at the man. "My ladylove?"

"The one you met in Cornwall."

"You even know that much?"

"I know a lot more than you give me credit for, Your Highness."

Alex nodded. He didn't doubt that. "I'm meeting her at midnight at Vauxhall."

The man paused. "I see." Another pause. "Do you think that's wise?"

"It's a necessity." And if he was brooding, he wouldn't be brooding for much longer. However, the thought of Vauxhall Gardens filled him with equal parts hope and dread. He couldn't not show up. The idea of disappointing Sera—or worse, never seeing her again—was unbearable. But what if she didn't come? What if he was clinging to a dream, a memory that had grown larger than life in her absence?

He glanced at the clock. How many minutes until midnight?

He tugged at his cravat.

"Where is my brother?" Alex asked Charles.

"He and your sister already left for the ball, Your Highness," the man replied. "Does your family know about your midnight meeting?"

"They do not," Alex said, giving the man a look. "I wish for it to stay that way."

"I live for your discretion, Your Highness. If I may be so bold as to ask, does your ladylove have a name?"

Alex hesitated. The valet was more than just a servant; he was a confidant. Of sorts. "Sera," he said softly. The name felt like a prayer on his lips.

"And does Miss Lyndon know about your Sera?"

"She doesn't," Alex admitted. "And she never will."

"That's probably wise," the valet replied. "I hope she's worth your effort."

The man stole the words straight from Alex's heart.

"Well, sir, if that's the case, I'd say you're braver than most. But bravery doesn't mean you won't get hurt."

Alex shot the man an odd look. "Thanks for the depressing warning." He slipped on his gloves and prepared to leave.

"Wish me luck," he said as he reached for the door.

"Good luck, Your Highness." The valet's expression was uncharacteristically sincere. "You may need it."

Let's hope I don't.

But midnight couldn't come soon enough.

Chapter Twenty-One

THE CHANDELIERS IN Lady Anna Ashford's townhouse blazed with what seemed like a thousand candles, casting their golden glow over the crush of London's elite, each whisper and sidelong glance brimming with anticipation of the engagement ball unfolding beneath their glittering light. Yet, Sera had never found it more difficult to breathe.

"Smile," her mother commanded through gritted teeth as they stepped into the ballroom. "You look like you swallowed a lemon."

Sera cast a quick glance at her father and whispered, "You didn't tell Papa."

"I tried but it would have sent him to an early grave. It would break his heart to see years of business collapse because of a rebellious child." Her mother scoffed. "You will do what is best for the family. Nobody needs to know."

"Mama—"

Her mother's fan snapped open beside her, the sound sharp and deliberate. "Hold your head high, Seraphina," she said with a warning look, "and for our family's sake, try to enjoy yourself. Or pretend to at least."

"It's a lie! I'm not—"

"Stop it! An omission isn't a lie. And when you feign surprise on your wedding night, you don't need to lie either. Just leave out—" Her mother tsked. "I'd rather not name what you did. Get it together, child. You're not in Cornwall anymore. This is London, and you'll be a princess."

"I'm not doing this," Sera hissed, clearing her throat when her father's gaze fell on her, but he must have been out of earshot from his position near the buffet.

"Your father will formally announce the betrothal in exactly two hours. Behave until then."

Behave?

That wasn't going to happen.

This was her moment to act—to find the prince, break the engagement, find Alex at Vauxhall, and finally take control of her future. She couldn't—wouldn't—fail. But it wasn't so simple anymore. Not with her mother's gaze drilling into the side of her head, likely doing so for the rest of the evening.

Her mother leaned closer, her voice a low hiss. "Do not embarrass this family, Seraphina. This is a ball with royals in attendance. Whatever foolish ideas you've concocted, I suggest you bury them now and forever."

Sera didn't respond. She couldn't, not without igniting the argument that would ruin all her plans for tonight. Instead, she scanned the room, her eyes flicking over the crowd of faces, searching for the one man she had no interest in finding, and yet she had to speak to him. Surely, the prince was here somewhere, and she needed to get this over with as quickly and quietly as possible.

First, escape her mother.

But another face lingered in her mind, distracting her, pulling her focus like a siren's call. Alex. Would he be thinking of her right now, too? Was he pacing somewhere, counting the hours until midnight as she was? Or was she merely fooling herself, clinging to a dream that had no chance of becoming reality?

She would never find out if she allowed the situation with the prince to proceed. Plus, if Alex knew, he wouldn't want her, right?

Stop it! No more doubts! Just action!

She had imagined this moment a hundred times—what she would say, how she would say it. But the thought of delivering such a blow at an event full of watchful eyes made her palms sweat. Where was he? Wouldn't a prince hold court at a ball or was this only reserved for British royals?

"Sera!" Ashley called out before Sera could further examine the attendees. A secret sigh of relief escaped her lips as her friends presented her with an opportunity. She sent her friend a bright smile as Ashley approached with her fiancé, the Earl of Linsey.

An escape!

And a chance to move about the room and look for the prince.

Could she steal a dance? The quadrille would be next, and Sera looked toward the string quartet. Many guests were dancing. She glanced at Ashley, who had a sparkle in her eyes. Her friend understood, and she was ready to help.

Her mother suddenly fanned herself furiously. "Lord Linsey, what a pleasure."

"Linsey," her father greeted. "Congratulations on your engagement. It warms the heart to see young people forging such respectable paths together," Mr. Lyndon said to the earl.

The words sent heat bubbling under Sera's skin. Her voice came out stronger than she expected. "Why don't I get a chance to decide my path?"

Her mother froze, her hand ceasing its restless adjustments of her jeweled bracelet. "A chance to marry a prince?" she asked sharply. "By all means, my dear, that is precisely what we are here to confirm this evening." Her eyes flashed, daring Sera to push further.

But Sera couldn't stop now. Her chest heaved as the words spilled out. "What about love? Why hasn't that factored in?"

Mr. Lyndon released a low chuckle, shaking his head as though amused by a naïve child. His words prickled at Sera's every nerve. "You see, Linsey, these young women today—they don't quite understand the bigger picture we lay out for them. Love?" He waved a hand dismissively. "That comes secondary. Or not at all."

Sera sent Ashley a prompting glance. "I need your help," she mouthed at Ashley who came to their side with a knowing look.

Ashley nodded. "I know," she mouthed back.

Then tell your fiancé to ask me to dance!

Ashley nudged her fiancé lightly, her expression urging. However, Sera's eyes caught on the two gentlemen beyond her friends. There he was again. One of them in particular seemed familiar but she wasn't quite sure where she knew him from. His shoulders were broad, he was tall, and his hair was a light shade of golden-blond. The color of sand.

She blinked, but Linsey's voice drew her back to their group.

"Miss Lyndon," he began with a soft smile, extending a hand. "Would you honor me with another dance?"

Thomas's timing was impeccable, a lifeline before Sera could combust any further under her parents' scrutiny. She hesitated only a second before nodding, slipping her hand into his. She didn't care what anyone thought. She needed to escape.

This might be her last dance in high society if her plan worked and she could reunite with Alex. A simpler life awaited, and yet it beckoned sparkling with love rather than superficial lavishness. Sera placed her hand in the earl's and allowed him to lead her toward the dance floor.

There was no return.

The orchestra struck up a waltz as the earl guided her into the steady rhythm of the dance. His calm, measured steps offered surprising comfort to her trembling limbs.

After a moment, he looked down at her, his expression unreadable, though his tone was warm. "Sera," he said softly, "don't let anyone or anything get in your way if you've found love. If you have, I can tell you—it's worth any risk."

Her breath hitched.

She tilted her head up, catching the sincerity in his eyes as he glanced briefly at Ashley, his expression softening.

Sera's heart warmed. Despite everything, she had good friends. "Thank you."

From the corner of her eye, a figure caught her attention—a man standing by the far wall, his posture sharp and commanding, a silent authority in the easy way he held himself. Her gaze lingered, curiosity unfurling in her chest, but the next step drew her away before she could focus more on him.

Sera's pulse quickened, more from distraction than exertion.

Then she saw him again.

Dark hair, taller than most men in attendance, standing just beyond the crowd. Striking, yet different. He wasn't looking at her, not directly, but something about him prickled at her memory. A shadow of familiarity danced in her thoughts, just out of reach. Had she seen him before? Her mind whirred, but the tempo quickened, forcing her attention back to partner and the ordered rhythm of the dance.

She dipped her head, trying to shake off the tension creeping up her neck. A sense of foreboding suddenly gripped her heart.

ELEVEN O'CLOCK. ALEX had one hour to untangle his future from Miss Lyndon and find the pavilion at Vauxhall. He'd asked his valet to circle the block and remain ready to take him there at a moment's notice. But nothing was dropping here besides his patience. He stood near the edge of the ballroom, his gaze drifting over the elegantly dressed crowd, with Stan at his side. The ballroom was resplendent, candlelight reflecting off crystal chandeliers, casting patterns of light that danced across the polished parquet, but he felt dread rising in his chest. Everywhere he looked, he saw Sera.

As if the strangers here in London were no more than waves

in the ocean. Oh, how he wished he could turn back time and kiss her that day. Hold her again. Because one thing was certain: he wouldn't let her go again.

But he'd been on the wrong path all along, consumed by ideals of duty when it was love he'd truly saved himself for. Because of his principles, his station, and his responsibilities, he'd dismissed that sentiment for years. How wrong he'd been, because all that mattered was love—his love for Sera *and* his love for his family. He didn't need to serve his country out of duty; he loved Transylvania and had vowed to protect his heritage. But that wasn't all that mattered in life.

But also, he couldn't regret his path, for then he wouldn't have met Sera.

"Isn't it rather grand, Alex?" Stan's voice was light, carrying an edge of excitement. "Lady Anna's ball is the event of the season, and I don't think I've seen our sister happier."

"Yes, Lady Anna Ashford seems to be a dear friend to Thea." Alex was glad Thea had found Lady Ashford's support and friendship, but he couldn't shake the sense that something was amiss. The hairs on his neck pricked up again, just like they had when he'd first arrived in London and met the Earl of Langley at his house. He looked over his shoulder but couldn't see anything suspicious.

The ballroom hummed with life, the swirls of gowns and coats forming a swirling chaos of movement. Alex gripped the edge of the window frame, his eyes scanning the room with precise efficiency. Somewhere among the sea of faces were the Lyndons. And her.

"Stan," Alex said tightly, turning only slightly to where his brother lingered near the refreshment table. "Where are the Lyndons?"

Stan's gaze slid over him, cool and calculating. He took an unhurried sip of champagne. "Why?"

"You know why." Alex's chest tightened. His fists strained at his sides, and he forced himself to relax his fingers, inch by inch.

"Where are they?"

Stan arched a brow and set down his glass. "You've been brooding over them since you arrived in London. What do you plan to do when you see them? Better still, how do you plan to manage the fallout?"

"I didn't ask for your commentary. Just tell me if you've seen them."

"I have." Stan's jaw tensed. "But before you go charging ahead and saying something foolish, you should consider carefully who you're dealing with." He glanced pointedly across the room. *"Lyndon Fleets and Transportation* aren't just any business, Alex. They're the gateway—our gateway—to expanding Transylvania's presence in Europe."

"I'm aware," Alex growled. He pressed his palm against the windowsill, the cool wood a meager relief against the heat building in his chest. "That's why I'm handling this quietly. You don't need to—"

"Handle what, exactly?" Stan cut him off, his voice razor-sharp. "You've got two hours to explain to Mr. Lyndon why you're reneging on a perfectly advantageous alliance. Two hours to convince him not to bury us when he's the only one capable of transporting gold from the mines to anywhere that matters. And, most importantly, two hours to decide what we'll do about von List if he gets wind of this. What if he simply sides with the Lyndons—"

"Why would he do that?"

"I don't know! He always finds a corrupt way and gets away with it. And if he does, then he's not just stealing the gold from our mines but shipping it quickly and efficiently all over Europe."

The threat hit Alex like a blow to the gut, although he already felt down. He turned fully to face Stan, his expression faltering for just a moment. "von List isn't something I can fix tonight."

"No, he's not. Just be warned, Alex—this could go two ways: Either von List works with the Lyndons to deplete all our natural resources and riches or, if von List keeps siphoning gold from the mines, the entire operation collapses. And if the mines collapse, everything crumbles—starting with Lyndon's transportation contracts. So, you'd be the one who ruined their daughter's prospects and their business. Look around you, Alex. They are well-connected. All England would turn against us."

Alex's hands flexed at his sides. He inhaled deeply through his nose, the scents of punch and an overpowering mix of the guests' perfumes clogging his senses. "I know all this," he said, his tone clipped. "And still—there's more than one way to save this."

Stan's laugh was low and humorless. "Is that what you tell yourself? That risking the only stable alliance we have is a repositioning of priorities. Not exactly comforting."

Alex's throat tightened. He hated Stan's calm, logical tone when his own thoughts were a mess of guilt, panic, and simmering anger. Stan didn't need to understand. No one needed to understand. He only had to act. Quickly. His heartbeat drummed heavily in his ears, drowning out the din of the ballroom. Dancers spun gracefully out of sync with his thoughts.

"It's not just about the mines," Alex said finally, his voice low and dangerous. "Father always said you have to see the big picture. The bigger arrangement."

"And what picture do you see tonight?" Stan's lips pressed into a thin line. "A collapse? A gamble? Or just one reckless fantasy that will cost us everything?"

Alex met his brother's gaze. Stan's eyes were steady, unyielding, but Alex's resolve hardened in kind. "No. It's not a collapse. It's a shift. A better foundation, even if it looks messy at first."

Stan sighed, shaking his head. "Miss Lyndon and her father aren't just 'messy,' Alex. They are the lynchpins of this arrangement. If you—"

"I know," Alex snapped.

Stan leaned closer, his voice dropping to a whisper. "Do you? Because all I see is someone prioritizing his heart over his people. If you can't separate the two, you have no business leading anything."

Alex's chest burned, a corrosive mix of frustration and truth tearing at him. He glanced across the ballroom again, his eyes moving urgently from one face to another. He needed to find the Lyndons. He needed to find her. And then what? He'd rehearsed his words a hundred times, but none of them seemed adequate now.

"Enough," he said finally, though it sounded more like a plea than an order. "I don't have time for this."

Stan's gaze lingered for a beat too long before he stepped back, smoothing his waistcoat. "Then I suggest you make it count, brother. Because two hours isn't nearly enough time to clean up the kind of mess you're about to make."

"I'm going to make this right." *Although I don't know how.* "If I marry for love, I can be stronger for our family. And we will be stronger against anything that our enemies send our way, von List or whoever will come next."

Stan sighed but Alex's mind was already elsewhere, splitting in too many directions at once. He surveyed the room, forcing himself to focus. The distant strains of the orchestra filled his ears, but they felt like static. Somewhere in the crowd was Miss Lyndon. Somewhere in London was the woman he was meant to spend his life with—and somewhere among the tightly wound facades and carefully placed smiles was the woman he couldn't.

Less than two hours now. He straightened his shoulders, trying to drown out the gnawing guilt in his gut and the cold, calculating voice of his brother. Whatever the fallout, he would face it. After all, love—real love—wasn't supposed to be easy. But tonight, it felt like a battlefield where every choice could mean the difference between ruin and redemption.

His mind raced, caught between disbelief and the undeniable recognition that blasted through him.

"Ah, Linsey has arrived," Stan said, his tone casual as he gestured subtly toward the tall man bowing to a woman on the dance floor. "You met him at Langley's, remember? We didn't get to talk much, but it's worth noting he owns some of the finest horses in England."

"I remember," Alex replied curtly, his jaw tightening. His brother's words barely registered. Horses didn't matter. Linsey didn't matter. Nothing mattered outside the fact that something about the scene unfolding on the dance floor set his nerves humming in warning.

"Just saying," Stan continued, with a flick of his wrist. "With your level of distraction lately, one never knows."

But Alex was no longer listening. His eyes had locked on the couple as Linsey straightened and extended his hand, claiming a dance. The woman moved with poise, her figure draped in flowing fabric, the pearls on her gown catching the low light. He could only see her in profile as Linsey led her into the center of the room, the crowd shifting like waves around them.

Something clawed at the edges of Alex's awareness, faint and insistent. The slope of her neck, the way her hand rested lightly in Linsey's—it all felt too familiar. His pulse started to race even before he could articulate why. He blinked, willing the sensation away, but it only grew.

No, he thought. It can't be.

His fingers curled into his palms, the air thickening around him as he waited for her to turn just enough. The music swelled, and a cluster of spectators blocked part of his view. His breath quickened, chest tightening, the rational part of his mind clinging to the impossibility of what he suspected. And yet…

When she finally turned, even slightly, his heart stopped. It was like being struck, the impact reverberating through his chest as her face came into full view.

Sera.

It was her. There was no room for doubt now, no chance for his mind to reason it away. Her hair wasn't loose, as he so often saw it in his memories, but piled in elegant curls. Her gown wasn't the simple daywear he'd associated with her, but an elaborate ensemble more befitting of a princess. And yet it was her all the same. His Sera.

Time seemed to warp, the din of the ballroom fading into a muffled hum. Every muscle in his body locked as he followed her movements with his gaze—graceful, practiced, altogether foreign. This Sera wasn't the woman he'd held in his arms as they walked along the cliffs of Cornwall, laughing at the unruliness of her wind-swept hair. She wasn't the one who whispered her fears and dreams to him when no one else could understand.

This Sera was a stranger. Yet, she wasn't.

Alex's stomach churned as Linsey twirled her, a polished smile on his face. The earl led her with a natural confidence, and she followed with equal ease, her expression unreadable. How could she be here? And why was she with him?

"She shouldn't—" The words barely escaped his lips, no louder than a breath. He forced himself to unclench his fists, though his nails had already bitten into his palms. Pain spiked briefly before another wave of disbelief hit.

A hundred questions cut through Alex's mind like shards of glass, each one more disorienting than the last. Why hadn't she told him? Why was she at this ball? Would she still come to Vauxhall? And most pressing of all—was this his love he'd risk his family's safety and his country's future for?

The thought tightened a noose around his chest.

Linsey leaned in closer, murmuring something that made Sera glance down, her lips pressing into a tight, polite smile. Whatever the earl had said, Alex couldn't hear it, and he hated that.

"Alex?" Stan's voice broke through the haze. He must have been speaking for some time, but the words were a blur of background noise.

Alex shook his head slightly, his lips parting but no sound emerged. He wanted to look away, to reclaim control of his scattered thoughts, but his body betrayed him. His gaze remained fixed on her, every movement of hers intertwining with the memories of all the moments they had shared.

And still, she was unreachable.

The orchestra's crescendo seemed to mock him, matching the chaotic rhythm of his heart.

"Linsey is quite the dancer," Stan remarked, oblivious to Alex's inner turmoil. "They must be very good friends for him to leave his fiancée looking on, I'd say. What do you—"

"Enough!"

Alex clutched at his chest, his eyes locked on Sera as she moved onto the dance floor with the earl. Their steps were steady, each movement practiced and perfectly timed. It was as if she'd been made for the dance floor.

Sera.

She was truly here.

How? But then, they never told each other their full identities.

They never questioned each other's lives.

They just… accepted.

He watched them dance, unable to tear his gaze away.

The cotillion, with its lively pace, seemed to slow around them, each turn and spin emphasizing the undeniable connection between Sera and her partner. Alex's mind reeled. Who was she to be friends with the earl? Would she leave the ball, like him, in time to meet at Vauxhall? He didn't know how he should feel.

Memories of Cornwall flooded his mind—days spent by the sea, laughter carried on the wind, and the brightness of her smile that had become his refuge. Those moments now felt like a distant dream. He felt as if the very ground beneath him had shifted, leaving him adrift in a world where everything he had believed was suddenly uncertain.

You didn't tell her either.

She didn't know he was a prince.

Right.

She. Didn't. Know.

Stan's voice sliced through his thoughts, a lifeline amid the chaos. "We should find the Lyndons before it's too late for you."

He nodded mechanically, though every fiber of his being

screamed otherwise. How could he be all right when the woman he loved was in the arms of another? He forced himself to stay composed, even as his heart shattered with each beat.

"You're nodding but not moving," Stan said. "Who's the woman you're staring at?"

Alex wanted to tell his brother, but he couldn't find the words.

His feet were rooted to the spot, watching as the earl and Sera shared a laugh. The realization settled over him, heavy and inescapable. He had lost her. Or perhaps he had never truly had her to begin with.

Was this a dream? Would he wake up if he pinched himself?

The room buzzed with the energy of the ball, yet Alex felt detached from it all, a spectator in his own life. He longed to approach her, to call her name aloud, to demand answers to the sudden questions that tormented him. She was so close, yet impossibly distant.

But Stan was right.

He could do nothing before he ended his engagement. He certainly couldn't approach Sera to demand anything while still engaged.

"Yes, let's find the Lyndons."

Chapter Twenty-Two

THE VIOLINS SOARED, their lilting notes threading through the ballroom as Sera twirled under the Earl of Linsey's guiding hand. But the music, the laughter, even the rhythmic steps of the cotillion seemed distant. It all faded to a dull hum, overtaken by the pounding of her pulse.

Alex.

He was here.

Her mind stumbled over the realization as her heart lodged itself in her throat. The moment their eyes met across the sea of glittering dresses, she knew. Even if he no longer looked like her carefree Alex, the man whose laughter had filled the cliffs of Cornwall, she knew. There was no mistaking him, no hope of denial.

And yet, her head swam with questions that raced too fast for answers. What was he doing here? How had he come to stand in this space, polished and stiff, so far from the world they'd shared? Did he know? Did he know she'd been promised to another? Had he come to find her? Or perhaps he wouldn't want her anymore?

Her knees almost gave in, but the earl's firm hold kept her upright, guiding her through the movements of the dance with ease. She clung to the rhythm mechanically, the steps ingrained in her muscle memory. But tonight, every figure, every turn, felt as though she were wading through mud.

"Your attention is waning," the earl said lightly, his sharp eyes catching her fleeting glances. "You're hiding something."

Her laugh was empty, brittle. "Am I?"

"You've glanced toward the same man half a dozen times," he teased as he turned her. "Who keeps your attention so engaged, Miss Lyndon?"

Her stomach twisted into a tight knot. She couldn't look away, though every instinct screamed at her to do so. Alex hadn't taken his eyes off her either, his gaze hauntingly steady, as though he were searching her soul.

Her Alex was here.

How could he be though? This was not a place he could just attend unless…

"Who is he?" she managed to say, her words breathy, uneven, betraying her. She motioned toward Alex, though it nearly killed her to say so.

Thomas tilted his head, his brow furrowing slightly as he glanced in the direction she indicated. "Who? Him? Surely you know. That's Prince Alexander von Hohenzollern-Sigmaringen."

Sera almost tripped, her foot faltering mid-step. "The prince?" Her voice was strangled, faint. The world tilted precariously.

Thomas steadied her, his hand firm at her waist. "Yes, the prince you've been promised to marry. Why? Did you not realize?" He spoke with faint puzzlement, studying her with a concern she lacked the strength to address.

Promised. To marry.

That night in Cornwall seemed so far away and so terribly long ago. And the distance between her and Alex was now a cleft as steep as Cornwall's cliffs.

The words thundered through her mind, louder than the violins, louder than the excitement of the attendees tonight.

Her Alex. Her Alex—the man who had stolen her heart beneath the summer sun, who had made her feel more alive in days than she had in years—was the prince. The prince. The very man she was bound to marry by her family's decree.

The man she'd been trying to tear herself away from.

No.

"It can't be," she whispered, though she wasn't sure if the words were for Thomas or herself.

Thomas's concern deepened. "Are you unwell?"

That was an understatement. Her entire world was unraveling before her eyes, yet she couldn't bring herself to look away from the man who had lied to her—or had he? What had Alex known? How much of their shared days had been truth, and how much a carefully constructed facade?

Had this all been a test? Did he know who she was all along and—Sera clasped her chest with her hands—did she fail the test because she showed the prince that she gave her heart too easily to a sailor boy she didn't know? Not only her heart but... Sera nearly cast up when she considered what she'd done and how stupidly naïve she'd been.

Her breath quickened, and beads of pearls gathered on the palm of her hands. Every moment between them played back in her mind, now tainted with new meaning. His accent, his guarded words, the documents she'd glimpsed in his bag. She should have known. She should have seen.

A sharp, humorless laugh broke from her lips before she could stop it, drawing a startled glance from Thomas. She recovered quickly, masking her wild thoughts with a brittle smile. "Forgive me, my lord. I seem to have much on my mind." *And no good mind of my own, I suppose.*

The thought struck her like a dagger. She felt the sting of it bloom in her chest, spreading with every labored beat of her heart. How had she been so foolish? How could she pride herself on cleverness and independence, yet stumble so blindly into this tangled mess? The answer was painfully clear—she had allowed herself to dream.

Her pulse thrummed in her ears as her gaze slid away from Thomas, who smiled kindly, oblivious to the storm within her.

She could feel the weight of his steady presence, so polite, so composed, in stark contrast to her unraveling thoughts. A lump rose in her throat, bitter and sharp.

If anyone could see inside her now, they would only find a chasm of self-disappointment. She had thought herself capable of bending the rules, of grasping some elusive, gilded thread of happiness. But all she had done was weave confusion and heartache into an already knotted web.

Her hands trembled subtly.

For the first time in all the carefully choreographed dances of her life, she was utterly out of step—with herself, with her future, with him. She blinked against the heat rising behind her eyes, willing herself not to falter now, not here.

But even as the music swirled around her, lifting the crowd on its joyous tide, she felt herself sinking under the weight of her own choices. What freedom she had thought to claim now felt like nothing more than folly, leaving her most disappointed in the one place she had relied on—herself.

"I'd say," the earl mused, though his smile was warm, gracious. "Perhaps you need air."

What she needed was clarity. Answers. She needed Alex, alone, without the weight of titles, expectations, and family obligations suffocating them both. But more than anything, she needed to know why.

Why hadn't he told her who he was? Why had she allowed herself to fall for him so completely, when all along, fate had already dictated their paths?

Her heart twisted painfully as she cast one last glance at Alex.

He hadn't moved, still watching her, unmoving, unflinching.

No, she couldn't wait.

She'd wanted to confront the prince and longed to speak to Alex—here was her chance. Everything was different than she'd dreamed—or was this a nightmare after all? Could she wake up? She turned her attention back to the earl, forcing her lips into a smile she didn't feel.

"I won't keep you much longer." She was neither a pawn nor the prize of a business deal. And she was especially not a naïve girl to be seduced at the beach and then... well, she was. Fine! But clarity was necessary now, so she had to confront him.

Alone.

Everything would become clear then. But then, could it be any clearer? They had both chosen to remain mysterious, and this was the result. Should she just head home and lock herself in her room?

Perhaps that would be for the best.

THE BUZZING BALLROOM faded into a muddled backdrop as Alex's gaze locked on her.

Sera.

Even amid the glittering crowd, she stood out, her form poised yet achingly familiar. His chest tightened with the blow of recognition. She moved with a grace different from what he remembered—more polished, more precise.

But it was her.

He knew it as surely as the rapid pounding of his heart. But why was she here, at this ball, dancing with that man?

"Alex." Stan's voice cut through his thoughts, steady and brusque. "Mr. Lyndon is ready to speak with you now. I passed your request on to him."

Alex barely turned his head, his attention still fixed on the dancers as they shifted positions. "What?" he muttered absently. His pulse thundered in his ears, drowning out his brother's words.

Stan exhaled sharply beside him. "Mr. Lyndon, the man you've spent a lifetime preparing to meet? He's waiting. Do try to act like you weren't just swallowed whole by a memory."

"Memory?" He snapped his gaze at Stan but darted it back just as quickly, searching the crowded ballroom for her again.

Panic prickled at the back of his neck as he realized she was no longer where she'd been seconds ago, dancing with the Earl of Linsey. His stomach churned. "Stan," he said, his voice low, "did you see her?"

Stan tilted his head, frowning. "See who?"

"The woman with Linsey. Dressed in pale-blue and pearls. Did you see her?"

Stan sighed, his patience clearly thinning. "I have no idea who you're talking about." He scanned the dancers with vague interest before his lips pressed into a flat line. "No sign of her now. Why?"

Alex clenched his fists at his sides, forcing himself to take two measured breaths. This wasn't the time. It couldn't be. Sera appearing here, in this room, was the last thing he should be thinking about with everything hanging in the balance. But his mind refused to grasp anything else. "No reason," he lied, voice clipped.

"Your Royal Highness." The new voice was smooth but carried a weight Alex immediately recognized. Turning, he found himself facing an older man—average height, slightly stocky, and impeccably dressed. The man's presence radiated wealth, even with his friendly smile. "What a pleasure to finally make your acquaintance in person."

Stan stepped in smoothly. "Mr. Lyndon, may I present Prince Alexander."

Alex straightened, forcing himself to pull his scattered thoughts into some semblance of order. This was Mr. Lyndon. The man who held the future of *Lyndon Fleets and Transportation*—and by extension, Transylvania's fragile trade independence—in his hands. The man who could unravel everything with a simple handshake denied. Alex's mind screamed at him to focus as he returned the man's gesture, feeling its measured grip.

"Mr. Lyndon," he said, his voice even despite the chaos beneath it. "The pleasure is mine, and I hope this will be the first of many such conversations."

"I certainly hope so," Mr. Lyndon replied with a knowing smile. "Though I do feel this evening may prove significant for more than just business, wouldn't you say?"

The pointed yet casual remark tightened the knot in Alex's stomach. Careful, he told himself. His pulse pounded as he tried—and failed—to keep his gaze from wandering over Mr. Lyndon's shoulder. The dance floor was a shifting blur now, the couples twirling too quickly to distinguish one from another. His chest hollowed with frustration when he didn't see her.

I need to find Sera.

"Your Royal Highness, I trust you understand the importance of our families' connection," Mr. Lyndon continued, his tone polite but edged with unmistakable expectation.

Alex nodded absently, his lips pressing together as he fought to meet Mr. Lyndon's gaze fully. The older man's expression was friendly but shrewd, his eyes calculating. Alex knew this conversation was critical, that von List's corruption of the mines and a potential collapse of trade hung precariously in the balance. Yet even as he acknowledged it, even as he prepared to respond, his mind was already slipping back to her. To Sera.

She had looked over at him. Seen him. He was sure of it. But where had she gone? And why had she been here at all?

"Your Royal Highness?" Mr. Lyndon's voice came again.

Alex blinked, his focus snapping to the man in front of him. "Yes, of course," he said quickly, though he wasn't entirely certain what he was agreeing to.

Beside him, Stan suppressed what Alex was sure was a groan of frustration. Mr. Lyndon tilted his head, eyes narrowing slightly, as though measuring the younger man before him.

Alex's throat tightened. This was one of those many situations in which even a royal title didn't help.

"I certainly hope," Mr. Lyndon repeated after a beat, his voice measured but deliberate, "that our alliance becomes more than just a family connection."

Alex swallowed hard, his fists curling momentarily at his sides before he forced them to relax. The words hung heavily in the air, the implication clear. His gaze darted back to the floor, searching desperately for some sign of her.

Of Sera.

"Perhaps you're unwell, Your Highness," Mr. Lyndon said. "I was hoping to announce the engagement tonight, but shall we revisit this tomorrow—when you're recovered?"

"No," Alex replied, steady but firm. His gut churned, every word costing him. "There can be no misunderstanding. I cannot marry your daughter. It would be wrong—for both her and for me."

Stan shifted beside him uneasily, a muscle feathering in his jaw. He looked ready to intervene, to stem the approaching storm, but Alex raised a hand, signaling he could handle it. Even if it was tearing him apart inside.

"Wrong?" Mr. Lyndon's voice rose an octave, his calm veneer beginning to crack. "Do you think I'd put forward a match unworthy of you? My daughter is a treasure, Prince Alexander! A treasure! What could possibly compel you to act so recklessly, to humiliate her, to humiliate *me*?" A shade of red darkened the man's cheeks.

Behind him, the room carried on as if oblivious—music swelling, guests laughing and sipping punch—but Alex could feel every set of eyes that had begun to glance their way. The scrutiny scraped against his skin, but he didn't flinch.

"My heart," Alex said simply, his words measured yet heavy, "belongs to someone else."

The admission left his lips, and with it came a quiet clarity. He'd known this; it had been true long before tonight. But saying it aloud—here, in this moment to this man—made it irrevocable.

Mr. Lyndon blinked, stunned into silence, and then leaned forward slightly, his expression almost venomous now. "Your heart? What *exactly* do you expect me to tell Seraphina? What am I to tell the people counting on this alliance? Do you intend to gamble your entire country's trade future on this… whim?"

Alex forced himself to breathe through the fury beneath the words, to remain unwavering. He swallowed against the annoyance of that question. "There's nothing whimsical about it. I promise you. Just as I promise this decision wasn't taken lightly."

"Oh, it seems light enough to me."

"Alex," Stan cut in, his voice taut, pulled in sharp contrast to the music lilting in the background. "We can't—"

"What time is it?" Alex interrupted suddenly, his gaze snapping to Stan in a way that made his brother hesitate mid-sentence.

"What does that—" Stan started before exhaling harshly. "I don't know, almost midnight? But that's not—"

"That's all I need to know." Alex turned back to Mr. Lyndon, his shoulders set but his voice softening slightly. "I beg your forgiveness for this, Mr. Lyndon, but I need to leave. This moment doesn't allow for explanations, but you deserve them, and I'll offer them as soon as they can be given. Please. Trust that my every action tonight is guided by honor. That hasn't changed."

"Honor?" Mr. Lyndon's voice was sharp with disbelief, but Alex didn't wait for more.

He moved, maneuvering swiftly through the throng of silk and laughter, past curious eyes and murmurs shadowing his wake.

Sera.

His mind fixed on her exquisite profile, on the way she'd moved across the floor with such quiet elegance. Could she have gone to Vauxhall after all? Every second felt like a grain of sand slipping through his fingers, and the sheer weight of possibility pressed against his chest. If he didn't act now, if he didn't reach her…

Breaking into the crisp night air felt like plunging headfirst into fire. He scanned the row of waiting carriages frantically, his breath visible in the cold, but his was nowhere to be found. Swearing under his breath, he started down the street, gravel crunching beneath his hurried steps.

The sound of hooves clashing against stone drew his attention, and he flagged down a hack as it came into view. "To Vauxhall," he ordered, his voice tight, catching slightly on the words.

The driver—a surly man with drooping shoulders—gave him a hard glance. "At this hour? Past midnight soon, it is. My rates double after midnight. What'll you pay?"

"Whatever you ask." Alex stepped forward, nearly shoving himself into the rickety carriage. "Just don't waste another moment."

With a sharp pull of the reins, the coach set off, wheels rattling as they left behind Lady Ashford's glittering estate. Alex sat stiffly on the edge of the seat, his hand gripping his knee so tightly it ached. The streetlights flashed by in an uneven rhythm, the damp air seeping cold through the thin material of his jacket, but he barely felt it. Every fiber of his being was ablaze, a searing torrent coursing through his veins, fanned by an unyielding resolve.

Ten minutes. That's all the time he had to save an entire future—to find her and make her listen, to fix a life in flames that seemed irreparable. Sera. It was always Sera. His mind refused to consider the alternative—because if he didn't, if he failed tonight, there may be no rebuilding what they'd begun.

The hack jerked forward suddenly, rattling him in his seat, but he welcomed the discomfort. Each jolt pushed him further into the realization of what he had to do. When they reached Vauxhall, there'd be no time for second-guessing.

He had made his choice long ago; now, he would live by it or lose everything he truly valued.

Chapter Twenty-Three

ALEX REACHED VAUXHALL and found the tree with lanterns with the driver's helpful directions. The gardens stretched out before him, muted shadows and pale pathways dimly illuminated by scattered lanterns. They should have been beautiful—peaceful, even—but instead they felt like the exact opposite, resembling a stage set for the ruin of something precious. The revelry had faded. Only faint echoes of laughter lingered, as distant as the memories of the tryst at the beach—or could it be more?

Alex ran a hand through his hair.

Never had he expected that.

How could this have happened?

Now, in the summer heat and in the heart of London, in what was meant to be a romantic setting for even more romantic moments, Alex felt more alone than he ever had on the open sea. Alex stood beneath the tree, his gloved hands pressed against the cold iron railing, as though the firm grip could still his restless thoughts.

He tugged at his cravat, his whole body feeling stifling.

Would she come?

He looked toward the path once more, hope still burning faintly, madly, that she might emerge from the shadows. She was just late, he told himself. Only delayed. But so was he. By each other. He shook his head trying to understand how this could have happened. But even as the thought formed, he felt its hollowness. The bells of St. Paul's Cathedral had already rung when he was on the way. How many minutes past midnight it was, he could not say.

I missed her.

His chest was so heavy, the air didn't seem to fill his lungs as he breathed the hot night air.

And yet he lingered.

He could not bring himself to leave, foolish as it was to stand there like a fool for a woman who might not show. But this was still Sera. Each moment stretched the tension within him to an almost shattering point but leaving—leaving would mean admitting the truth. That she wasn't coming.

He closed his eyes briefly, exhaling a long breath. Regret always came too late. Another man might have told her everything about himself. But he had delayed, selfishly hoarding their stolen moments, leaning into the mystery of just being a girl and boy in Cornwall, treasuring the way her smile lifted the burden of his responsibilities.

But hadn't she done that?

Yes, it wasn't the same.

Now she must know he is the prince. An engaged one at that. If he had told her from the beginning, he could have won her heart the proper way.

His lips twisted into a grimace.

Just days ago, he had replayed all her different laughs in his mind. Sera. She was summer's glimmer of joy in a life shaped by duty, expectations, and sacrifices. He had given so much, restrained so much. But when it came to her... she was the only gift he had ever wanted for himself. And he just couldn't let her go.

Yet, if she didn't come tonight... he didn't want to think it.

I lost her.

Couples laughing filled the spaces around him, mocking him. What had he expected? That she would come here, to honor a moment shared in innocence, when all her trust in him had surely been shattered? When his own trust should have been shattered? And yet it wasn't. Not at all. He should have known.

He dragged his hands through his hair and turned toward the pavilion, glancing at the crowded benches as though they might offer an answer he hadn't yet considered. But there was nothing. Just him. And the tree with lanterns.

A simmering frustration boiled under his skin as he started to pace. His booted steps scuffed against gravel and flagstone, sharp even amid the noise.

"Fir-ar să fie!" Blast it, he murmured under his breath. His brow furrowed. This wasn't the life he was meant to lead. His life had rules, expectations, and outcomes laid like paving stones long before his birth. He knew how to follow paths and bear the weight of them.

But none of that had mattered when he was with her.

And yet here she was—absent.

Who could blame her? Her absence spoke as loudly as his regret for not revealing who he truly was. He exhaled sharply, his back rigid with effort as he forced himself to glance at the path one last time. A man in his position shouldn't bend under emotion. Yet he was chained by it. And the path was empty. Just like last time. Just like every time.

She's not coming.

He turned, fists curling. It took all the control he had to keep from punching his fist into the bark of the tree, from letting his emotions spill out unchecked. What would his brother say? Princes didn't act rashly. And yet his heart snarled against the press of reason as he pinched the bridge of his nose.

Please, Sera, come.

Come and demand answers!

More curses hissed from his lips in Romanian, the language of his ancestors heavy with frustration. Another twig met its fate under his heel. He would snap them all if he could!

His head tilted back briefly toward the faint shimmer of the stars above. They stared back, distant and unfeeling, indifferent to the torment of princes and commoners alike.

She wasn't coming.

He should go.

He sighed and walked away, leaving the spot behind with one last sweep of the area.

It was over.

⭆⭆⭆✶⭅⭅⭅

IT WAS ALL a great mess! She had been Alex's fiancée from the very beginning! The irony was almost enough to make her bang her head against the wall. Instead of leaving her, he should have come to London with her. They should have gone together.

Sera rushed through the hallway of Lady Ashford's home. *He's not getting out of this. He's not just slipping away.*

Am I late?

She hoped she wasn't too late. Would he still be there? Would he even go to Vauxhall? She had to tell him that it didn't matter. Oh, why, oh, why had she thought to collect her breath first?

Perhaps he'll forgive me?

The marble tiles gleamed beneath her silk slippers, her reflection fractured as if the world itself had splintered. She paused just long enough to drape her shawl over her bare shoulders—modesty preserved but barely, as her heart raced ahead of her.

Outside, the air was stifling hot. It felt suffocating compared to midsummer in Cornwall. There was no sign of her family's carriage. She had sent her footman ahead with instructions to return promptly—yet the spot where it should have waited loomed empty.

A flicker of panic surged through her.

Not tonight.

Not when every unresolved emotion and unanswered question between her and Alex boiled within her like a kettle left on the fire too long.

A shadow emerged near the gate. Sera hadn't noticed him at first, but there he was—a man standing beside another carriage, its glossy black paint reflecting the scattered light from the house's torches. The golden crest emblazoned on its door glowed unmistakably, regal and bold. Her heart hitched, recognition dawning too late. She recognized that crest. *The carriage that left when Isabella spoke to my prince...*

The prince.

Her prince.

The man stepped forward, silhouetted by the carriage lamps. "Miss Lyndon," he addressed her with a small bow. His face entered the light as he straightened—a vaguely familiar one, though not enough to soothe the flutters in her belly.

"You," she breathed, narrowing her eyes as memory clung to the edges of her thoughts. "I've seen you before, haven't I? You lingered in which scene?"

The man nodded once, his expression professional yet edged with something she couldn't quite name. "Indeed, Miss Lyndon. My name is Charles Brown. I am Prince Alexander's valet."

"Oh," she said, blinking, though her mind reeled to pin him down. "And his driver as well?"

"If he so desires, yes."

She arched a brow, recalling the picnic with those maps. "And his secretary?"

"Exactly," he replied without hesitation.

"Well, he must trust you quite a bit," she murmured. "But you'll have to excuse me, I'm a little pressed for time."

Mr. Brown nodded slightly. "May I take you to him? Vauxhall, is it?"

Sera glanced at the door he held open for her. She didn't need to ask. It was his carriage—the one with the crest of a prince. Alex's crest.

"You know about Vauxhall?"

"I do," he said simply. "Yet I only now pieced together another few things."

Meaning her identity, but that wasn't important. "So, he went? To Vauxhall? But with what? If you're here with his carriage."

"That, I cannot say. However, I had his entry token ready, Miss." He offered her the token.

She nodded, and her breath trembled as she stepped up into the shadowed interior, sinking against the velvet cushions as the door shut with a crisp finality. The wheels began to turn, the faintest lurch as the coachman urged the horses onward.

The ride to Vauxhall was an agonizing half hour or perhaps half a century; she measured it in the unspoken weight filling the carriage. Mr. Brown did not speak, nor did she. What could either of them say? The silence suited her mood. Every moment, every breath brought her closer—and yet farther. Her mind danced uneasily between the hope of mending what they had severed and the deepening dread that she might already be too late.

I should have told him.

She shouldn't have leaned so heavily into the romance and mystique of spending time with someone without knowing who they were to the world. But this was also why she knew, having met Alex as a mystery sea man, she didn't want to lose him.

It didn't matter who he was to the world. It only mattered who he was to her.

The pavilion of Vauxhall came into view after what felt like hours, standing pale and still under the soft haze of moonlight. People were still roaming about despite the hour, and she hoped one of those people was Alex.

Sera stepped down before the carriage had even come to a complete stop. Mr. Brown's protest lingered wordlessly behind her as she smoothed her gown, her shawl clutched tightly to her chest, and dashed for the entry, her slippers whispering against the gravel. Forward, she thought. Forward, always forward. If she stopped now, she might shatter entirely.

But her steps faltered as she approached the spot they had agreed upon.

It was empty.

No shadow of a man waiting for her arrival, anticipating her like she had envisioned in her heart. No sign that he'd ever been there. Only absence.

I missed him.

Her hands formed into fists, her knuckles tightening with the force of it. The reality seeped into her all at once, sharp and bitter.

She was too late.

Her heart pounded with the violent tide of loss. Alex, her Alex, the man she loved beyond words. A laugh—tight and humorless—escaped her as tears blurred the edges of the tree. She was a fool, wasn't she? Of course he wasn't here.

Of course she had lost him.

He must think she wasn't worthy of him. A liar. An imposter. He couldn't know.

After all, they were engaged, and she'd given her chastity to another man, even if that man was him—did he know?

How much did he know?

Sera's head was spinning with questions for she wasn't clear about it herself any longer. When had it all gone so terribly wrong? She turned slowly, the edges of her vision spinning, her throat tight with the hollow weight where desire had once lived. She turned to walk back to where she had left Mr. Brown. Each step she took away from the tree hanging with lanterns felt heavier than the last.

She had barely crossed the threshold from the gardens when a voice—low, rough, unmistakable—shattered the silence.

"Sera."

Her name cut through the darkness. She whipped around as her breath stopped, frozen on her lips. And there he was.

Alex.

Her sea man.

Prince Alexander von Hohenzollern-Sigmaringen stood not even five feet away.

Her lips parted, but no words came. She could only look at him, tears burning her cheeks and his name resting in her heart like the faintest whisper of hope.

He came.

Chapter Twenty-Four

I T HAPPENED. AFTER all this time, he saw her again. He could finally smell her again and her closeness was all that mattered even though there was so much more.

The night. Her. Life.

His senses, dulled by worry, roared back to life. The faint murmurs of people grew lively. The soft breeze cooled the otherwise warm air. He could practically taste the delicate scent of her skin that seemed to linger in the atmosphere. All around.

Her name burned in his throat.

Sera.

Alex inhaled sharply, closing his eyes for the briefest of moments. When he opened them again, she was still there. Standing just a few steps away, her pale-blue dress catching the faint glow of the gaslights behind her. The sight of her hit him with the same force it had earlier, his chest tightening as though the air had evaporated between them.

"You came," he said, his voice rough, barely steady.

Her gaze didn't waver, her expression unreadable. "I did. And so did you."

He hesitated, his feet rooted to the ground despite every instinct telling him to close the distance, to take her in his arms, to assure himself this wasn't some cruel figment conjured by his frantic mind. But the weight of everything he'd just broken—his promises, her world, their tangled history—kept him cautious, his confusion and longing warring for control.

"You're the prince."

"I am," he admitted blunt.

"We're engaged."

"We are." Wait. "What? No, I mean, I was engaged. I'm not anymore."

"You are or were engaged to me." The words came out certain, deliberate, like an anchor thrown against the storm swirling inside him. "I am Seraphina Lyndon."

Alex couldn't process what he was hearing. She… *She* was his betrothed from the very start? She'd been his all along and he didn't even know?

A curse flew from his mouth.

"My sentiments, exactly."

A flicker of panic licked at his composure. He stepped forward, his posture firm, his voice leaving no room for argument. "This is a terrible mess, but first of all, despite what happens, we *are* still engaged, and we will remain so if you wish."

"If I don't?"

Pain. "If you don't, then nothing needs to be done further. I already spoke to your father."

"And yet you claim we are still engaged?"

"My heart will always be engaged to you, Sera. No matter what you decide."

But the truth still burned his mind. He still couldn't believe that *Sera* had been his from the start. Only hours ago, he'd been prepared to dissolve this engagement without a second thought. Back then, Seraphina Lyndon had been nothing more than a name—a vague, faceless obligation thrust upon him.

Now, standing before him, she was *Sera*. The woman whose smile had once lit something inside him. The woman he hadn't known he'd been searching for until he'd found her. The woman he had almost walked away from, unknowingly.

His heart twisted.

For a prince who claimed to be smart, he surely was a confounded fool! How had they managed to miss each other so entirely?

"I didn't know," Alex admitted, his voice quieter now but no less resolute. "I didn't know it was you, Sera. I didn't know this—us—was what my future held." He swallowed hard and stepped closer, his pulse pounding. "If I had known…"

He couldn't explain it but a flash of Anton struggling in the water rushed back. He should have saved him back then, but it was too late. He didn't want to be late now and felt utterly at sea.

Sera crossed her arms, her guarded stance betraying the turbulence in her own eyes. "If you had known? What, Alex? Would you have done anything differently? Because from where I stand, it feels like you were ready to end this—until now."

Her words stung, sharp and direct, but he couldn't fault her for uttering them. She wasn't wrong. And still, he refused to shy away. He took one more step, leaning closer, his voice low yet steady. "If I had known it was you, Sera, I would've moved heaven and earth to find you sooner. I would have never wasted a single moment letting you believe otherwise."

Her lips parted slightly, and for a moment, her expression softened. But just as quickly, her shields rose again. She uncrossed her arms, stepping forward too, matching him in defiance. "And yet, you didn't. You didn't know, Alex." Her gaze bore into him, unyielding. "How could we have been so oblivious?"

Alex shook his head, frustration flickering in his eyes. "I don't know. Somewhere along the way, we lost each other. But I am telling you now, I won't lose you again."

She hesitated, her fingers curling loosely into her skirts as she finally looked away, her composure faltering. "You're the prince," she murmured, her voice tight. "The very same one engaged to Miss Seraphina Lyndon. You knew about her, didn't you?"

His stomach twisted as he recalled their first meeting—the teasing glint in her eyes as she'd thrown out that question, 'Are you a prince, then?' If he'd just admitted it, if he hadn't been so careful… He ran a hand over his jaw, exhaling sharply. "I couldn't have known it was you, Sera."

"I know," she said with a heavy sigh. "I didn't formally introduce myself, after all. Neither did I demand an introduction. Honestly, if you had told me who you were, I'd probably have run."

"Will you run now?"

She looked at him, truly looked at him, and in her eyes, he saw the battle playing out—the hurt, the uncertainty, and something deeper. Something unyielding. Finally, her fingers relaxed at her sides, a soft, hesitant whisper escaping her lips. "How can I? But I don't know what to do with this. With us."

He nodded slowly, his heartbeat steadying for the first time all evening. "Then give me a chance to show you," he said quietly.

"We were meant for each other all along. Even without our parents' meddling, we fell in love, didn't we?" she said.

"Yes, we did. I'll never love another, never have. It was you. Just you and me, Sera." Even though it had become so complicated, at its core, the matter was so simple.

His gaze fell to the shawl slipping from her shoulders. She looked as beautiful as ever, in a different way than he was used to, but still breathtaking. His eyes met hers again. "It must have been a shock, right? I'm not the smuggler you hoped I'd be."

A bubble of laughter escaped her. "How silly you must have found me."

"I never once found you silly, Sera." Alex's voice was steady, but his heart pounded like a drum in his chest. She hadn't cursed him yet. Hope bloomed daringly again. "Perhaps a bit too bold. But never silly. What about me?"

She took another step closer, and he followed suit. Her shawl slipped farther, exposing the delicate curve of her collarbone. She didn't bother adjusting it, her focus locked entirely on him. "You? I never found you silly."

"Are you angry?"

Another step. "I don't know. I'm not sure how I should be feeling right now." Another step.

"I'm not."

"I wanted to break our engagement. Are *you* angry?"

"How can I be?" Alex smiled then. "To be with me."

"Yes," she murmured. The final steps brought them before each other. "For two people who don't find each other silly, we sure were a bit silly."

"You didn't want to marry me," Alex asked, finally voicing the question in his heart. This wasn't just about her meeting him on the beach; this was before then. "May I ask why?"

"I don't want to leave England."

Ah.

"Is that the only reason?"

"There were other small reasons, but that was the biggest one."

He nodded. "So, do you never want to leave, or do you just not wish to leave permanently?"

"Permanently," she said without hesitation.

At least that wouldn't be a hurdle for them, then. He didn't want to drag anyone across the continent against their will. "Then we won't."

"We?"

"I am where you are," Alex said firmly. There was no other option. Even if she refused to see him, he wouldn't leave England while she was still there. "Do you not want me anymore?"

She sighed. "We're standing here, and everything is... different. Everything has changed. A prince who pretended to be a common man. A man who makes me feel things I shouldn't. Are you truly not upset?"

"First of all, I'm only upset with myself for not paying more attention to my fiancée. You have just as much right to be upset as well. And finally, Sera, everything has always been different. We just didn't realize it yet. Even if I had turned out to be a pirate and you, the princess, it would still have been different."

Her gaze faltered, dipping to the ground before flicking back to meet his. "I told my mother I wanted to break off the engagement."

"Like I said, I told your father, but it doesn't matter." He closed the small, remaining gap with one decisive step. He was close enough now to see the faint rise and fall of her chest, to catch the smallest wrinkle between her brows. "I have no desire to separate from you. Things may be different now, but some things have stayed the same. Like the way I feel about you. Like the fact that we are engaged, no matter what happened in that ballroom. Do you still feel the same?"

"I do, but..." her voice trailed off.

His heart sank.

She inhaled deeply, exhaling slowly before she continued, "The last time we saw each other was before I knew who you really were. Before you knew who I really was. But none of that changes what we are to each other."

"My heart nearly failed." He clutched at his chest, his eyes on her, almost moodily. "Couldn't you just have thrown yourself into my arms?"

Her smile widened. "I could have, but I needed to stay that way then."

"How about now?" Alex asked, opening his arms. "Can you throw yourself into them now?"

OF ALL THE emotions swirling within Sera's breast at that moment, relief was the strongest. He looked handsome in the dim light—too handsome for a man who had thrown her entire world into momentary chaos. She didn't hesitate. She stepped into his arms, nearly choking as he enveloped her.

She'd missed his scent.

The warmth of his body.

Him.

Her mind still reeled. Seeing him tonight in all his princely glory, she hadn't been able to connect him with the man on the beach. But in his arms… He was still the same Alex. And that was everything.

"I never saw this coming."

"Neither did I," he admitted.

Sera shivered despite the heavy warmth in the air. She turned her gaze outward toward the darkened line of the garden, where the shapes of trees beckoned couples to trysts. Beyond them, she knew, the city pulsed, especially Lady Ashford's ball.

They would have to return to reality soon.

"Do you really believe that everything will be okay? We left quite a mess at the ball. My parents are furious."

"Yes," he said without hesitation. "I believe it, Sera. I believe in us. I have since the very beginning. Sera and Alex are stronger than their positions in the world. We have something unexpected."

"Love?" She laughed at the realization because it was either too mad or too perfect, she didn't know which. She could just picture her mother's expression, though she should be pleased. "You make it sound so simple." She would never be able to live it down in the future. Even just thinking about Isabella's response made her stifle a groan.

"It's simple," he said, his tone softening. "The hardest part was waiting here and thinking you weren't coming." He kissed her forehead. "You have no idea how happy I am."

"I'm happy too."

His arms tightened around her. "I've never wanted anything as much as I want you. I want you and everything you desire."

"But what do you want, Alex?" she asked, her voice breaking slightly. "There must be more than just everything I want."

He didn't hesitate. "I don't know about that. I want you, Sera. All of you. Your boldness, your fire, your fears. Everything, my sweet tigress. All of you! It doesn't matter where we live. Besides, England has grown on me."

Sera couldn't help it. She lifted onto her toes and kissed him.

The moment their lips touched, Sera knew she had come home. She traced her tongue over his lower lip, prompting him to take charge and deepen the kiss. He didn't disappoint. Immediately, their tongues danced together. It quickly turned playful when Alex grinned against her lips and then chuckled mid-kiss.

"What's so funny?" she demanded, pulling away just enough to narrow her eyes at him.

"So eager."

"Of course, I'm eager! Are you telling me you're not?"

He laughed outright then. "Eager," he hurriedly said.

Sera reached up, brushing a stray lock of his dark hair from his forehead. "Good."

Before she could say anything else, he kissed her again. How dangerous. She could lose herself in this man. Correction, she had already lost herself in this man. The kiss was brief, but it still left her reeling. He stepped back. "Come, we need to go."

"Back to the ball?"

He nodded. "We need to explain to your parents why I made a mistake."

"Not explain all of it!" Sera groaned. But he was right. And yet, for the first time since the big reveal, Sera felt like everything might just be fine.

A loud crack sounded through the air, and the bark of the tree exploded next to them.

Sera screamed.

Chapter Twenty-Five

THE SILENCE SHATTERED like glass. The gunshot ripped through the stillness, sharp and violent. Alex's heart seized, but his instincts moved faster. Before the last echoes faded beneath the heavy veil of night, he pulled Sera into his arms, his palm cupping the back of her head, cradling her against his chest. Whatever anger still lingered between them dissolved in an instant.

Someone had fired a shot.

But the moment the thought landed, he knew the truth.

It had been aimed at them.

All around them, people cried out in alarm, scattering.

"Stay low," he whispered urgently, his breath barely stirring the strands of her hair. He scanned the dark expanse of the gardens, his sharp eyes picking out the vague outlines of shadowy hedgerows and empty paths. No one in sight posed a threat. But whoever had fired the shot was out there, watching.

Probably reloading.

Sera's breath came quickly against his collarbone, and her hands clenched the fabric of his coat. For all her bold wit, she trembled. Guilt twisted low in his gut—she should never have been here, unguarded, and he blamed himself bitterly for leaving her in danger. But this wasn't the moment for regret. He shouldn't have let them linger here.

"We can't make ourselves a still target," he said, his voice steady and low, the calm authority of his naval years cutting through both doubt and fear. "Let's go. Stay close to me."

She nodded against him, her chin digging slightly into his chest before she lifted her gaze. Her wide green eyes, filled with unspoken questions, met his for one suspended, fleeting second. Then she nodded again, more resolute this time.

"What is happening?" she asked worriedly.

He didn't want to scare her more. "I don't know. Let's first get out of here." Alex tightened his grip on her hand. His chest tightened. He didn't know London as well as she did. "Where can we run, Sera?" he asked, his voice urgent but measured. "There's no clear ground—it's all hedges, trees, and traps. We're sitting ducks here."

On a ship, I can navigate by the stars.

But London's a maze.

Her breaths came faster. She squeezed his arm as though anchoring herself. "Vauxhall Bridge," she said finally, her words hurried but confident. "To the south bank, across the river."

"South bank," Alex repeated, his eyes narrowing as the words tried to fit into a map of a city he did not yet know. The sharp spike of helplessness clawed at him—he'd navigated half the Mediterranean, even around the Greek Isles, but in London, he was adrift. His jaw tightened, and he caught her gaze again. "Lead the way."

Her fingers twitched in his as though she barely trusted his reliance, but there wasn't time for doubt. She gave a quick nod and took off, pulling him with her. Alex followed without hesitation, his longer stride quickly aligning with her swift pace as they broke into a run.

The night seemed darker now, shadows stretching long fingers to ensnare their hurried steps. Every crack of a twig beneath their boots sent shivers down Alex's spine, though he fought to maintain his focus. Behind them, faint but unmistakable, came the muffled pound of footsteps matching their rush.

"They're following," he growled under his breath, cursing when she tensed beside him.

Sera glanced back before Alex tugged on her arm, urging her forward. "So, you do know what's going on?"

"I'll explain later. Keep going. Don't look behind you."

"Alex!"

"I'm here. I won't leave you." *Never.*

Their footsteps—hers lighter, his heavier—echoed in scattered bursts, weaving through paths barely lit by slivers of moonlight. At last, those chasing steps seemed to fade away. Alex pushed them forward still, not trusting the eerie silence that followed.

When they finally emerged onto the riverbank, the vast water shimmering faintly under the night sky, Alex stopped them short. The land opened wide here, far too exposed. At this time of night, the city was eerily quiet. Danger seemed to prickle in the air. He cursed under his breath.

"This is open space," he muttered grimly. "Too dangerous."

Sera turned, her cheeks flushed from the run, her chest rising and falling heavily. "What now?"

His eyes darted to the water. The sight of a small, roughly moored sailboat caught his attention like a beacon. He didn't hesitate. "The boat," he said, pulling her toward it.

Sera stiffened, resisting the pull. "A boat? No, Alex—"

"Trust me," Alex said sharply, looking down into her terrified face and tugged at her hand. The urgency in his voice cracked like a whip against her hesitation. "I need you to trust me, Sera. Do you? Please!"

Something flickered in her gaze, equal parts fear and something softer, something reluctant but yielding. She froze.

The sound of footsteps crushed the moment. A second shot rang out, jolting through the night. Birds startled from nearby trees in a flurry of wings and panicked cries.

"Sera!" His tone cut through the chaos, desperate but firm.

He reached for her waist and clasped it tightly. "You know who I am, who I truly am. I will protect you with my life. Forever." Then he jumped onto the boat and reached his hand out. "I'll catch you!"

Her eyes fixed on his, her breaths shallow and quick, but the doubt finally melted from her face. She gripped his hand, stepped onto the edge of the rocking boat, and allowed him to lift her in.

Alex crouched low, untying the moor with one hand while keeping her steady with the other. The boat swayed slightly as he pushed them free, the dark water lapping against its sides as they drifted into the unknown.

Alex crouched low, fumbling with the knotted moor as Sera's breath rasped beside him, shallow and quick. The river's surface shimmered like black glass under the moonlight, but its tranquility only tightened the knot in his chest. Every splash of water against the boat's sides felt deafening, a beacon ready to betray them. Somewhere behind, the footsteps had ceased, but he wasn't foolish enough to believe they were alone for long.

"Hurry," Sera whispered, her voice strained to a threadbare edge. She clutched the edge of the boat, her gaze darting to the shadows on the bank. The rustle of leaves felt too loud, too close.

"I know," he muttered, teeth gritted against the stubborn rope. It was coarse in his hands, damp and unyielding, as if conspiring to keep them tied down. His fingers trembled, slick from sweat, and with each failed tug, his heartbeat grew louder, thundering in his ears. "It's this or swim—ah!" Finally, the knot slipped free.

The boat rocked violently as it began to drift. A surge of relief broke through him before the rope, forgotten in his haste, went taut. The boat jerked back, its lurch nearly throwing them sideways. Sera stifled a gasp, gripping the edge harder as her wide eyes snapped to his.

"*Draci!*" Alex clutched at the hull, barely saving himself from toppling overboard. Fingers scrambling, he snatched at the rope, hissing under his breath. Behind them, shouts erupted, echoing over the water.

"Alex," Sera choked, panic slicing through her whisper. The voices were closing in now, boots striking dirt, urgency breathing down their necks. Torches flared in the distance, their light chasing shadows across the reeds.

"Oh, brilliant," Alex muttered. "Nothing like an audience for one's blunders." He wrestled with the rope, its fibers burning against his palms, refusing to yield. "Remind me to write a treatise on the art of theatrics during a daring escape."

"Perhaps less muttering and more escaping?" Sera snapped, her knuckles white against the wood.

A sharp crack echoed, a warning shot splintering the stillness. It pierced the air before hissing into the river just yards away. Alex's breath stopped. He yanked the rope with one final, desperate pull. It didn't give.

"There! I found them!" A voice from the distance—but it wasn't far enough.

SERA'S INSTINCTS SCREAMED at her to turn, to see where the shots had come from. Her heart pounded, her breaths shallow as she glanced over her shoulder. But before she could catch a glimpse, the flutter of startled birds exploded in the quiet, their wings carving sharp crescents into the dim light of the moon. The sound jolted through her like the rocking of the boat.

A shot had been fired somewhere behind her.

Alex's touch was firm and sudden. His hand pressed against her shoulder, forcing her down with an urgency that brooked no argument. The coarse, musty fabric of an old blanket enveloped her as he tucked it over her head with a sharp whisper.

"Stay hidden, Sera."

As if safety were an option.

"What is going on here, Alex?"

"Shh, I promise I will tell you later."

On all fours, with the wooden boat swaying beneath her, she gasped at the warmth of the night seeping through the planks from where Alex's body had settled moments ago. But then her hand brushed against something cold and slick against the wood—a sensation that sent a shiver racing up her spine. Was this… Her fingers instinctively tightened around the object as her stomach churned beneath the blanket.

A fish knife of sorts.

She could feel the rust covering the blade. It might be small, but it was still a weapon. Still deadly. Still something she could use for protection. Her heartbeat settled a bit. Just a bit. It still pounded far too loudly in her ear. But not enough to drown out all the noise. From the shore, she heard voices—low and harsh—carried across the tide. They weren't speaking English—of that much, she was certain. The syllables rolled in guttural tones that made her hair stand on end.

"Nichtsnutz!" Good-for-nothing.

"Hier sind beide wie auf einem Präsentierteller!" Here they both are, served up on a silver platter! Another voice that seemed somewhat familiar.

"Draci!" Alex cursed under his breath.

His movements shifted against the shallow hull of the boat, the tension of those motions rolling off his body and prickled at her like a palpable force. She imagined his sharp profile, his serious expression, and pride as he protected her from their unseen adversaries. But there was a tightness to his voice, a measured control that told her he was being cornered.

The tether.

The knife burned cold in her grip like a promise. "Alex," she whispered his name under her breath, a prayer carried to the heavens, before she moved.

With one sharp motion, she pushed herself out from under the blanket.

The outside air hit her, charging her senses, feeding the pulse pounding through her blood. She didn't look to Alex—didn't look at the faces beyond him that she was too terrified to see.

Instead, her whole body lunged toward the line.

The coarse rope stretched taut beside the boat, an anchor dragging them backward into danger prevented them from leaving the dock. Her chest swelled with determination, her fingers shaking but sure as she brought the knife to it.

They would leave, or they would die.

Chapter Twenty-Six

T HIS WAS NOT safe.

No, this was a disaster. Colossal. When Sera lunged for that rope, knife in hand, Alex felt like his heart might just stop. He tightened his grip on the edge of the boat, fighting the urge to lunge at her.

"Ich sehe sie!" I see them. The first voice again. *"Da auf dem Boot!"* There on the boat!

Baron von List's voice and his Prussian lilt were unmistakable.

Alex yearned to return Sera to the ballroom's comforting embrace, where she was shielded from harm. His instincts rebelled against the sight, against the danger, and the exposure to his enemies in that moment, but there was no chance to stop her. It was impossible for him. He prepared himself for the rope breaking. He cursed, alert, his eyes never once leaving her.

"Sie haben Ihre Aufgabe nicht vollendet." The voice was smooth, calculating—almost conversational. The haughty Prussian tone. Alex didn't miss the threat that lingered beneath Baron von List's words. You didn't finish your task, hm? Alex watched as Brown stiffened at the accusation, the faint moon highlighting the sweat beading on his brow.

"Doch, habe ich!" Brown shot back, his voice sharp as a blade,

defensive but quaking at its edges.

Alex's blood ran cold.

That's why he was always there, his valet, waiter, driver… and the questions. His curiosity wasn't interest, it was spying!

This traitor!

He had dared to believe they had stumbled into something worse than hired mercenaries, but there stood Baron von List himself, his cloak sweeping behind him like a shadow of his treachery. Next to him was Brown, the man Alex had once dismissed as nothing more than a meddlesome footman hovering near him. Now he understood why…

A Prussian lilt tinged their words, and Alex was familiar with the German dialect. The words chilled him, their weight heavy with betrayal.

From beneath the blanket, Sera's hand continued to move, slicing the blade against the thick rope tethering them to the pier. Her progress was slow, but he could see the rope fraying in the dim light. Alex's heart skipped a beat—he could see the determination in her movements, but Brown's pistol was swinging in her direction.

And then Alex saw it.

Baron von List, holding a double-barreled flintlock firearm. The man had two shots. *Draci*! One had already rung out, but the second…

He needed to stall.

"Mist!" Crap! the Baron cursed.

Alex's breath was barely audible, but his jaw tightened. His mind raced through his options, weighing them against the barrel of that deadly weapon.

Stall!

"What do you have to gain from hurting her?" Alex's voice cut clearly across the river's hum, steady yet edged with purposeful defiance. He knew von List; such a call, such provocation would throw him off. He shifted his weight, tightening his grip on the line that held the sail to the mast. It kept him moving, making him a harder target for a gunman's aim, but it was more than that—it was essential for their escape. He needed that escape to be possible.

"If one desires a task done well, one must see to it personally." Baron von List tilted his head slightly, as if surprised by Alex. Then came the answer, full of venom and quiet malice. "It's her father's ships I've been using for the gold." von List's words dripped with self-assured smugness. "If she falls under your influence, your 'sense of justice' will take away my entire infrastructure." He nearly spat the words. "You're just as righteous as your brothers and father."

Alex stilled.

The ripples of this revelation seeped into his chest like icy water. He had long known that powerful people—seeking economic alliances—had orchestrated his engagement to Miss Lyndon, but now this realization painfully crystallized before him. This wasn't merely about their families or Europe's balance; it had always been about control.

Sabotage.

"You've been diverting our gold. None of it belongs to you."

"What do you want to do about it?"

"Return it to the people you stole it from." Alex's eyes darted to the rope that was about to snap.

"That'd be you and your royal family, hmm?" The words sounded like insults in von List's voice—their royal status.

"No. Other than you, we serve and protect the locals. They deserve to be paid for their work, reimbursed for the natural resources—"

"That's unnatural! Finders keepers! Isn't that what they say in English?"

"It's not finding if you're mining for it." Just a little more, Sera. You can do it.

"You and her together," von List continued, voice darkening, "would be the worst possible obstacle to my business."

"It's not business," Alex shot, furious now, "if you exploit the mines and the people for your own enrichment."

"And is that why you hired a spy?"

The baron only laughed, sharp and grating. He turned his gaze to Brown, who flinched. "Someone needed to keep an eye on you, Prince Alexander. But, in hindsight, I overestimated the simple footman from Cornwall."

Brown's lips pressed into a thin line, but he didn't refute it. Anger flickered in his eyes, quickly buried in shame.

Alex held his breath as he watched.

The baron handed Brown the pistol with almost casual disdain. "Finish this."

Alex clenched his fists.

Charles raised the pistol. Alex noticed it in the slight tremor of his arm and the twitch of his jaw. Whatever drove Brown—whether it was a shadowed past or unseen loyalty—remained a mystery to Alex, a muddled puzzle he didn't have time to solve. The man stood rigid, his jaw tight, his hands twitching at his sides as if they wanted to move but couldn't find a compelling reason. His gaze was fixed on von List, and for a moment, Alex thought he saw something flicker there—a hesitation, a crack in the stone facade.

von List didn't miss it. He stepped closer, his voice low but insistent, the words too soft for Alex to catch completely. Whatever he said cut through the tension like a knife, his tone sharp with purpose, his movements deliberate.

Brown's posture shifted, almost imperceptibly. His shoulders dropped a fraction, his stare no longer sharp as steel but dulled, worn at the edges. Alex could swear the man's hands steadied, their restlessness replaced by an uneasy stillness. He clenched his teeth, the muscle in his jaw jumping like it was trying to lock down whatever emotion brewed beneath.

Alex tightened his grip on the tiller at his side, unsure whether to brace for violence or mercy. No matter what game von List was playing, it was weaving itself between Brown's silence and stance with a skill that Alex couldn't comprehend.

"Whatever it takes," von List murmured abruptly at last, his voice carrying just enough for Alex to catch. His tone was a lash, and it landed.

Brown exhaled sharply, his head sinking a fraction before he straightened again, resolute. Alex couldn't tell if it was surrender or defiance. Maybe it was both. But when Brown finally moved, it wasn't toward the gun on his belt. It was toward von List, his expression forged with something Alex still couldn't place.

"I know your girl needs the papers to stay in England," von List said, "and I will procure them so you can marry her."

Brown twitched, startled. His hard gaze returned to Alex's direction.

And then Alex's heart froze. Brown glanced at Sera, his eyes lingering. Alex panicked. "You might be Prussian," he shouted, his voice rising forcefully, "but this is England. You don't have to obey him. von List has no authority here."

The baron's sharp laughter sliced through the air. "I may not have authority," von List drawled, drawing another pistol from beneath his coat with a flourish, "but I do have another pistol." Brown aimed the pistol at Sera. Alex froze. "Get your aim straight," he growled.

Silence descended like a noose. Alex's grip on the sail line tightened, his pulse roaring in his ears. His eyes flicked quickly from the corner of his gaze to Sera. She just needed more time. One more saw.

Alex planted himself between Brown's aim and Sera.

"You're a fool if you think this ends with her blood on your hands," Alex said, his voice steady as stone.

Just one more second.

SERA'S NERVES WERE as frayed as the rope, stretching but holding on. The dull scrape of the knife against the rope filled her ears like a curse word. Her heart pounded so loudly that she almost couldn't hear the low murmuring behind her—the sound of men arguing in German. Their voices rolled like distant thunder, sharp at the edges, incomprehensible yet oppressive in their tone. What were they discussing? Would they notice her? The blade bit deeper into the thick, unyielding rope.

Her hands trembled with the effort; her fingers slipped on the hilt as sweat slicked her grip. The fibers began to fray under the sharp edge, but it wasn't fast enough. Each second felt like a lifetime. She pressed harder, her teeth clenched, the knife stubbornly resisting. Then, suddenly—a sharp jolt.

Sera gasped as the knife slipped from her hand, clattering onto the wooden floor of the boat. The boat lurched violently away from the dock, sending her sprawling to the side. Fingers scrambled for purchase, and she barely caught the edge before she could fall completely. Her knuckles went ghost-white, her breath catching in panic as the rope finally snapped with a deafening crack.

"Sera!" Alex's shout cut through her panic, raw and desperate. The blanket was ripped away from her, the musty fabric replaced with the crisp night air. Moonlight spilled across her face as Alex grabbed her shoulders, his eyes wild, scanning her features.

"Are you all right?" he demanded, his voice trembling with an emotion she couldn't quite name. Sera blinked up at him, struggling to assess her own state as her heart thundered within her chest. She wanted to say yes—that she was fine—but her voice failed her. Then she froze, the telltale sound of a gunshot cracking in the air. Her head whipped around toward the pier.

Framed in the moonlight and growing smaller by the moment as the boat drifted downstream, Mr. Brown grappled with Baron von List. Their figures swayed in a deadly struggle, his movements less certain, less controlled. A sudden twist, a desperate shove—then a splash. Sera winced as Baron von List disappeared into the dark water below. Mr. Brown stumbled but caught himself, leaning heavily against the pier, the pistol hanging limply in his hand as if the fight had drained the strength from his body.

"What just happened?" Sera whispered, more to herself than to Alex. He didn't answer. Instead, he gathered her into his arms, pulling her against him more protectively as the small boat drifted farther from the chaos they had left behind. The voices faded, replaced by the soothing lap of water against the hull and the occasional chirp of insects carried on the night breeze. They escaped immediate peril.

"You reckless, magnificent fool," Alex muttered, his voice low and sharp near her ear. His arms tightened around her as though he feared she might slip away even now. "That knife could've been the end of you."

Sera drew back slightly, meeting his stormy gaze with one of her own. Her breath rattled still, but her chin lifted defiantly. "And staying still would've been the end of us both."

Alex's lips parted—whether to argue, or perhaps to admit defeat—but instead, a faint, ragged laugh fell from them. Disbelief and pride mingled in the sound as he shook his head, almost as if in surrender.

Silence fell; distant city lights shimmered. Only when those lights became faint pinpricks did Alex speak, his voice softer this time, heavier with emotion.

"This," he said, gesturing faintly at the dark expanse of water around them, "is exactly why I wanted to protect you in Cornwall—from my life. It's all danger, Sera. Spies. Gunshots in the night. Threats that never cease." His words hung heavily in the air, weighted with both frustration and a pain he couldn't hide. Sera hesitated, the threads of his confession wrapping tightly around her heart. She could feel his anguish, his longing to shield her—but she wouldn't allow it. Not now. Not after everything. Her voice, when she spoke, was steady, resolute.

"And that's exactly why I was raised for this," she said firmly. "It's my family's business—my father's fleet. This isn't just your fight, Alex. It's mine, as well." For a moment, he said nothing, his gaze lingering on hers, searching for something. Then Sera sighed and looked down at her hands, flexing her fingers to ease the lingering tension. A flicker of regret crossed her face as the boat drifted across the Thames.

"For the first time," she admitted quietly, "I regret skipping my German lessons. If I'd studied properly instead of collecting seashells in Cornwall, maybe I'd understand what they were saying back there." Alex's lips quirked at the corner, a faint and unexpected smile breaking through his solemn expression.

"If you hadn't nearly drowned," he said gently, "I wouldn't have found you." Sera blinked, startled by his warmth. A memory surfaced, unbidden but vivid, painted with sunlight and the salty scent of the Cornish coast. Her cheeks flushed faintly.

"It was the bird," she confessed, her words quiet but deliberate. "A seagull. It was tangled in a fishing hook, and I…" She trailed off, her eyes dropping briefly. "I fell into the water trying to free it. That's when you saved me."

His fingers lightly brushed her cheek, grounding her as his gaze burned into hers. "I'm glad I could," Alex said, his voice softening. "Because it's your heart that I love—the heart that said, 'I couldn't just leave that injured seagull behind.' "

Her breath caught as he leaned closer, and for the first time since the chaos began, she felt something other than fear—a fragile, fleeting moment of peace. Darkness their only tether, they drifted together.

For now, they were together. And for now, it was everything.

But they had to go back to the ball.

Chapter Twenty-Seven

THE HACKNEY RATTLED through the cobbled streets, its worn wheels creaking over uneven stones. Sera clutched Alex's arm, her damp gown a cold weight against her legs. She was grateful for the cover of darkness as they approached Lady Ashford's estate where the ball was still in full swing, telling from the soft glow of lit windows spilling onto the road ahead. Somewhere beneath her exhaustion pulsed a ripple of nerves— what exactly would they find upon their return?

The carriage jerked to a stop, jolting her from her thoughts. Alex descended first, his steady hands guiding her out, careful to keep her upright despite the ache in her limbs. Sera lifted her tattered hem, glancing down at the mud caked around the skirts of her dress. The sight reignited her shame, a hot flush creeping into her cheeks. She hadn't exactly envisioned her return to the ball like this.

Before she could dwell further, the side door of the estate swung open. Ashley's face appeared first, her expression of relief quickly melting into bemusement. "Thank heavens," she said, stepping forward. "Do you both have any idea the stir you've caused? And more importantly, what happened to your poor dress?"

"Stan?" Alex said. "This is Prince… ahem… My brother."

"Lady Ashley filled me in. Let's keep the formalities for later. Come inside. There's a crisis only you can address," the man said.

Sera recognized him. He looked like Alex, with darker hair. He was the man she'd seen. It all came together now.

But there was no moment lost on idle thoughts. Ashley all but dragged them through the servants' staircase and upstairs. Prince Stan followed behind her, his tall frame momentarily blocking the light. "Lady Ashley's been pacing," he said with a grin. "She practically wore a trail into the floor—and here I thought I'd seen everything."

Sera managed a shaky smile despite herself. Her dear friend, as unruffled as she seemed, swept into action like a polished team of accomplices with Alex's brother.

"We'll get you sorted. Trust me." She shot Alex a pointed glance. "You, too."

Prince Stan rolled his shoulders, gesturing for Alex to follow. "Come on, you're tracking dirt all over the hallway."

They hurried through a side passage into lavishly adorned quarters, where warm water waited in steaming basins. Ashley fussed over Sera's dress, muttering protests about the state of her once-pristine gown as she helped peel the damp fabric from her arms. Prince Stan returned with a clean cravat for Alex and a comb to tame his wild, wind-stiffened hair.

It wasn't a complete transformation—they didn't have time for that—but enough was done to make their return acceptable, if not entirely dignified. Ashley draped a shawl over Sera's shoulders, a soft gray that subdued the remaining wrinkles in her borrowed dress.

"It'll have to do," she said quietly, smoothing the fabric down. Her tone softened. "You'll be fine, you know. Together."

Sera nodded, unsure what to say other than a whispered "Thank you." A warmth settled in her chest at the sight of Ashley's light-hearted wink.

By the time they stepped through the back entrance together—both slightly less ragged and a bit more presentable—the din of the ballroom filtered through heavy doors. The sound pricked at her nerves, her heart thumping harder with each step closer to their re-entry. Alex must have sensed it; his hand found hers as they reached the threshold.

And then, they were inside.

The ballroom glittered, every sconce and chandelier casting light over the elegantly dressed crowd. Sera's gloved hand rested in Alex's, and despite the storm of unease that had brewed earlier in the evening, her heart felt oddly light. Until the doors swung open, showing a wet, bedraggled valet in the center of the room.

"Him! See?" Mr. Brown pointed at Alex.

Gasps rippled across the crowd.

Mr. Brown's coat clung to him like a second skin, dripping water onto the polished floor. He shouldn't have been here at all—not in this state and certainly not with what he'd done. Conversation faltered and then hushed completely as all eyes turned toward the spectacle.

Sera's cheeks burned as her father's gaze locked on her and Alex, his expression darkening. Father wasn't a man used to scandal, and this—this spectacle—was exactly that. He strode toward them, his boots clicking sharply on the marble floor, authority and fury in every step.

"What is the meaning of this?" he barked, his sharp eyes darting between Sera and Alex. "And what," he added with a pointed glance at their joined hands, "is this?"

Sera tilted her chin, a spark of defiance flaring in her chest. She tightened her grip on Alex's hand and smiled, far too sweetly. "My engagement ball, is it not? Shouldn't I be allowed to hold my fiancé's hand?"

Father stiffened, clearly torn between annoyance and disbelief. Before he could respond, the valet stumbled forward, his soaked boots scuffing against the floor as he pointed a trembling finger.

"They've done worse than holding hands," he stammered loudly, eyes flicking nervously over the crowd, "at the beach in

Cornwall!"

A collective gasp swept through the room. Sera's mother froze mid-fan, then resumed fanning herself with renewed vigor.

"Sera!" she hissed, her voice sharp with feigned shock and disapproval.

Before Sera could speak, Ashley and the Earl of Linsey came to her side, their faces determined and reassuring.

"Is there a problem, Your Royal Highness?" Linsey asked smoothly, his arm brushing against Sera's as if to shield her and his gaze fixed to Alex.

"Hardly a problem," Alex said.

"Merely a… misstep in protocol," Ashley added, her tone light but her gaze shrewd as it swept across the gathering.

The murmurs in the ballroom edged into an apprehensive quiet, every gaze fixed on her and Alex. Sera could feel the weight of her father's disapproval pressing down on her, his gaze sharp and unwavering. The valet's soaked figure, still dripping and shivering near the threshold, only added to the unbearable tension. Her grip on Alex's hand remained firm, her fingers curling tighter as her pulse hammered in her ears.

Alex drew himself up, his shoulders rigid. Sera braced herself for another reprimand—she could see it brewing in the hard set of his jaw. But instead, the valet spoke, his trembling voice barely disguising the fear vibrating in every syllable.

"I need to say my piece," he stammered, his eyes darting anxiously around the room before they landed briefly on her. "I— I beg your forgiveness, Your Highness."

Sera's chest tightened as the man directed his plea toward Alex. Her gaze flicked to his face, but he gave no immediate reaction. The valet forged ahead, his words a frantic tumble. "I threatened your love. Instead of seeing what was growing between you two, I acted out of fear—and jealousy." He paused, swaying slightly before steadying himself. "von List has my wife. I didn't know—if I'd known what my meddling could bring, the danger it could cause, I would never have done it."

Sera caught her breath, the air around her suddenly stifling. The valet's confession filled her with unease, a crawling sensation under her skin. She tried to read her father's expression, but his face remained closed, the weight of their shared family responsibility heavy in the stern lines of his features.

Thomas shifted beside her, his presence solid and unmoving. His voice cut through the suffocating silence like the crack of a whip. "You cannot expect to face no consequences after threatening the lives of a—"

"Enough." Alex's voice interrupted, firm and steady. Sera's stomach clenched at the sound of it. Alex released her hand gently and stepped forward, his posture commanding the gathered onlookers' attention. His words, though calm, carried an authority that left no room for argument. "I'll hear him out."

The valet exhaled harshly, his hands trembling at his sides as he continued. "von List… von List is trying to stop this union," he said, his voice quieter now but filled with a plea. "He wants the Lyndon fleet. Your family's ships, Miss Lyndon—he would take them with no regard for the cost."

Sera's heart sank, a cold dread pooling in her chest at the mention of her family's fleet. She felt her father's sharp gaze on her once more, and when she looked at him, she thought— impossibly—that something like regret softened his features, though he masked it quickly.

Father straightened his back, his voice low, but weighted. "Sera—forgive me," he said. "I did not mean to risk your life for this alliance. If you do not wish to continue—"

"I do." She said the words quickly, interrupting him before she could think better of it. Her voice, though steady, sounded distant to her own ears. She turned back to Alex, their hands interlinked again as she met his unwavering gaze. His presence filled her with a steadiness she hadn't realized she needed. Her next words came with more conviction. "I do."

Her father's sigh broke the silence, a heavy sound of resignation that filled the room. He hesitated briefly, then gave a slight nod, almost imperceptible, toward Alex. "A clean break will suffice," he said. "A truce between our families." The formality of his words couldn't hide the subtle resignation settled into his expression. Without waiting for Sera's reply, he turned to her, extending his hand with an unspoken intent.

Sera froze. There was an offer in her father's outstretched hand, but the weight of a choice hung heavily over her. She cast a hesitant glance between him and Alex—her past and her future. Stilling herself, she tightened her grip on Alex's hand and turned back to her father. She met his gaze with a determined smile, tilting her chin just slightly in a gesture of quiet defiance.

"I think I'll stay right here."

⤜⟫⟫⟫✕⟪⟪⟪⤛

THE MURMURS OF curious onlookers faded to a distant hum as Alex looked down at Sera. Her small hand, velvet-soft in his own, now rested alongside her father's larger, steadier grasp. Father's expression was a tumult of resignation and grief, his gaze flickering between Alex and his daughter.

"Let go, love," Mr. Lyndon said, his voice quieter now, weary. "I'm sorry you won't be a princess, but I'd rather have my daughter alive than titled."

Alex's pulse quickened. He stepped forward, standing shoulder-to-shoulder with Sera. The earl's hand might have rested on hers, but Alex wasn't relinquishing his place. His voice, low but certain, filled the taut air between them.

"She's already my princess. Whether she carries the title officially or not, she holds my heart. And I will not stop until I can share my life with her."

Mr. Lyndon drew back slightly, his brow furrowed, but Sera, with a strength that never failed to stagger Alex, tightened her grip, linking the three of them more firmly. In the background, Alex saw his brother and sister. Thea's brow was furrowed as she whispered to Stan, "Wait—Miss Lyndon? The girl from Cornwall?"

Alex nodded.

But her father tried to tug her away. "He said he didn't want you. Now he's missed his chance."

"It was a misunderstanding," Alex said.

Mr. Lyndon squared his shoulders, his voice cutting through the tension like the crack of a whip. "Mis—" He paused to clear his throat, his tone tightening into something sharp and unyielding. "With all due respect, Your Royal Highness, this is my daughter. I only have two. There are no misunderstandings. Take as many ships as you wish from my fleet, but Sera is going home with me."

Alex's jaw tightened, and his free hand curled into a fist at his side. The words struck like a deliberate blow, but he forced himself to remain steady. He felt Sera's slender fingers still clasped in his, her touch like an anchor tethering him to this moment. If her father thought he could simply command her life, dictate her destiny, he had clearly underestimated the strength she had shown Alex time and time again.

And then she proved it again.

"Enough," Sera said, her voice carrying effortlessly through the ballroom. Alex's focus snapped to her, startled by the light, almost teasing quality in her tone. Before Mr. Lyndon could respond, she yanked them both closer together, her hand holding firm between Alex's and her father's. "I'll decide for myself."

Alex couldn't help the faint tug at the corner of his mouth, admiration flickering in his chest as a ripple of murmurs passed through the room. Even now, even here, she was her own force of nature, pulling every ounce of attention toward her.

Sera turned her face toward her mother, a small, serene smile gracing her lips. "It was him I had chosen all along," she stated. "Even before I realized he was the prince."

The room crackled with barely contained whispers and gasps, yet Alex hardly noticed. His world had narrowed to the woman beside him, standing there as if she wielded all the power in the universe in the palm of her hand. He felt it too—that undeniable pull she had, that determination that had shaken his carefully ordered life.

If the crowd judged them, it didn't matter. He cared about only one thing—Sera. His grip on her hand remained steady, his thumb brushing lightly over her knuckles, a silent promise meant for her alone. Whatever came next, whoever stood before them, Alex wouldn't falter—not for a second. She had chosen him, and that unwavering truth filled his chest until there was no space left for doubt.

Her father stiffened, clearly prepared to argue again, but Alex's resolve surged stronger with every beat of his heart. Sera had already spoken for herself—and whether Mr. Lyndon was ready to accept it or not, she was no longer standing alone.

Alex felt his chest swell, a rare and foolish giddiness threading through the moment's tension. His fingers wrapped more firmly around hers, his love for her too fierce to temper.

"I meant what I said," Alex added plainly, his gaze locking with the Earl's. "I would never—will never—allow anything to happen to her. Sera's safety and happiness will always come first."

Before Mr. Lyndon could respond, Stan and Thea stepped forward, their presence solid, grounding. It was Stan who spoke first, his deep and steady tone punctuating the charged atmosphere. "When someone joins our family, she doesn't stand alone. We all protect her."

Thea's hand rested lightly on Alex's arm as she nodded. "We take care of our own, Mr. Lyndon—always."

Mr. Lyndon looked unconvinced, his expression tightening. "No thanks," he muttered, his tone laced with wary sarcasm. "I'd rather not put her in this danger to begin with."

But Sera, true to form, refused to back down. "It's too late," she said briskly, drawing all eyes to her. A rare flash of hesitation crossed her face, but then she pressed onward. "I may already be carrying the prince's child."

Alex's breath hitched. The words hung in the air, shocking and irrevocable. A gasp rose from across the room, followed by the faint flutter of a dropped handkerchief. Mr. Lyndon groaned loudly, dragging both hands over his face.

"I hope," he muttered, his voice filled with wry misery, "you mean a by-blow he foisted upon you."

"No, Father," Sera replied evenly, placing her hand deliberately over her abdomen.

A much louder groan followed, and Alex resisted the urge to laugh—*Draci*! He couldn't reveal how much he admired her audacity in this moment. Instead, his gaze softened, and he reached out to rest a hand over hers.

"I'll go wherever you go," he told her, his voice steady, the words low and meant only for her. "Whatever comes, I'll stay by your side."

Sera's expression broke into a small, uncertain smile before her father interrupted them with a sharp clearing of his throat. "Be that as it may," he began, clearly poised to continue his protest.

But Alex wasn't finished. He turned fully to Mr. Lyndon, shoulders back, voice unwavering.

"There will never be by-blows," he said firmly. "There will never be anyone else. I love your daughter, Mr. Lyndon. Whether she's the girl from the beach, Miss Lyndon, or Seraphina, I'll spend my life proving it. If she'll have me, I'll be her servant, her partner, whatever she needs—and above all, I vow to keep her safe for as long as I live."

Stan stepped up beside him, his expression fierce with approval. "You've my word as well. We'll all protect her."

Thomas joined them next, a quiet but steadfast presence. "And mine," he said simply.

With a nod, the Earl of Langley and his countess stepped forward too, placing themselves firmly at Alex and Sera's side right next to Ashley and Linsey.

Mr. Lyndon hesitated, visibly outnumbered, visibly overwhelmed by the display of unity.

And then Ashley appeared, threading her arm through Sera's and pulling her into a warm hug. "Well," she said lightly, offering a pointed glance at her father. "It seems the decision has already been made."

Alex exhaled, a quiet relief washing over him as he turned to Sera. But just as he reached for her hand again, a servant appeared with a flourish, a grand bouquet of roses in hand. The vibrant red blooms stood in stark contrast with the quiet tension of the moment, and for the first time, Alex truly smiled. Taking the flowers, he knelt before Sera, his voice soft but clear as he spoke.

"Oh, the Viennese tradition!" Thea squealed and clapped her hands together.

"Miss Lyndon, Seraphina—" He looked up at her with a love he didn't bother to hide. "Will you grant me the honor of your hand in marriage?"

Sera froze for a moment, her wide, luminous gaze meeting his. Then, with a smile that outmatched even the roses in brilliance, she took his hand. "Yes," she said simply, the word carrying all the weight and joy of the moment.

The music resumed then, a joyous overture that swept through the ballroom as murmurs turned to cheers. Sera's mother grasped her shoulders gently, though her voice carried its usual commanding tone. "You, my dear," she said firmly, "need to change into a fresh dress before your first waltz."

The room buzzed around them, the tension breaking like a dam as Alex remained where he was, his eyes still on Sera. Whatever trials awaited them, here, in this moment, she was his—and he would face them all for her.

Chapter Twenty-Eight

T HE EVENING PRESSED on, the engagement ball unfolding around them in light of the extraordinary that had occurred. Laughter and music filled the air once more, though whispers still trailed behind Sera and Alex wherever they moved. Mr. Brown, soaked through and visibly pale, had been quietly ushered out of the ballroom. Stan, his expression set in practiced calm, followed close behind. The weight of what would come from that confrontation lingered on, but Alex knew his brother would handle it.

For a while, they had done what was expected—danced, greeted guests, and engaged in the conversation required of them. Sera's smile never slipped, though she could feel exhaustion tugging at the edges of her composure. Alex, she noticed, wore his princely role well, offering charming remarks to those who approached and standing steadfastly beside her. There was strength in his quiet gestures—a hand pressed lightly against her lower back, his touch brushing hers when no one was looking.

But even his patience had limits.

After the final set ended, Alex leaned in close, his breath warm against her temple as he murmured, "Sera, come with me."

She blinked up at him, startled by the quiet intensity in his tone. "Now?"

A faint grin tugged at the edges of his lips. "Now."

Before she could protest—or agree—he took her hand in his,

weaving them both through the crowd with practiced ease. The grand entry hall loomed ahead as they left the full, glittering warmth of the ballroom behind. She cast a quick glance over her shoulder, catching her mother's gaze from across the room, but Alex didn't slow his pace.

Once they had slipped beyond the main doors, the cool air of the corridor kissed her flushed skin. "Alex, we can't just leave," she whispered, glancing around to ensure no one had followed.

"Why not?" His voice carried that same lightness she had come to crave, the easy confidence that made her heart flip at the most inconvenient moments. "What are they going to do, make me marry you?"

Sera choked on a laugh, turning her face toward him as a smile broke free. "You're insufferable."

"And yet, here you are," he replied, a spark of mischief bright in his gaze as he tugged her forward.

Their steps quickened as he led her down a shadowed side hall and toward the cool night beyond. Sera felt a giggle rising in her chest, though it wouldn't do to give themselves away with the sound. Still, she could hardly help herself. The scandal, the rush of it, the sheer audacity of being pulled away from her own engagement ball—every part of it felt exhilarating, dangerous, and entirely right.

Alex paused before a side door, glancing down at her with a rare softness that caught her off guard. "Come on," he said quietly, his eyes searching hers in the dim light. "We'll only be gone for a little while."

Her breath caught, and for one heartbeat, she stilled. Then, without another word, she nodded, slipping her hand into his more securely. Whatever awaited them, for now, she would go. Wherever Alex was concerned, she always would. The stairs creaked softly beneath her slippers, but Sera barely noticed. Alex's hand was firm around hers, pulling her forward, his steps quick and determined. Her breath faltered, caught halfway between laughter and the swirling anticipation that coiled low in her belly.

The grand staircase curved upward, each step dimly lit by the glow of silver candelabras. The music from the ball—fading now—played faintly below, an echo of a world she no longer cared to be part of. Not when he was leading her somewhere else entirely. Somewhere that felt like just theirs.

"Where are we going?" she whispered, her voice barely more than a shaky breath. His urgency made her giddy, made her cling tighter to him as they rounded the second landing and hurried up toward the third.

"I don't know," Alex said, tossing a glance back at her with a smile that was all mischief, all heat. "But I can't wait anymore."

Something about the way he said those words sent a thrill through her, pulling at memories of long ago—the alley in Cornwall, when the night had hidden them, and the salt-kissed air had made her head spin. But this… this was different. This was better. Here, the settings were finer, softer, the smell of fresh wood polish and roses chasing the air. It felt illicit but far more elegant. It felt like them, now.

Before she could form another word, Alex spun abruptly, tugging her into the shadows of the corridor. Sera gasped as her back met the plush damask wallpaper, the impact cushioned but the jolt sending her pulse racing. Her hands, which he had been holding, were lifted—high above her head, over her curls—by the strength of one of his capable hands. His body pressed close, so close she could feel the hard planes of him against her softer curves. Her breath hitched.

Alex's lips met hers with a force that started like desperation but gentled within heartbeats. That gentleness unraveled her, pulling her apart even as it stitched her back together. She melted beneath the press of his mouth, her sigh captured between them. His other hand, the one not pinning her arms above her head, slid—slow, deliberate—from the edge of her jaw, down the graceful curve of her neck until it rested at her shoulder. Then it lingered before continuing, tracing her through the fine fabric of her gown, until he barely brushed the swell of her chest.

"Are all these rooms occupied?" she whispered against his lips, speaking only because words were all she had left to steady herself.

"Does it matter?" Alex's growled response shot straight through her, tightening the air in their shared small space. His hand around her wrist loosened suddenly, but before she could mourn the loss of his restraint, his arm slid quickly around her waist. He pulled her so sharply against him that the breath left her body in a dazed little gasp. Reflexively, her fingers reached out, skimming the damask walls as they stumbled farther down the hall.

Then Alex opened a door. Just like that—one twist of a handle, and the world around them disappeared.

Moonlight poured through the room's tall windows, washing the space in soft, bluish light. The heavy curtains had been drawn only halfway, and the gleam of the city reached faintly inward, reduced to a muted whisper in the quiet sanctuary of the chamber. It was a simple room—clean, elegant, a single bed against the far wall dressed in crisply folded linens. Perfect. More than perfect.

"This is better than a cave, isn't it?" Alex said, his voice low, teasing, as he glanced back at her.

Sera couldn't respond. Not with words. Her gaze drank in the room's surroundings, but all that mattered was him, the way he looked at her as though she was all he needed, all he'd been searching for. And when he stepped inside, pulling her in alongside him, she realized she would follow him anywhere—no matter where the path twisted, no matter how dark it may seem. If this is what privacy meant—being alone with him, unburdened by the world—then she wanted nothing else.

Alex pressed her back against the door and locked it with an audible click. The sound of it, sharp and final, made her shiver. His hands didn't hesitate this time; they framed her waist firmly, holding her as though he might never let her go.

"Finally alone," he murmured, his breath lighting against her ear, his lips grazing the sensitive skin just there.

Her heart stuttered, then sped, a glorious rhythm that echoed through her body. Alone had never felt so complete.

THE LOCK CLICKED beneath his fingers, and Alex inhaled, sharp and deep, as though the sound had punctured something inside him. He couldn't have stopped himself if he tried. The urgency burned too hot, too close. He turned back to Sera, Seraphina, Miss Lyndon—as long as it was her, he didn't care what she was called.

She was his.

Her breath unsteady, the moonlight catching on strands of her hair and making her glow like a vision long dreamed of but never truly real.

But she was real. She was here, and he reached for her—not gently, no, not now. His hand found her waist, warm silk under his fingers, and he pulled her to him as if the ocean itself might drag her away if he didn't hold her tight enough. Her body gave against his, pliant and perfect, and when she tipped her face up to him, lips parted, it undid the last fraying thread of his restraint.

Alex kissed her—or didn't just kiss her. He claimed her, his mouth crashing into hers with the force of everything he couldn't say. And yet even as his hands pressed against her back, sliding up, tracing the elegant curve of her spine, his touch softened. She tasted of something sweet and heady, something that reminded him of late summer and stolen glances. Something that made his chest ache with the sheer immensity of it all.

This was them, truly and completely. For the first time, Alex understood what it meant, truly meant, to be beyond the watchful eyes of the world. To be free to love her, wholly and without hesitation, without the weight of expectation pressing on his shoulders. Here, there was no crown, no duty—only his love.

The realization hit him so forcefully that he broke the kiss, his forehead resting against hers as they both fought for air. She smelled of roses and faintly of candlelight, delicate and intoxicating.

"Sera," he murmured, her name barely audible, reverent and rough all at once. His hand, still firm on the curve of her hip, slid upward, grazing her ribs. Her breaths shuddered against his palm, and he had to close his eyes for fear of losing himself entirely in the way she was looking at him.

Her fingers found the lapels of his coat, trembling only slightly as she tugged him closer, and any willpower he'd clung to dissolved instantly. He stepped forward, pressing her gently yet completely against the door, his hands framing her face now as he searched her eyes. She held his stare, unflinching, and what he saw there made every sacrifice, every regret, every moment of torment worth it. It wasn't just desire; it was trust, fragile and whole all at once like she was handing him a piece of herself and daring him to break it.

He wouldn't.

I won't.

His lips found her neck this time, moving slowly, reverently, down to where her pulse thrummed and leaped beneath his touch. Her bare skin was impossibly warm against his mouth, and every sigh she gave was a melody that unraveled his careful composure. He could stay here forever, lose himself completely in her touch, but he needed more. Needed her.

His hands slid back down her waist, catching at the fabric of her gown as he pulled her with him, away from the door. Her laugh—light, breathless—was the most beautiful sound he'd heard in years. He led her across the room, his lips finding hers again, softer this time, a slow burn rather than a blaze. The moonlight fell across the bed, illuminating a space too small for two but perfect for them.

"Better than a cave," she whispered, her voice lilting and teasing, though it trembled slightly, and Alex knew it wasn't from fear.

"Far better," he replied, his own voice dark with feeling, his smile ghosting against her cheek. But his hands were steady as he slid them lower again, anchoring her, grounding himself in the feel of her in his arms. He would never have enough of her. Never.

He sat on the edge of the bed and pulled her to stand between his knees, looking up at her now, devouring the delicate flush on her cheeks, the way she bit her bottom lip as if to keep from saying something. His hands ran lightly, reverently, up and down her arms as if committing her to memory, though he already knew he'd remember this night for the rest of his life.

"Sera," he began softly, unsure of how to put into words what was threatening to overflow inside him. But she leaned forward, silencing him with a kiss, and he pulled her down to him, consuming her completely as the world beyond them ceased to exist.

The room dissolved around him. There was no damask wallpaper, no moonlight pooling over the polished floors. There was only her—soft, yielding, and utterly his. Alex had never known touch could feel like this, like every nerve in his body was tuned to hers, like her breath over his skin could stir volcanic fervor within him. His lips whispered over her collarbone as he bent with her onto the bed, his hands roaming with reverence, urgency, and something too tender to be named.

Sera clutched at him, her fingers threading through his light sandy hair, tugging as she pulled his face back up to hers. Their mouths met again, desperate now, consuming, her moan a stifled melody that made his very spine shiver with need. He cradled her face as though it might splinter under the wildness between them, his thumb brushing her temple even as his other hand swept down, anchoring her by her waist, as if holding her in place might keep the night from crumbling into nothing.

The rhythm between them built, a perfect storm of shared gasps and whispered names shattered into fractured syllables.

"Alex, oh Alex," she cried, meeting him exactly where he needed her.

"Sera," he rasped, her name guttural and fractured, dragged from depths he hadn't known existed. Her leg shifted—her thigh pressing against his hip—as she arched into him, and Alex thought briefly that heaven must feel like this, if he believed in such things.

When she looked at him—her gaze impossibly dark, impossibly luminous—it was his undoing. There was no coyness, no pretense, just raw trust and longing. His heartbeat thundered in his ears, drowning out everything but her. This woman. She was a force he'd underestimated, her love a treasure he'd once risked losing entirely.

"My prince."

Every touch, every movement grew sharper, amplified by the electric connection pulling them both taut with anticipation. Alex's hand smoothed across her shoulder, down the dip of her spine, his fingertips memorizing each and every curve as if this moment were their last. Sera trembled beneath him, her breath catching, her hands clutching at his back, pulling them closer until there was no space, no air, nothing but the tether between them snapping taut.

The wave crested with the force of inevitability, and Alex buried his face in the crook of her neck, his groan low and shattered as the storm inside him broke. Sera's cries mingled with the heavy air between them, her arms tightening around him, anchoring him even as the floor seemed to fall away. Together they collapsed, their bodies pliant and utterly spent as they tangled into one another, the quiet hum of their heartbeats the only sound in the world now.

His chest rose and fell against hers, their breaths mingling hot and uneven. Alex rolled slightly to the side, without relinquishing his hold on her, his hand gripping hers now, lacing their fingers together like a vow unspoken. Her head rested over his heart, the warmth of her cheek settling him, even as bliss still coursed faintly through his veins.

He wanted to say something, but words felt hollow compared to this.

Instead, he pressed a lingering kiss to her forehead, inhaling deeply. Sera exhaled softly, her body molding naturally against his, as if she had always belonged there. And for once, Alex allowed himself to believe that she did.

They lay there, cradled in the fragile cocoon of their privacy, wrapped in moonlight and the absolute certainty that they were none other than their truest selves for this brief, stolen moment.

"I thought…" She inhaled deeply. "I thought I'd lost you this summer." Her eyes shut, but a smile twisted her lips. "You might not understand this, but I truly thought for a minute that I lost my prince this summer. I'd have regretted it for the rest of my life."

"I'm here. For as long as you'll have me." Alex wiped a tear off her cheek. "You didn't lose your prince; I found my princess."

Sera's Entry in Matters of the Heart

Notes by Princess Seraphina Lyndon von Hohenzollern-Sigmaringen For the Enlightenment of Young Ladies of Distinction and Refinement

On Matters of Churning Feelings

When you find the gentleman who causes your composure to falter, whose every glance sets your thoughts awry—such a meeting is no accident. These feelings, though unsettling, are the very essence of life's greatest joy. Hold them dear and do not allow society's expectations or prudence to part you lightly from their source.

On Following the Whisper of Emotion

Should your heart beckon you to stray from the path well-trodden, take heed. Slip away, if only for a stolen moment, to explore the tender bloom of your sentiments. For it is in these quiet interludes, away from prying eyes, that true understanding can be found. Be neither reckless nor hesitant—but curious, brave, and true to yourself.

On Love and Matters of Station

Though titles may gleam, and coins may shine, they will warm neither hearth nor heart on a cold and bitter night. Remember this, dear reader, as you weigh the merits of a union. Follow your heart and its inclinations; the truest fortune is companionship founded on affection rather than gold or rank. While the world may scoff, true happiness has no price.

May all young ladies, in reading this, be guided toward the felicity of love unmarred by compromise of the soul.

When we set out to create Prince Alexander von Hohenzollern-Sigmaringen, we knew he needed to embody the kind of complexity that draws us into history's most intriguing figures. Inspired by Sara Adrien's masterfully crafted fictional royal families from the *Miracles on Harley Street* series, where we meet his brother Stan and his sister Thea, each of whom get their own love stories, Alex gets his story here. He shares a fascinating parallel with Prince William of England, the third son of King George III. Like Prince William, Alex is a third-born royal who, while unlikely to inherit a throne, possesses a spirit of adventure and a sense of destiny that takes him far beyond the expectations of his privileged birth. Prince William IV, born on August 21, 1765, as the third son of King George III of the Royal House of Hanover, had little expectation of inheriting the throne. Instead, he pursued a dynamic career in the Royal Navy and later served in the House of Lords. During his time as a midshipman, he stationed in New York during the American Revolution, making him the only British royal to visit the American colonies. A foiled plot to kidnap him by American forces bears testament to his presence in the conflict. Afterward, he rose through naval ranks, eventually serving under the esteemed Admiral Horatio Nelson in the British West Indies.

Prince Alex has naval duties and instead of facing the American Revolution has to help Stan and Thea defeat Baron von List, who's trying to exploit Transylvania to weaken its trade power.

That same power is what the liaison with the Lyndon family, Sera's wealthy father, should solidify.

But Alex's story goes beyond historical parallels. He comes from a fictional Transylvanian royal family, tied to the Hohenzollerns of Austria, which was the Imperial German Empire—a creative "what if" that allows us to imagine him in a time and place rich with untold stories. Imagine a prince born in a land of breathtaking beauty and immense wealth, one that history all too often overlooks. Transylvania, with its rolling hills, shimmering forests, and deep veins of natural resources, offers the perfect backdrop for a royal hero whose heritage is as vibrant as his heart is noble.

While his roots are tied to a family bearing the future name of Hohenzollern-Sigmaringen, Alex already embodies the heroism that history sometimes lacks. What might it have been like, we wondered, to have such a prince emerge from this land—one who could protect, love, and challenge the world while honoring a culture brimming with strength and depth? What would it mean for him to carry not only the weight of royal duty, but also the yearning to forge a path his ancestors never dreamed possible?

Through Alex and the stories of his siblings their books, Sara Adrien hopes to transport you into a world where history and imagination blend seamlessly—a world of Regency romance shaped by tradition, but alive with passion, wonder, and the promise of a hero unlike any other.

Read Princess Thea's story in "A Touch of Charm" and Prince Stan's story in "The Sound of Seduction" by Sara Adrien.

For more information about these stories and a complimentary copy of the *Handbook on Seduction and Matters of the Heart*, please visit www.SaraAdrien.com.

About the Authors

Sara Adrien

Bestselling author Sara Adrien writes hot and heart-melting Regency romance with a Jewish twist. As a law professor-turned-author, she writes about clandestine identities, whims of fate, and sizzling seduction. If you like unique and intelligent characters, deliciously sexy scenes, and the nostalgia of afternoon tea, then you'll adore Sara Adrien's tender tear-jerkers.

For more information and exclusive sneak peeks, new releases, and more books, sign up for Sara Adrien's newsletter at www.SaraAdrien.com.

Tanya Wilde

Award-Winning and International Bestselling author Tanya Wilde developed a passion for reading when she had nothing better to do than lurk in the library during her lunch breaks. Her love affair with pen and paper soon followed, after she devoured all their historical romance books! When she's not meddling in the lives of her characters or pondering names for her imaginary big, white greyhound, she's off on adventures with her partner in crime.

Wilde lives in a town at the foot of the Outeniqua Mountains, South Africa. You can read a bit more about her at www.authortanyawilde.com.

ACKNOWLEDGEMENTS

Special thanks go to Fil Reid, our author friend and expert on all things Cornwall. She and her husband introduced us to the idea of Shrub, a brilliant recipe that had Sera and Alex fooled it wasn't alcoholic. We are also so grateful to Dominique for her keen eye to help us chase typos and to the brilliant edits by Dianne.